A Curse of Shadows and Ice

A Curse of Shadows and Ice

CATHARINA MAURA

FOREVER

New York   Boston

This book is a work of fiction. Names, characters, places, and incidents are the product of the author's imagination or are used fictitiously. Any resemblance to actual events, locales, or persons, living or dead, is coincidental.

Copyright © 2025 by Catharina Maura

Cover design by Catharina Maura and Daniela Medina. Cover images by Deposit Photos. Cover copyright © 2025 by Hachette Book Group, Inc.

Hachette Book Group supports the right to free expression and the value of copyright. The purpose of copyright is to encourage writers and artists to produce the creative works that enrich our culture.

The scanning, uploading, and distribution of this book without permission is a theft of the author's intellectual property. If you would like permission to use material from the book (other than for review purposes), please contact permissions@hbgusa.com. Thank you for your support of the author's rights.

Forever
Hachette Book Group
1290 Avenue of the Americas, New York, NY 10104
read-forever.com
@readforeverpub

First Edition: October 2025

Forever is an imprint of Grand Central Publishing. The Forever name and logo are registered trademarks of Hachette Book Group, Inc.

The publisher is not responsible for websites (or their content) that are not owned by the publisher.

The Hachette Speakers Bureau provides a wide range of authors for speaking events. To find out more, go to hachettespeakersbureau.com or email HachetteSpeakers@hbgusa.com.

Forever books may be purchased in bulk for business, educational, or promotional use. For information, please contact your local bookseller or the Hachette Book Group Special Markets Department at special.markets@hbgusa.com.

Print book interior design by Taylor Navis.

Library of Congress Cataloging-in-Publication Data has been applied for.

ISBNs: 978-1-5387-7582-0 (standard hardcover), 978-1-5387-7297-3 (deluxe limited edition), 978-1-5387-7299-7 (ebook)

Printed in China

APS

10 9 8 7 6 5 4 3 2 1

*This one is for those who hide their inner strength for fear of how their environment might respond.
Don't let them cage you. Don't let them throttle your growth for their own comfort.
Unleash your magic.*

CHAPTER ONE

Felix

If I could end my life right at this instant, I would. There are no weapons I haven't tried, no poisons I have yet to consume. Without fail my body mends itself. This curse refuses to let me leave its clutches—there is no escape, not for me, and not for my people.

Despair seeps deep into my soul as I approach the tall mirror hidden in the depths of the east wing, icy winds whipping across my skin as my footsteps echo ominously in my moonlit palace. Dark magic clutches at the tarnished silver mirror, wispy tendrils of black smoke swirling around the edges, threatening to knock off the icicles that have formed around the delicate golden floral ornaments that disguise what lives within.

When I look into the mirror, it isn't my reflection I see. Bitterness claws at me as I stare into the milky-white eyes of the seer that inhabits it. "Show me the girl."

Pythia smiles, her expression eerie and foreboding as she slowly fades from view, her image replaced by that of a young woman sitting in the corner of a dark room, a book in her hands, something akin to wistfulness written all over her face. Long dark hair falls to her waist, and even in the dim lighting, her light-brown eyes shimmer with hope. Every time I've seen her, her eyes have held that same expression. *Hope.* It's something that's rarely seen in Eldiria.

The girl smiles to herself as she flips the page, and my heart squeezes tightly. She is unaware that none of her dreams will come to pass. Arabella of Althea has yet to realize that sorrow beyond anything she's ever known is to befall her. After all, her fate is entwined with mine.

"You're certain it's her?"

The image blurs until once more, Pythia stands before me, her unseeing eyes keeping me pinned in place. "Only she is capable of breaking the curse," the seer confirms. "Arabella of Althea is destined to become your empress."

My gaze roams over her pale face, doubt taking root deep inside my chest. Seers are known to be deceptive, but I've come to believe that Pythia is different. The decades in torment have worn her down as much as they have me. She's as tied to this curse as I am. Until it's broken, she's trapped in the mirror dimension—in this very mirror.

"She's so young," I murmur, my mind drifting back to Arabella. "She looks weak."

The edges of Pythia's dark-red lips turn up into a semblance of a smile. "She's twenty-three, Your Excellency. Hardly a child."

I fail to understand how Arabella of Althea could possibly set us free, but if there's even the slightest chance, I owe it to my people to try. Perhaps I should rethink the plans that have been in the making from the moment I learned of her, three months ago. I could have her captured and brought to me before dawn. Had she been anyone else, that's exactly what I would've done.

"She must come of her own free will," Pythia reminds me, her tone sharp. I raise a brow in surprise, instantly wondering whether it's my expression she read, or my thoughts. Fates, it wouldn't surprise me if it was the latter.

I nod in acquiescence and take a step back, resisting the urge to question the seer further. This is the first time she's given me any hope that this curse could be broken. It's unfortunate that it'll be at the cost of Arabella's future.

Arabella of Althea.

My future wife.

She's a glimmer of hope in an otherwise dark and bleak world. She'll save us all, and it'll cost her everything.

My heart feels heavy as I walk toward the palace's atrium, the walls filled with blood-red roses—my mother's favorite flower. The mere sight of them nearly brings me to my knees, shame and regret coursing through my dark veins. I can't help but wonder if my mother's spirit is looking down on me today. If so, she's no doubt enjoying my misery. Her curse played out exactly as she wanted it to.

"So you'll go through with it, then?"

I look up to find Elaine standing to my side, her fingers gently caressing the frozen petals of a rose, her gaze filled with longing. "I have no choice."

She averts her face, but for a moment, I'm certain I saw a hint of anguish in her expression. "There is always a choice," she says, her voice soft yet firm. "You will not endear yourself to her if you see this through. Love cannot bloom under threat of force."

"*Love*," I scoff. It's a common myth among those that heard Pythia's prophecy—they believe true love will break the curse.

A true union between the emperor and the woman fated to wield from within shall set you free.

Elaine is certain that *true union* must mean true *love*, but she should be more concerned about the *wield from within* part. Neither she nor I have been able to decipher those words, and time is running out. Everyone knows that magic can only be drawn and controlled from the ether, and never from *within*, so it isn't a sorceress we're looking for, nor an alchemist. If Arabella of Althea truly is the prophesied one, what does she *wield*? I've watched her for months, and I have yet to see anyone weaker than she is.

"Yes. *Love*," Elaine repeats, her tone firm, unyielding.

I sigh as I raise my face to look into her eyes. I never understood how Elaine holds on to hope despite everything this curse has taken from her, from *us*. Why does she still believe in love so fiercely? There is nothing I won't try, but love is not the answer to the curse that plagues us.

I force a smile for her and cup her cheek, my touch gentle. Elaine is the only one who doesn't shirk away from the vileness that I've become, the only one that looks at me and sees more than just a monster. My black, vile, poisonous veins don't faze her. She should hate me for all I've taken from her, but she's never once blamed me for the effects of the curse. She's never given up hope.

"If only that were true. If I had a choice, I'd have taken my life and freed those that were cursed alongside me." I wouldn't be getting *married*.

I was too young to comprehend my mother's words, but I've heard them repeated back to me all my life. She cursed me to live in the shadows the way she always did, bathed in inescapable darkness that would encompass our entire kingdom. I was to bear witness to her destruction helplessly, and to live with the misery that lies in knowing I would never experience true love. She cursed me to live the life she did.

I didn't know what that meant until the rolling green hills I'd known in my teenage years withered away, right along with my father. By the time I was fifteen, his body had become riddled with poisonous black veins, an unknown illness making him rot away and beg my mother for mercy each day, until he became bedridden and so delirious, the only thing he could utter was her name. Not long after, the sun set and never rose again. By the time he passed away, days short of my twentieth birthday, the entire empire had become covered in treacherous ice, making growing crops impossible. The forest had begun to close us in as though it wished to trap us, making trade equally impossible, and our people were perishing at a rate higher than I ever could have imagined.

If only that'd been the worst of it.

Because of my mother, I'll have to douse Arabella of Althea's flame and pull her into the darkness with me. Another sacrifice in our endless battle against this curse.

One more victim.

I hope she's the last one.

CHAPTER TWO

Arabella

"Father will kill us if we're caught," I murmur, my trembling voice betraying my building anxiety.

My little sister merely lifts her index finger to her lips, amusement dancing in her eyes. "If we're careful and quiet, Father will never find out," Serena promises, reaching for my hand. My heart thumps wildly as she pulls me into a long-forgotten hallway that leads to a set of stairs in dire need of repair. "No one comes here," she reassures me, "and this is the perfect vantage point. Don't you want to find out if the rumors are true?"

I hesitate before following her up the long winding stairs, unable to cast aside the unease I've felt all day. I'm used to sneaking around, and even when I'm not, I'm mostly ignored, my existence barely registering to the castle staff, let alone anyone else. It's different for Serena—she's almost always accompanied by her personal guard and her ladies in waiting. It won't take them long to realize she isn't in her bedroom. Then what? I'll be punished for getting her into trouble, no doubt. I'm always the one to blame, even if I have no hand in her mischief.

The wood creaks under my weight, and my breath hitches. "Nearly there," Serena says, looking over her shoulder. She pulls me along the last remaining steps until we're standing in front of a small window that overlooks the castle's courtyard, the view stretching for miles beyond it.

"*There*," she whispers, raising a trembling hand to point out the unmistakable army marching toward us, each and every soldier dressed in an unnatural shade of black. They look as inhuman as they're rumored to be. "It's really him."

"The Shadow Emperor," I whisper, my voice tinged with fear. I'd hoped the rumors were just that—rumors.

"What do you think the Shadow Emperor is doing here? Why would he come here of all places—and without notice, too," Serena whispers, excitement slowly bleeding from her voice, leaving nothing but the same fear that courses through me.

I force a smile for my younger sister, uncertain how to answer her question truthfully, without causing her to descend into a panic. How am I to tell her that there is no positive reason for him to come here?

The Shadow Emperor is the most powerful man in the world—the last alchemist in a world that has largely outlawed every form of both magic and alchemy following the plague that spread across the world five decades ago and killed hundreds of thousands of people, yet never a single magical being. It wasn't long before a sorceress handing out potions to aid with some of the symptoms was blamed for the plague, and then another, until they were all burned alive for fear they'd summoned the plague to rid the world of those less powerful than them, or to profit off those wealthy and desperate enough for a cure.

Though the plague is gone, they remain hunted. It is widely taught not only that they are deceptive, but that magic has begun to bring misfortune to its users and those around them. It is said that magic itself has turned against its users and cursed them, as repayment for bringing forth a plague that disrupted the natural order of life. Those who possess magic are to be reported to the authorities and condemned to a lifetime of captivity, where they can do no harm.

Just within the last decade, the Shadow Emperor has conquered most of the countries surrounding us, exploiting their natural resources and trade routes under the guise of creating magical safe havens. It's not hard to guess what might bring him here, but it's no easy feat explaining something like that to my sheltered sister, who knows nothing of politics, despite being only three years younger than me. I have often envied her naïveté, but today is one of those rare days that I don't. "I dare not guess," I tell her, being as truthful as I can be.

She leans into me as we stare out the small window in the tower. I can see the Eldirian flags waving in the distance, a delegation drawing closer to our castle with every second that passes.

Even from afar, it's easy to recognize the Shadow Emperor's uniform. He looks exactly as the history books portray him, his clothes darker than black ink, embroidered with gold that moves along his clothes, magically crafting the Eldirian insignia over and over again. I once heard that every bit of gold on his uniform is real gold, spun so thin that it could be used as embroidery thread, and I'm starting to believe it. A matching cloak flaps in the wind, his hood keeping his face hidden. There isn't a single image of his face in any of our books, and I have always wondered how that could be possible. How can it be that no one has ever seen and documented his face?

"His horse looks... *demonic*."

There's fear in Serena's voice, and I wrap my arm around her shoulder in reassurance. "The horse's name is Sirocco. No one knows how old the Shadow Emperor is, and the same goes for his horse. They've always been mentioned together, and both first appeared in our history books over a hundred years ago. Sirocco has always been described as unnaturally black, with black eyes that lack any white. I thought it was an exaggeration, but it appears not." I've never seen a horse like Sirocco. Rumor has it that he came straight from the underworld, alongside the Shadow Emperor.

"They're here," Serena whispers, her voice shaky, the confidence that led her up here depleted. She grabs my hand, and I entwine our fingers, holding on to her tightly. If anything goes wrong, I'm taking my sister and getting her far away from here.

We watch as my father and members of his court step forward to welcome the delegation from Eldiria. Even from all the way up here, I can tell that everyone is tense. But then again, how could they not be when receiving a man as unnatural as the Shadow Emperor? For years, I've been hearing that he's a monster, a creature that escaped from the deepest crevices of the underworld. I can't help but wonder if it's true.

My heart skips a beat when I spot Nathaniel standing behind my father. Deep concern for him eradicates every hint of butterflies when the Shadow Emperor's soldiers come to a stop and begin to dismount. "Come with me," Serena whispers as I watch Nathaniel disappear from sight, along with the members of my father's court. He's begun to shadow his father lately, in preparation for his own role as one of the kingdom's strategic advisers, so it shouldn't surprise me to see him here. Even so, I can't shake this niggling feeling that it would've been better for him to stay out of the Shadow Emperor's sight. "They've entered the castle far sooner than I expected. I was hoping to see more from here," Serena adds. I hesitate, but she pulls me along before I can object. "We can try going through the kitchens. Their corridors lead to most rooms, including the throne room. That's probably where Father will take them, isn't it?"

The staff gasp as we walk in, their outrage mostly reserved for my sister. They're used to seeing me here, but never her. I'm invisible in this castle despite being a princess, but Serena is not. Where I am the one they fear and call cursed, she is the golden child. Quite literally, with her long blond hair. She's light where I am darkness, she is grace whereas I leave destruction in my wake, and she's a blessing, while I am without a doubt a curse on my kingdom. If I didn't love her so dearly, I would despise her for it.

I carefully push the service door ajar, just wide enough to see, but not wide enough to draw attention. Much to my surprise, Father isn't seated on his throne. I have never seen him receive guests the way he does today, seated at a long table alongside everyone else, and I suspect that it's because he knows he is powerless against the Shadow Emperor. He is not even attempting to assert his authority like he usually does, and his usual pride and arrogance are notably absent today. So is Nathaniel, much to my relief.

"Who is that woman?" Serena whispers.

I glance at the people at the table, my eyes settling on the Shadow Emperor. His hood still hides his face entirely, and even his hands are covered by black leather gloves. No part of him is visible, and it only heightens my curiosity. Is he truly as hideous as the books say he is? Could he really be a monster from the underworld?

I struggle to tear my gaze away from him—it's as though the air is buzzing around him, and my gaze remains fixed on him, as if I have no choice but to give him my full attention. My chest tightens, and the strangest sense of longing rushes through me as I draw a steadying breath. I bite down on my lip harshly and force myself to look away, my eyes landing on the woman seated next to him.

"That is Elaine," I whisper, taking in her jet-black hair and her piercing violet eyes. She doesn't look much older than I am, but I've been reading about her conquests ever since I was twelve. "She is his most trusted adviser. She commands his army in his absence, and she's the only woman in the world to have such a high-ranking position." It's hard to keep the awe out of my voice. In a world where women have no rights, Elaine has defied all odds.

"She's beautiful," Serena sighs, and I huff. Elaine is so much more than her beauty. If what the books state is true, she's a brilliant strategist and a powerful sorceress. I read that she once took on fifty men who raided her army camp and killed them all. She never leaves witnesses.

Before I even realize it, my gaze is drawn back to the Shadow Emperor—Theon Felix Osiris is his name, but no one ever refers to him that way. I wonder if they do in person. I can't see his face, but I can feel the energy surrounding him. I've never felt such power before. As far as I can tell, he hasn't spoken a word, yet it's clear that he is the most powerful man in the room.

I jump when he turns his head in my direction, and for a moment I swear I can feel his gaze on me. It lasts only a moment, and a sudden sense of loss washes over me when his attention is drawn away.

"Arabella!" Serena grabs my arm, her grip tight, and I turn to look at her in confusion, only to find that part of the wooden door is on fire.

I gasp and try to use my dress to put the flames out, but that only makes it worse.

"*Cursed*," I hear one of the maids mumble under her breath as she rushes toward us, trying to douse the flames with a bucket of water. Shock crashes through me as I stumble back, my eyes roaming over the disarray the kitchen is in. It's clear the fire spread quickly, and had the maid not been there to douse the flames, Serena and I would've been in danger.

"Don't listen to her," Serena tells me. "I'll ensure that you'll never see her again. Come. Let's go back to our rooms before Father finds out." I snap out of it and let her lead me away.

"She's right," I whisper as we round the corner, my heart heavy. "I'm cursed. Misfortune befalls me wherever I go, Ser. I'll be the downfall of us all."

Serena shakes her head, but I think deep down she knows it's true. She knows it as well as I do.

CHAPTER THREE

Arabella

My steps echo in the empty hallway, and though I keep my chin high, I'm shaking as I walk toward the throne room. It's never a good sign when my father calls me to this room. If Father found out I was once again nearby as an incident occurred in the castle, the consequences would be dire, especially because Serena was with me this time. She could've gotten hurt.

Nausea takes hold of me as my breaths become more shallow the closer I get to the wide wooden doors. The fact that there are no guards to let me in makes me even more anxious. I inhale deeply and push the doors open with trembling hands, surprised to find my father sitting in the seat he was in this afternoon, instead of on his throne. He lifts his head to look at me, and I stop in my tracks. I've never seen him look at me this way before, like he really sees me.

I've always been the daughter he despises, the one he wishes was never born. He has told me so on more than one occasion. All I am to him is a constant reminder of my mother, the sorceress he claims enchanted him. Father has ordered for her name to be stricken from our records, but he doesn't know about the archives kept hidden in a forgotten tower. If those records are to be believed, he fell in love with her at first sight, and the two were married within a year. Every portrait that he's hidden away and every record kept about them indicates they were happy—until the night I was born, six weeks sooner than anticipated. My mother used her healing magic to ensure I'd live, and she paid for my life with her own.

Father had her executed, certain she'd bewitched not only him but his court, too. He feared she had him under her spell, that her ultimate aim was to gain power in order to aid those just like her—magical beings who sought refuge. He was convinced she'd been funding a rebellion with his coin, and the magical attacks on our kingdom following her death only further fueled his beliefs.

To my father, I'm nothing but a shameful cursed being with cursed blood, one that is to blame for my stepmother's illness and subsequent death. He won't acknowledge the fact that she died of a failing liver, or that I was never alone with her and couldn't possibly have caused her harm.

Perhaps it would've been easier if I'd possessed my mother's magic, but I don't. The only thing I was born with was a penchant for misfortune, a curse that my father continuously reminds me befalls those of magical lineages. I've always been taught that the endless prosecution and eventual death that follows is a fair price to pay for the harm done by those who came before me, especially since our mere existence still brings illness and misfortune to our loved ones. But how could that be? I didn't choose to be born this way, and unlike the many sorceresses that have been burned all over the world, I don't have powers of any kind.

"Arabella," Father says as I curtsy, his voice soft. My heart starts to race nervously as I look at my father. He looks pained and tired. *Weak.* My father has never once looked regretful or anguished. According to the recordkeepers, he was impassive when he executed my mother for possessing magic, and I'm still haunted by the expressionless look on his face when I was pulled out of the lake

I nearly drowned in a year ago. He'd looked at me like he'd been disappointed I survived at all. So why does he look so troubled now?

"Sit," he tells me, pointing to the seat opposite him. I do as he asks, barely able to keep from shaking. Every fiber of my being is telling me to be terrified, and my intuition has never failed me before. Most nights I'm haunted by the memory of each form of punishment I have suffered through due to my curse. What will it be today? Will he succeed in breaking my spirit at last?

Father inhales deeply, as though he's bracing himself. I've never once seen him look conflicted, but he does now. "The Shadow Emperor asked for your hand in marriage." I stare at him, the words not quite registering. "He requested a swift ceremony. It will take place tomorrow."

Marriage? It can't be. Father knows. He *knows* Nathaniel is only a few days away from asking for my hand. Serena has been teasing me about it incessantly.

"You will do your duty as Crown Princess of Althea. This is the last we'll speak of this matter. Your hand in marriage in return for leniency for our kingdom."

I look up, my eyes filling with tears. "Father," I whisper, my voice breaking. "It can't be me he asked for. It can't be me he wants."

Throughout the years, this kingdom has taken everything from me. My mother. My happiness. My voice. Nathaniel is the only light in a world that's rapidly descending into darkness. I've never fought for anything. I've performed my duties, never asking for anything in return. I endured the rumors, the whispers, the pain.

"It's that curse of yours," my father says, sneering. "Why else would the Shadow Emperor's attention fall to our small kingdom?"

My eyes close as I inhale deeply. I'm well aware that the kingdom is better off without me. I am misfortune personified—yet I can't help but try to reach for happiness. I've never been this close. "*Please.*" My voice breaks, and I know that this moment of weakness has cost me any chance I had of getting out of this engagement. My father has always punished weakness in his children and his court, and this is the ultimate punishment.

His head snaps up, and I cower in fear when he rises to his feet. "You *will* marry him," he warns, his eyes filling with malice. "So help me Fates."

I lower my head, terror and despair battling for dominance, each adding to my mounting distress. Words elude me, yet I can't help but wonder if he's glad to be rid of me. I'm a thorn in his side, a relic of the sorceress who deceived him. The only thing that's keeping me alive is the fact that his blood, too, runs through my veins.

For a moment, I wonder if Serena was ever considered for this match, but then I smile wryly. Not even the power that comes from an allegiance like this is worth sacrificing a beloved daughter to a monster. They would never ask this of her. I inhale deeply as I rise to my feet and bow to my father before stepping away, well aware that changing his mind is impossible.

I'm resigned as I walk back to my room, my steps loud on the stone floor. I should've known better than to expect kindness and understanding from a man who has always wished I didn't exist. I should've known that there would come a time when he would sacrifice me.

"Arabella." I pause when I hear Nathaniel's voice, my heart constricting painfully. I can't face him. Not now. "Is it true?"

My eyes fall closed when he places his hand on my shoulder and turns me toward him. I swallow hard and look up into his golden-brown eyes. The hurt I see in them breaks what's left of my heart. "Yes," I whisper.

He tenses and takes a step back, his hand falling away. His expression mirrors my every feeling. Shock. Disbelief. Heartbreak. My throat burns with unshed tears, but I do my best to hold on. I can't break down now.

"When?"

I open my mouth, but the words won't come out. It's almost like I can't get myself to acknowledge it, like part of me hopes that not speaking of it will make the issue disappear. If only it were so simple.

"Tomorrow," a soft voice behind me sounds. I turn around to find Serena standing in the corner. I instantly take a step away from Nathaniel, knowing that we're too close for propriety.

"Serena," I murmur.

"I just heard the news." She pushes away from the wall and takes a step toward us, her eyes filled with the same emotions I just saw in Nathaniel's eyes. It oddly brings me a small amount of relief to know that there are people who will miss me, people who will mourn me.

"You don't have to do this," she says. I smile at my naïve little sister. She's never had to do anything she didn't want to do, so there's no way she could possibly understand.

"It's okay, Serena," I tell her, knowing in my heart that it's true. If I don't do this, it's the only other Princess of Althea he'll take. I could never watch my little sister marry a beast—not when I can take her place. I'd do anything for Serena. I just wish someone would do the same for *me*. Just *once*.

"She's right," Nathaniel says. "You don't have to do this."

He looks at me, a calculative glint in his eyes. Growing up, that look has always meant trouble, and I can't help but smile. "You can't save me," I tell him, knowing that it's true. "Not this time."

He and I have gotten into incessant trouble throughout the years, and marriage was meant to be our greatest adventure of all. Instead our story will come to an end before it even had a chance to truly begin.

Nathaniel straightens his shoulders and starts to speak, but I shake my head and take a step away. I can't do this today. I can't humor anyone else. I can't provide the consolation he's looking for—not when I need it so badly myself.

CHAPTER FOUR

Arabella

I flip through the pages of the oldest history books in the castle, each portraying Theon Felix Osiris as a cruel monster. No one knows how old the Shadow Emperor is, and for a while there was some speculation that he wasn't a person at all, but a myth whose mantle was passed down from one generation to another. After all, no one lives forever. Fates, no one lives as long as the Shadow Emperor seems to have. It should be impossible, yet it isn't.

I browse through the accounts of his conquests, each tale more gruesome than the last. He's conquered half the world, yet it never seems to be enough. Based on what I'm seeing, he mostly conquers lands with fertile grounds and crops, but we don't have any of those. Althea is known for its trade, and compared with the countries already under his command, there isn't much we can offer him.

I don't understand what he wants with us. With *me*. According to historical records, the Shadow Emperor has never been married, nor are there accounts of mistresses or concubines. The only woman he has ever been mentioned alongside is Elaine, who seemed to appear by his side a decade ago. She is as shrouded in mystery as he is. Why would he take a wife now? And why a Princess of Althea?

I'm trembling as I reach for yet another book about the Shadow

Emperor, fear chilling my skin. Will I survive? If I marry the monster, will I make it past our wedding night? Even if I fight him, I doubt I could harm him. My father won't avenge me, and I won't be able to protect myself. I don't stand a chance against him.

My eyes widen as I flip the pages and begin to read about his alchemy, my fear making way for intrigue. The Shadow Emperor is one of the last known alchemists alive, and according to this book, he's able to perform alchemy without needing to draw transmutation circles—circles that can be drawn on any surface, often with a pentagram inside, along with equations and ancient written text that allow an alchemist to channel the energy required to perform alchemy. It's unheard of, and if it's true, his alchemy wouldn't just look like magic to bystanders. It'd make him even more powerful than the rumors suggest.

> Alchemy is a forgotten science—it's similar to magic, yet different in its nature. While sorceresses can often conjure things out of nothing but the energy in our atmosphere, alchemy relies on the laws of equal exchange, which dictate that something cannot come out of nothing. For example, gold must be transmuted from another type of metal, and cannot be conjured with energy alone. The law of equal exchange is different from the natural balance sorcerers are subject to, which dictates that magic cannot be used for nefarious purposes without a hefty personal sacrifice.
>
> Magic is limited by spells, potions, and a caster's natural ability to channel and manipulate the life-force that magic utilizes, but alchemy is limited only by the alchemist's environment. To create a spear, an alchemist would need metal, yet a sorceress might be able to use energy in the ether. The difference, however, would be that the sorceress's spear is only as strong as her powers, and eventually, the spear would

return to the ether, often at a most inopportune moment.

An alchemists' spear would remain forever.

I bite down on my lip harshly as I continue to read about the Shadow Emperor's ability to manipulate sunlight into hot beams that cut straight through people, his command over the shadows that surround him, and his rare ability to use alchemy as a means of teleportation, moving objects at will. It appears he has found a way to weaponize even the most mundane things in ways magic users are simply incapable of, such as the air we breathe and the blood that courses through our veins.

If he so chose, he could suffocate me without so much as blinking, or render me completely immovable without the need for spells. All he'd have to do is displace the air in my lungs, or solidify it around me. My life would end before I even realize what's happening.

"Arabella?"

I look over my shoulder to find Nathaniel standing by the library doors, a look in his eyes that I can't quite decipher. "What's wrong?" I ask, my voice trembling.

He walks over to me and drops a bag beside my chair. "Let's go," he says, his voice soft as he pulls me to my feet. "I can't let you do this. I can't watch you marry someone else—least of all *him*."

I freeze and stare up at him in shock. It hadn't even occurred to me that I could run away. For once, I could choose myself. "And go where?" I ask, a hint of hope blooming deep within my chest. "My father would find us wherever we go, and when he eventually does, he'll have us hung for treason."

Nathaniel runs a hand through his hair, exuding the same restlessness I feel. "You're dead either way, Arabella. The Shadow Emperor… do you think he'll let you live? And if he does, for how long? What kind of existence will that be, living with a man like him?"

A shudder runs down my spine. "I can't run," I whisper. "He'll just take my sister. It's one thing to live a life in exile, but it's something else altogether to live with Serena's blood on my hands."

Nathaniel shakes his head. "Arabella, he didn't ask for just any of your father's daughters. He asked for you specifically."

"Me?" That can't be. I've never met him—I would remember if I had.

"Yes. *You.*"

Nathaniel stares at me as his words sink in. "You don't think he'll take Serena if I run?"

He shakes his head. "I'm certain. My father was present when the decree was delivered. You are to marry him. You, and no one else."

I raise my hand to my pounding heart, trying my best to hold on to the sliver of hope Nathaniel is handing me. He takes a step closer and places his hand on my shoulder, his eyes on mine. "I don't need to tell you how I feel about you, Arabella. I can't think of a future that you're not in. If that means the only way I get to have you is in exile, then so be it."

My heart races as I take in the sincerity in his eyes. I inhale shakily, allowing my thoughts to roam for a moment, to a future where Nathaniel and I are living together in a small house in an obscure village, somewhere no one knows who we are. It'd just be the two of us, without any royal obligations, no rumors about me being cursed. We could even live somewhere where magic isn't outlawed.

"You're certain?" I ask. "I have nothing to lose if I go. My life is already condemned. But you? You're in line to take over as my father's strategic adviser. You'd be one of the highest-ranking officers in the country. If we run, you'll lose everything."

He shakes his head and cups my cheek. "I won't. I'll gain everything I've ever wanted. Don't doubt my intentions, Arabella."

He seems so certain that my own hesitation seems foolish. Nathaniel is one of the smartest people I know. If he's proposing this as a solution, then that means it's the only viable option.

"Okay," I whisper, trying my hardest not to overthink this. "Let's go." This is likely our only chance at a future together. It isn't what I expected, but I'll take any chance of being with Nathaniel.

He smiles at me and bends down to pick up the bag at my feet. "I've already had some of your essentials packed. You cannot go to your room and be seen leaving with luggage. You cannot say goodbye to your family, either. We must have left the borders by the time they realize that we're gone. We must leave at once."

He's trying to tell me that I can't bid my farewell to Serena. I'll never see her again, and her last memory of me will be the devastation in my eyes as I found out about my impending marriage. "She'll forgive me, won't she?"

Nathaniel entwines our fingers and tightens his grip on my hand as he nods. "She just wants you to live, Arabella. To be happy."

I nod hesitantly and squeeze his hand, and for the first time since my father told me the news, I'm filled with hope instead of despair. My mind is racing as Nathaniel pulls me through hallways I didn't even know existed, expertly leading me down to the tunnels within minutes. It's clear he's been planning this from the second he found out, yet somehow, I can't shake the unease I feel. "These routes are known by very few people in the kingdom," he whispers as we enter the humid stone area. It's cold, and it's dark, and all of a sudden I wonder what I'm doing. Is it even possible to run from the Shadow Emperor?

"He'll kill us if we're caught," I whisper, uncertain who I'm even referring to. Our lives are forfeit regardless of whether it's the Shadow Emperor or my father that intercepts us.

Nathaniel reaches for something by the wall, and before long, we're bathed in light from the lamp in his hand. "We won't get caught," he promises. He seems so certain that I want to believe in him, but there's a niggling feeling deep down that I can't ignore. My intuition has never failed me. We won't make it.

I choose to remain quiet, to ignore the voices telling me to stop and turn back, because I know there's nothing for me there. The unknown lies ahead of me, but all that lies behind me is certain death.

Nathaniel holds my hand as we walk together, and I take comfort in his touch. He's always kept a polite distance, but tonight is different. Just as I've convinced myself that Nathaniel and I will be fine, a soft voice sounds ahead of me.

"Arabella of Althea," a woman says. "You must turn back. Your father has been notified of your actions."

I whirl around, trying to find the source of the voice and finding nothing but emptiness. My eyes find Nathaniel's, and he looks as horrified as I feel. Before either of us has a chance to respond, we're surrounded by the sound of footsteps rapidly catching up to us, echoes ringing through the tunnel.

My heart sinks when I recognize the soldiers running up to us, our kingdom's flag stitched to their uniforms. Nathaniel's father is at the head of the group, but his eyes aren't on me. They're on his son.

"Nathaniel Orathis, you are under arrest on account of treason."

CHAPTER FIVE

Arabella

Pure terror courses through my veins as I'm led to the stone tower my father has always used to imprison me whenever I find myself at the center of misfortune in the kingdom. This room holds nothing but horrible memories, yet I have a feeling that nothing I've been through compares to what is to come.

My head begins to pound in line with the hammering of my heart, and my vision begins to blur just as the two men dragging me up the tower begin to struggle to hold me down. The torches that illuminate the spiral staircase begin to burn brighter, courtesy of my curse, no doubt, and they tighten their grip on my arms, their movements becoming more frantic.

The soldiers let go of me to open the heavy metal doors, and neither of them looks me in the eye as they hold the door open for me. Part of me wants to beg them to save me, but I know I'm beyond salvation. I stopped begging years ago.

I'm not surprised to find my father standing in the room, a whip in his hands. Cold sweat licks at my skin, and bile rises up my throat. Magical objects are banned in our country, yet my father's army has a handful of torture devices I'm certain are magical. The thick leather whip in my father's hands is enchanted to heal the surface of your skin instantly, leaving you with pain but no visible scars. Of all my punishments, this is the one I hate most, and I suspect he knows it.

"You thought you could run from the Shadow Emperor?" He looks at me, his eyes blazing with a mixture of disgust and rage. "Who did you think would pay the price for your treachery?"

I gulp when my eyes land on the handcuffs he picks up from the floor, black tendrils of dark magic seeping out of the metal. For a moment I try to resist, wishing that I truly had my mother's magic, as he's always accused me of having. Maybe then, I'd be able to fight back. Maybe then, Nathaniel and I would've made it out alive and well.

My father binds my hands together using the enchanted cuffs, and I'm instantly immobilized, my body stiffening unnaturally. I have no doubt he'd make me wear them every day if it weren't an item he shouldn't even possess.

Father smiles as he pushes against my shoulder until I tumble onto a cold metal stool, my movements stiff and unnatural. I've been here countless times, yet it never gets easier. I used to fight him, before he acquired the cuffs, but in time, I learned that my punishments only get worse if I do.

I try my best to brace myself for the inevitable pain, but it doesn't come. Usually my father can't wait to get started with disciplining me, hoping to beat the curse out of me, but today he just stands and stares at me, his gaze burning. "Answer me."

It takes me a moment to even remember his question. Fear controls my every thought, and I feel sick to my stomach. "I *wasn't* thinking, Father. I was terrified of marrying a monster and dying at his hands... I just wanted to *live*."

My father laughs, the sound in contrast with the swishing of the whip. It comes down on my back with such force that I struggle to stay in my seat. It feels like fire burns underneath my skin, coursing its way through to every last nerve ending, and I clench my teeth to keep from screaming. It's futile, but it's the last bit of control I hold.

"It's our entire kingdom you put at stake. You were to be traded in return for leniency for our kingdom."

The whip comes down again, and this time I don't manage to stay silent. I cry out in pain, and that only makes my father more angry. He hates weakness. "I'm sorry," I beg. *"Please*, Father." I say the words without thinking. Years of this should have taught me that my father knows no mercy, yet each time I try.

"Did the Orathis boy touch you?" he spits, raising his whip all over again.

"N-No! I swear it, Father. He had nothing to do with this. It was all me," I tell him, praying he'll have mercy on Nathaniel.

He hits me again, and this time I nearly choke from the air that suddenly rushes through my lungs. Much like the fire that flooded my body earlier, burning me from the inside, the air I breathe is now trying its best to suffocate me. The whip's powers are so reminiscent of what I've read about the Shadow Emperor that I can't help but choke out a laugh, the irony not lost on me. I'm moving from one tyrant's household to another. I won't die here tonight, but if I'm lucky, I'll die at the Shadow Emperor's hands tomorrow. Maybe then I'll finally know real peace.

"You *will* marry the Shadow Emperor tomorrow, and you'll do it with a smile on your face. Hesitate for even a second, and I'll have the boy hung."

I nod as tears fall down my cheeks. The whip stings, but physical pain is bearable. It's the heartache that has me shedding tears. I feel foolish for thinking that I could get away. For thinking that my father might understand, or that he might console me.

"You're just like your mother," he says, his voice radiating with anger. "She'd have condemned this kingdom to ruin by welcoming in those who bring misfortune if she'd had a chance, and you're just as selfish. You, too, would condemn an entire kingdom for your own selfish desires."

Part of me is tempted to argue with him. No territory that has been conquered by the Shadow Emperor has suffered, provided that it didn't resist, nor have there been reports of misfortune befalling the countries he's established safe havens in. It's not the kingdom my father is trying to protect. It's his position as king. He knows failure to comply with the Shadow Emperor's demands means being replaced.

"Did I ever mean anything to you, Father? I know you never loved me, but did you ever care at all?" I turn my head and stare up at him through teary eyes. He pauses as though caught by surprise. I have always endured the punishments he gave me for merely being who I was born as, never daring to ask for his love. But now? Now I have nothing left to lose. He can't hurt me any more than he already has.

"You are my daughter," he answers, evading the question. That in itself should tell me enough.

"If it was Serena that he'd asked for, would you have agreed?"

His eyes widen in anger, and when he raises his whip again, I have my answer. "Don't even dream of asking your sister to take your place!"

I shake my head to deny the allegation, but I should know better by now. There's no reasoning with my father. When it comes to me, he only hears what he wants to hear. Nothing I do or say will ever be right.

Except this. This marriage. Walking down the aisle tomorrow might very well be the only thing I'll ever do right in his eyes. The whip comes down on my back again, and this time I fiercely wish it truly could burn me until I'm nothing but ashes. My vision begins to swim as my father's last hit makes me fall off my seat, and my eyes fall closed as I welcome the darkness, my broken heart bleeding out on these cold stone floors.

CHAPTER SIX

Arabella

Light seeps through the bars by the window, and I stare at the wall as the shadows fade, my cheek pressed against the cold stone floor. I haven't moved from where my father left me last night—I know better than to try to escape this room. Besides, I won't be left here for long this time. Today is my wedding day, after all.

I inhale shakily and curl into a ball, relieved to find that at least my hands were uncuffed before Father left me here. If this is how I'm being treated, then how must Nathaniel be doing? Did they lock him up? Will he face punishment for what we did? I was selfish when I said yes, and I should've known better. I should've known I could never get away, and that I'd drag Nathaniel down with me.

Before long, I hear the sound of footsteps coming up the stairs. They're light. Handmaidens, most likely. I don't sit up when the door opens. I used to—I used to pretend I was fine, that my father hadn't hurt me. After all, there was never any evidence. Today I don't have it in me. Besides, it doesn't matter. Today is likely the last time I'll see anyone in this castle.

"Your Highness," one of the girls says. She bends down and helps me up, her face marred with concern. Mary, I believe her name is.

I will myself to fake a smile for her, but I fail miserably. "Oh, Your Highness," she whispers, squeezing my hand.

She helps me down the stairs, to the bedroom that will no longer be mine after today. I pause in the doorway and stare at the bags in my room in shock. All of my belongings have been packed—there's nothing left in this room that indicates it once used to be mine. It took only a few hours to erase all proof of my existence, and I have no doubt I'll be forgotten before long.

Mary grabs my hand and leads me to my vanity silently, her expression filled with the same sorrow I'm feeling. "We're going to make you look so beautiful, Your Highness," she says, clearly at a loss for words.

I nod at her and will myself to keep it together. When I fell asleep on the cold stone floor last night, I knew my life was over. I just need to learn to accept that now.

"Nathaniel," I murmur, my voice hoarse, and Mary freezes.

"I don't know, Your Highness," she whispers. "I've heard rumors about him being in the dungeons, but I can't be sure."

I nod and let my eyes close. If he's in the dungeons, then at least he's alive. That's all I can ask for.

"Your sister has been told not to leave her room until the ceremony. There are guards posted at her bedroom door," Mary tells me as she leads me to a steaming bath.

I'm numb as I let Mary perform her duties. My father is keeping the only two people I love hostage. If I attempt to escape, if I so much as veer off course, it's Nathaniel and Serena who'll pay for it.

I never thought my father would involve Serena. The fact that he has proves that this union means more to him than his beloved daughter does. I'll need to be careful today if I want to keep them out of harm's way.

I'm absentminded as Mary starts to apply my makeup, my heart aching in a way it never has before. I don't think this type of pain will ever heal. It makes the pain in my back pale in comparison. I've never felt so abandoned, so discarded.

"Take a look," Mary says as she leads me to a mirror. I stare at my reflection in confusion, barely recognizing myself. There is not a single blemish on my face. She has somehow managed to make my skin glow the way I imagined it would have if I were marrying Nathaniel today instead. There are no bags underneath my eyes, though weariness seeps through my bones.

The intricate lace my wedding gown is made of must have been costly, especially on such short notice—but then again, that is a small price to pay in return for safety from the Shadow Emperor's savage army.

Intense loneliness blooms from my chest, pushing tears into my eyes that I attempt to keep from falling. I've never hated my reflection more than I do at this moment. I look like a happy bride, nervous with pre-wedding jitters, when in reality, I'm terrified.

"You look beautiful." I swallow down the anger crawling up my spine and force a smile onto my face at the sound of my father's voice. Years and years of biting my tongue are all that's keeping me together today.

I hate you for doing this to me, is what I want to say. "Thank you, Father," is what escapes my lips.

He smiles, genuine glee in his eyes. This is what I imagined he'd look like on the wedding day of my dreams. I imagined him smiling at me with pride on his face, and my heart would overflow with love instead of resentment, as it does now.

He offers me his arm, his smile slipping when I hesitate. "Don't make this any harder on yourself than it needs to be," he warns me. A shiver of fear runs down my spine and I straighten, the fabric of my dress brushing against my injured back tauntingly, a blatant reminder of the consequences I'll face if I deviate from the path my father carved out for me. Nathaniel is only safe for as long as I cooperate.

I drop my eyes and take his arm, the two of us silent as he walks me down the hallway that leads to the ballroom. This might well be the very last time I walk these halls. This might be the last time I see my father, and I despise that part of me hopes it is.

Would he care? If the Shadow Emperor kills me tonight or in the days to follow, will my father live with regret, or will he move on and see me as but one of his many chess pieces? A soft huff escapes my lips as I smile to myself mockingly. If I could guarantee Nathaniel's and Serena's safety, I'd try to burn this entire castle down.

Father is likely glad to be rid of me, one way or another. At least this way, my demise benefits him. At last, I've made myself useful to him. We pause in front of the doors to the ballroom, and he turns to me as though he's about to say something, but then the doors swing open and the moment fades. His expression hardens, and he straightens as he leads me through the doors.

I tense when my eyes land on my betrothed. The rumors are true, it seems. He's as tall as they say he is, towering above everyone else. His signature dark cloak keeps him hidden from view, even today. Might he truly be as horrendous as the vilest of creatures? A beast on two legs?

And if he is, would it matter? It's not like I'll get to walk away from this union. If it had just been my father's life for mine, I would've left. My father doesn't deserve the sacrifice I'm about to make. But the people in this room? My sister? Nathaniel? Our citizens? They don't deserve to face the consequences of my selfishness.

Father pauses in front of the Shadow Emperor and, much to my surprise, bows low.

I stare at him in shock. I've never seen my father bow to anyone. He shakes me out of my stupor and pulls on my hand, forcibly dragging me down with him, the fabric of my dress rubbing against my injured back painfully. The surface of my skin has healed, but the wounds are still fresh just below view.

"Rise, Arabella." A shiver runs down my spine at the sound of his smooth, deep voice. It's not at all eerie or monstrous, as I expected. "You will never bow to me again."

A gloved hand appears in my field of vision, and I take it hesitantly. Part of me expected his touch to hurt, but his hand is warm even through his glove. He pulls me toward him, and I take a step closer hesitantly. He towers above me, and it isn't until I'm standing next to him that I realize he didn't wait for my father to place my hand in his, as is customary. I don't dare look back. Never before have I been this filled with fear. Fear of my father acting on the embarrassment he must feel, fear of the Shadow Emperor retaliating, fear of the life that lies ahead of me. He keeps his hand wrapped around mine, and that, too, scares me. His touch terrifies me.

I can barely focus on the ceremony, but part of me is glad that it isn't the altar we're standing in front of. It never even occurred to me that getting married outside the house of the Gods who abandoned me so long ago was an option. But then again, where else does one marry a demon?

I straighten when I hear my name and look up at the officiant, repeating after him word for word, acutely aware of the moment I sign away my life. "I do," I murmur, as though part of me is trying to keep the words in.

His voice doesn't break like mine did, nor does he hesitate. When he says "I do," it's with conviction. He sounds so certain, and I can't help but wonder why. Why me?

I tense when we're proclaimed husband and wife, knowing what comes right after that moment. The first kiss. The moment that most brides long for, and something I've dreamed of so many times. Except it wasn't the man standing in front of me I thought I'd kiss. I swallow hard as my thoughts turn to Nathaniel, glad he isn't here to see this.

Fear runs down my spine when the Shadow Emperor steps forward, bridging the distance between us. The air buzzes around him, almost like his aura is a living, breathing thing of its own, and my breath hitches when his gloved hand cups my face, his gentle touch entirely at odds with everything I thought I knew about him.

I look up at him, my curiosity outweighing my fear. I married the Shadow Emperor, and I still don't know what he looks like. It isn't just the cloak—it truly is as though he's cast in shadows. I stare at him, yet I can't seem to really see him. He seems covered in shimmery translucent energy that blurs his features.

"All in due time," he says before leaning in, his voice soft. The seconds begin to stretch, each moment lasting an eternity. My eyes flutter closed as I will myself to imagine Nathaniel, ignoring the way his hand slides into my hair, and the way he pulls me a little closer. I do everything in my power to forget who it is I just married, but the moment our lips meet, something I've never felt before rushes through my body, something exhilarating and freeing, and I can't help but lean into his touch, tilting my head just slightly.

My new husband groans, our bodies crashing against each other as he parts my lips, his tongue stroking mine for a split second, before he tenses and gently pulls away, leaving his hand in my hair. I look up, confused by my racing heart and the tenderness he showed me, only to be met with that same blurred image. Even so, I can't help but admit that for a few moments, he made me feel safe and wanted, two things I never expected to feel in his presence.

He turns and pulls me with him, and I try my best to collect myself as the two of us walk down the aisle hand in hand, the way any other married couple would. I try my hardest to smile, but it's to no avail. Despite the fraction of hope that kiss instilled in me, there's no denying that while this union is a beacon of hope to so many, it is a death sentence to me.

CHAPTER
SEVEN

Felix

The first thing I noticed about her was the sorrow in her eyes. It hasn't escaped my notice that the boy she's in love with is notably absent. No doubt he's facing the consequences of his actions last night. If not for the tracking and protection spells Elaine cast the moment the union was agreed upon, they might have slipped through my fingers, gone forever.

I tighten my grip on her hand, trying my hardest to suppress the hope her presence awakens within me. It's as if I took it from her to sustain myself.

Arabella of Althea. If the prophecy holds true, she'll be the one to break the curse. Two hundred years, and I'd almost forgotten what hope felt like. Until her. I always knew it would be a woman who would break the curse, but for years, Pythia was unable to see who it would be. Now that I've found her at last, renewed purpose surges within me.

I glance down at my newly wedded wife, uncertainty drowning out the hope she instilled in me. She's young, and she hardly looks powerful. If anything, she looks easily cowed. It wouldn't surprise me if she runs at the sight of me. She wouldn't be the first.

We enter the throne room together, and I struggle to keep my impatience in check. I must return to the palace soon. The longer and farther I'm away, the worse the effects of the curse. It's manageable now, but there's something about Althea that makes me feel more uneasy than usual—almost as though the curse knows I'm a step closer to breaking it.

Arabella seems tense beside me, her hand loose in mine, as though she wishes she didn't have to touch me at all. Her eyes roam over the guests in the ballroom, her shoulders straightening when her gaze lands on a blond woman just a few years younger than her. Her sister, I suspect.

The two women exchange a look of longing, and much to my surprise, Arabella smiles in reassurance. It's the first time I've seen her smile, and it's a sight to behold. When is the last time I saw someone smile in my presence?

It's obvious that Arabella had no real choice in this union, and she undoubtedly resents me for taking her away from her people under threat of violence. Perhaps Elaine was right. Winning her over won't be easy, and I won't do myself any favors if I make her leave seconds after the ceremony, without giving her a chance to enjoy her people's customs.

Arabella pauses in the middle of the room and turns to me, her smile vanishing. I tense when I realize what is expected of me. *A dance.* I haven't danced in decades.

I reluctantly place my hand on her waist, pretending not to notice when she winces. My touch repulses her, and she hasn't even seen me yet.

Her hand trembles as she lifts it to my chest. She's tall for a woman, but she's tiny compared with me. Something about her is surprisingly...endearing. I pull her closer, no doubt scandalizing her, and she winces again. I pause and study her face. She's not repulsed. *She's in pain.*

"You're injured."

Her eyes widen slightly and she looks up, a moment of confusion marring her beautiful face when she can't quite make out my features, courtesy of a spell Elaine cast for me. Arabella shakes her head and smiles tightly, but I see straight through her denial.

She and I move slowly, and I let my fingers trail over her back, noting the pain she tries so hard to hide. "Who did this to you?"

She shakes her head again and tightens her grip on my cloak, her eyes downcast. Anger rolls down my spine at her silence, and I pause, the two of us coming to a standstill.

"You *will* tell me," I warn her. "The question is, will you do it voluntarily?"

A shiver runs down her arms, and I inhale deeply, regret filling me instantly. Elaine has warned me countless times to be gentle with her, yet I've failed within an hour of marrying her.

"My father," she whispers eventually, her voice so soft I nearly missed it.

"Why?"

She looks up then, fire replacing the sorrow in her eyes. "I tried to run from you. From this."

The corners of my lips turn up into a reluctant smile as she lets her anger loose, her eyes dancing with fury. I've been wondering if the prophecy was wrong, because surely a demure girl like her can't be our savior. *Demure*... I see it now. She's all but.

I take a step away from her and turn to find her father already staring at us, a hint of fear in his eyes. He probably knows what's coming. I raise my hand, and just like that, the king is lifted into the air, hovering above the crowd, at my mercy. The music stops, and a hush falls over the ballroom.

"My bride is injured," I say, my voice soft. "Who touched her?" He opens his mouth to reply, but I shake my head and decrease the airflow to his lungs. "I'll have your tongue if you lie to me."

The king's eyes widen, and I loosen my grip just slightly, allowing him to speak. "Me," he says, sounding regretful. "It was me."

I pull the King of Althea closer and lower him to the floor in front of me, my jaw clenched in an effort to suppress my anger. This man dared to hurt the only person who can save my people?

Arabella instinctively takes a step away, as though she fears her father more than she fears me, and that's entirely unacceptable. I won't have anyone who carries my name fear a man like him. "Bring me the instrument you dared to harm my wife with." Only a magical object could have harmed her this way while under Elaine's protection spell.

The king stands in front of me, his eyes wide, seemingly in shock, and I snap my fingers. Just like that, the force of the air around his fingers compresses, until his little finger breaks. A loud scream escapes his lips, echoing through the quiet room as he falls to his knees in front of me. He clutches his hand to his chest in pain, true terror filling his eyes.

"I'll break a finger for every minute I'm left waiting. I'm not a patient man."

He finally snaps out of his self-pity and nods at one of his soldiers. I'm tempted to break another one of his fingers when it takes the soldier two minutes to get back, but I resist when I see the dark mahogany box being carried into the room, wild magic radiating off it. I frown and open it to find a black leather whip coated in malice.

"You dared use this against my wife after you promised me her hand?"

His silence speaks volumes. I flick my wrist and turn him around against his will, his back facing me as I lift the whip high before bringing it down hard. He screams, the sound echoing through the ballroom, his shouts even more shrill than the one before.

If this man is in that much pain, how would Arabella have

screamed? How much pain has she been in? How much pain is she still in? "How many times did he hit you?" I ask her.

She looks up at me, her gaze unfocused due to the spell marring my features. "I lost count," she whispers, her voice trembling. I'm scaring her, but it's better this way. I'd rather not hide my true nature. It's best that she sees me for who I am from the start.

I flick my wrist and have the whip move on its own, hitting down on the king over and over again, until regret is all he exudes, his tortured screams echoing through the room.

"Please," Arabella whispers.

I turn to her, surprised. "You'd ask for mercy on his behalf after what he did to you?"

She nods. "He is my father. I would bestow upon him the mercy I wish he had granted me."

I stare at her, taking in her features. Her eyes are filled with tears, and she's clearly terrified, yet she stands in front of me asking for my mercy when her father does not deserve it.

Arabella of Althea. She might surprise me yet.

"Very well."

I snap my fingers, and the whip falls to the ground. "Have that disposed of," I order. "I don't ever want to see it again."

Three of my men jump into action as I turn back to my wife. "We're leaving." I'm not willing to entertain her any longer. My outburst has brought the bloodlust I fight so hard to the surface. I don't have much time.

Arabella nods and looks back into the room, her eyes roaming over the crowd, settling on her sister for a moment. She smiles in reassurance before she turns and follows me, looking back once.

I have no doubt it's the boy she's looking for. He isn't present today, and if I have it my way, he'll never come near her again.

CHAPTER
EIGHT

Arabella

His cloak sweeps over the floor as the Shadow Emperor walks through the large doors at the entrance of our castle, my luggage floating behind him. I've never seen powers like his before. The way he broke my father's finger without a second thought and whipped him for all to see seemed effortless, as if it required little to no thought for him. If he's capable of doing that with such ease, then what could he do to me?

"You best hurry," a soldier tells me, a surprisingly friendly look on his face. "His Excellency doesn't like to be kept waiting."

I nod and force my trembling legs forward, willing myself not to look back at the castle I'm leaving my heart in. I have no idea if Nathaniel is safe, and no way of helping him escape punishment. I told my father that it was all my fault, but I doubt that'll be enough.

I might never see him again. He's in the dungeons because of me, and I can't even tell him how sorry I am. Fates, based on what I just witnessed, there's a chance I might not make it through tonight.

"You'll ride with me." The Shadow Emperor doesn't look my way, but it's clear that it's me he's speaking to. I glance at the giant horse with its unnaturally black eyes and shudder in fear. Sirocco is even more terrifying up close than he was in the horrendous illustrations I've seen. My eyes trail to the carriage and I try to work up the courage to ask if I can ride in that instead, but I fail.

"Theon."

I freeze at the sound of that voice. It's the same voice I heard last night in the tunnels. My heart hammers in my chest as I turn to look at the woman standing next to the Shadow Emperor. *Elaine*. She wasn't standing next to him mere seconds ago, but I'm certain it's her voice I heard.

"She can ride with me," she says.

Every instinct is telling me that I'm no safer with her than I am with the Shadow Emperor himself, especially if she knows I tried to run last night. Pure bitterness rushes through me as I take her in. I used to idolize her. Growing up, she was the only woman I knew of who was more powerful than her male counterparts. Once upon a time, I wanted to be just like her. Now I regret that our paths ever crossed. If not for her, Nathaniel and I might have been in a different country by now. Instead, he and I are both captives of different kinds.

"No," he says, and I tense. I might dislike Elaine, but I'd still choose to ride with her over riding with him. Before I realize what's happening, I'm lifted off the floor, the air around me solidifying. I gasp and flail out of fear of falling and stare down at the floor below me in shock, eliciting a chuckle from him. He moves his fingers, and as he does so, I move through the air, toward him. This feeling... feeling this helpless and weak... I *hate* it.

He lowers me on top of his horse and I instantly bury my hand through its dark mane, scared of being lifted off again. I've never felt anything like that before. I lost all control over my body and was entirely at his mercy, even more so than when I wore the handcuffs. Is that what the rest of my life will be like? Being thrown around at his every whim?

"Your Excellency," I say, my voice trembling. "I'm perfectly capable of getting on a horse myself."

He doesn't acknowledge me as he joins me on the horse, seating himself behind me. I regretted my words from the moment they left my lips, and I count my blessings when he ignores them. The few words I just uttered could result in endless pain for me. I could suffer like my father did.

"*Felix*," he says eventually. "You are my wife, Arabella. You'll call me Felix."

I stiffen when he reaches around me to grab the reins, entirely too close for comfort. His *wife*. The word and everything it encompasses terrifies me.

His chest brushes against my back, and I try my hardest to move away, to no avail. "Your squirming is futile," he tells me. "The force of our movement will have you pressing into me, whether you like it or not. You'd better get used to it."

I choose to ignore his words and hold on to Sirocco's mane, but the second we start to gallop I'm pressed into him just as he said I would be. Sirocco is much faster than any other horse I've ever ridden, and it's terrifying. Much to my surprise, Felix wraps one arm around my torso, keeping me securely in place.

"It's safer like this, Arabella. Carriages are always at risk, but nothing can harm you so long as you are with me."

There's a hint of concern in his voice, and I frown. I suppose I did just become the wife of the most powerful man in the world. I have no doubt that his list of enemies is endless. It hadn't occurred to me that I might become a target, too. "How far is it?" I force myself to ask, already barely able to bear the pain caused by the pressure against my injured back.

"It should take us half a day on Sirocco, weather permitting, but our entourage can't keep up that pace. Once we're on Eldirian grounds, we will leave them behind. It will take them a day and a half to reach the palace."

I nod and try my best to relax, to endure the pain, but the way his body presses against mine doesn't make it easy. My eyes fall closed and I inhale shakily, trying my hardest to focus on something else.

He terrifies me, but he doesn't seem to be the beast everyone says he is. He feels normal to me. I'm not particularly well acquainted with the anatomy of a man, but from what I can tell, he doesn't seem to be deformed. He seems strong and wide. Even his voice sounds normal—melodic even. Some of the things I've read about him are definitely true, but some might not be.

I glance at him over my shoulder, curious. "Why can't I see you properly?" I don't even realize I've said the words until they leave my lips. My stomach tightens as I wait for him to reply, part of me hoping he'll ignore the question altogether.

"It's an enchantment." He tightens his grip on me, and all it does is increase the pain in my back. "Why would you want to see me?"

I don't have an answer to that. I can't decide whether I'm better off keeping my distance from him or endearing myself to him—I can't decide what will keep me safer. "I'd like to know who I married," I eventually answer honestly.

I feel his gaze on the back of my head and tighten my grip on the horse's mane, refusing to let fear rule me. "You're in pain." It isn't a question, but I nod nonetheless. I have a feeling he'd see through any lies I try to tell him, and I'm not about to give him any excuses to punish me.

He slows the horse's pace until we're riding alongside Elaine. "We'll stop by the falls," he tells her, his voice soft and calm. The look the two of them exchange tells me they had no plans to stop so soon, and I can't help the gratitude I feel.

I'm concerned that the pain might cause me to faint, since it's not uncommon for that to happen in the days after one of my father's punishments. Fainting while on top of Sirocco would cost me my life.

By the time the horse comes to a standstill, I'm shaking and so lightheaded that I fear I might fall off at any moment. Felix jumps off the horse, and much to my surprise, he offers me his hand instead of lifting me off using his alchemy. I hesitate before slipping my hand against his leather glove. My eyes try to find his, but the spell on him makes it impossible to do so. It leaves me feeling disoriented as he helps me down with a gentleness that I'd never have expected of him.

He turns to Sirocco and grabs an apple from one of the pockets in the saddle, handing it to his horse with the same gentleness he just bestowed on me. It's on the tip of my tongue to ask if Sirocco truly is from Hell, but I value my life just enough not to utter those words.

I lean back against the tree he's tied Sirocco to and watch him groom his horse while his soldiers set up tents around us. For some reason, I didn't expect him to take care of Sirocco himself. There's something so human about him, but simultaneously I can't help but feel like that's all an illusion.

"I forget that you aren't a soldier. You're nothing like Elaine. I assumed you'd last until we made it back to Eldiria, but I should have known better."

I freeze and wrap my arms around myself, unsure of what to make of his comment. Is he chastising me or is he apologizing? Either way, he's got me feeling beyond confused. I was expecting fear and torture, but he hasn't hurt me. I'm relatively certain that we've stopped because he realized I was in pain, and his kindness throws me off. I turn away from him and watch the soldiers build up the tents at inhuman speed. What should take hours takes them only minutes.

"It's magic." I glance back at the Shadow Emperor, *Felix*. I can't quite get used to his name, not even in my head. To be on a first-name basis with him... it's strange. "Magic isn't banned in my empire," he tells me. His tone makes me feel like I'm missing something, like I should be reading between the lines. "We encourage the use and mastery of it. I do not believe that a sorceress was behind the plague, nor do I believe misfortune befalls those of magical lineages. That is merely a tactic that lets those who fear magic subjugate what they do not understand."

I nod hesitantly, my mind reeling. He doesn't believe the curse I was born with is real? I wish it were true, but there's no denying the countless fires that have started near me, or the typhoons and earthquakes that immobilized me each time I tried to run away after my father's punishments, fueled by rage and pain.

"Come." He gestures toward the small tent in the middle, and I hesitate before following him. It hadn't occurred to me yet that he'd expect his wife to share his tent. Despite the ceremony, I don't feel married.

I follow him through the doorway and gasp when I lay eyes on the interior. It's enormous inside, and everything is decorated decadently, with lush carpets and endless wide wooden doors. It looks like there are half a dozen rooms in what should be a small tent.

He walks through the door in the back, and I join him in what appears to be his bedroom. My nerves skyrocket, and for a moment, I almost missed the familiar woman standing next to the bed.

"Theon," she says, her eyes drifting over me in surprise, as though she hadn't expected him to bring me to his room. That in itself is a relief. It means he might just be showing me around.

"Elaine," he replies, his voice flat.

She straightens and smiles at me, her expression impossible to read. "It's an honor to finally formally meet you," she says.

I nod politely, wishing the circumstances were different. Once upon a time, I would have loved to meet her. I'd have been in awe. Now I find myself barely able to restrain my anger.

"Elaine is my most trusted adviser," he tells me. "She commands our army in my absence and plays a key role in facilitating trade among all our different regions."

I nod as though I didn't already know that, unsure how much to divulge. There's no way of knowing whether what I've read is truthful or not, after all.

"I wanted to check in with you about the unexpected stop," Elaine says, sounding worried. Her gaze is searching, and what she seems to find does not reassure her. Can she see through the enchantment? "I fear we will be at risk if we remain here too long."

Who would ever dare attack the Shadow Emperor? Surely no one would be quite so foolish?

"We'll stay an hour."

Elaine visibly tenses and stares at him, her brows slightly raised. It looks like a change in plans isn't common for them. "Very well," she says, turning to walk away.

My heart starts to race when the door closes behind her. I've never been alone with him before, and I'm terrified of what he'll do to me.

"Come here."

I swallow hard and take a small step closer to him. I'm shaking so badly that it's impossible to hide my fear.

"I hate having to repeat myself, Arabella."

I nod and step forward, letting my eyes close as I stand before him, like the coward I am. He moves around me and places his hands on my corset, untying it slowly, and I clutch my chest when it comes loose, scared of what he's about to do to me. I'm in so much pain that I don't have sufficient energy to even attempt fighting him.

I whimper when I hear the sound of my dress ripping, cool air brushing over my skin. He places his palm on my skin, and I gasp as a strange sensation washes over me, cooling down the invisible welts my father left. We stand there together for what feels like countless minutes, the pain slowly ebbing away, and I nearly collapse in relief. Usually, the whipping is the least painful part of my punishments. It's the healing of wounds that can't be treated that hurts the most.

"Better?"

I nod and turn to face him, only to recoil at the sight of him. The enchantment that blurred his face is no longer there, and I stumble back as I take in the thick black veins that move over his face like slithering snakes, obscuring his features. Pure horror rushes through me, and he rushes to pull his hood over his face, but not before I catch a glimpse of his turquoise irises, specks of gold illuminating his otherwise dark features. Somehow, I expected his eyes to be like Sirocco's, but they aren't. Something akin to dejection flashes through his eyes before he averts his gaze and pulls his hood farther down.

He reaches for me, and I wince instinctively, only for the fabric against my back to mend itself until, once more, my dress is whole again and my corset is tied. Remorse instantly rushes through me, and he sighs as he steps back farther. "We should resume our journey," he says, his voice weary as he turns and walks away, leaving me standing in his empty bedroom by myself.

CHAPTER NINE

Arabella

Felix's chest presses against my back as we resume our journey, his earlier actions still echoing through my mind. He treated me with kindness and took away my pain without punishing me for inconveniencing his soldiers and delaying the journey. I'm unsure what to make of him. My every instinct is telling me to fear him, to not lower my guard, and my intuition has never failed me. The sooner I figure out why he unsettles me so, the better. After all, the most powerful man in the world does not marry an unknown princess from a kingdom that's useless to him for no reason. The quicker I find out why he married me, the more indispensable I can make myself, and the safer I'll be.

Felix wraps his hand around my waist, and I gasp in surprise. His touch is intimate, and it startles me. Ever since he healed my wounds, he's kept as much distance as our positions allow us, keeping his hands on the reins.

"Look," he says, leaning in. His lips brush over my ear, and a shiver runs down my spine. His breath is so warm and so in contrast with the cold air around us. "Look closely."

I stare ahead, curious as to what I'm supposed to be seeing. We've been riding through the woods for hours now, following a nonexistent path that the horses seem familiar with. I tense when the forest gets thicker, the small path we were on disappearing into lines and lines of trees that absolutely won't let us pass, yet Sirocco keeps going straight ahead, straight into the trees.

Felix's grip on me tightens, and I feel his gaze on me, but I can't look away from our impending doom. Just as I'm certain we're about to crash into the trees, they part.

"Fates," I whisper as a wide path reveals itself in front of us, the trees locking us back in from behind. It's one of the most beautiful things I've ever seen, nature allowing us to pass through like that.

"Welcome to Eldiria," he says. "Welcome home."

Home. It's strange, but no one has ever said those words to me before. Not once. "Eldiria," I repeat. It's the name of his vast empire, but initially, it was just this. A small country surrounded by thick woods, cutting it off from most of the rest of the world.

The temperature drops rapidly within a matter of minutes, until the roads are covered with snow and ice, daylight fading as we ride deeper into Eldiria. I've never experienced anything like it. I shiver, and Felix brushes his hands over my shoulders. Warmth rushes through me, and I sigh in relief even as I begin to wonder where he's channeling the heat from. If he truly is an alchemist, as the books claim, there must be a heat source he's using. Magic crystals, perhaps? Surely it can't be his own body heat he's giving me?

Snow starts to fall around us and the trees thin until a beautiful white palace lies before us. As we get closer, I realize that the entire staff must have come out to welcome us. "They're here for you," Felix tells me.

There must be hundreds of people standing in the cold, all of them looking happy and hopeful, waving as we ride past them. I force myself to smile back and wave as best as I can. This I can do. I'm used to being a princess, a member of royalty.

"Ready?"

I nod, even though I'm not. I'm scared of what lies ahead of me.

Althea was never a place I loved, but I can't help but feel like things are only about to get worse in Eldiria.

Felix gets off the horse, but this time he doesn't grab my hand. He reaches for me and wraps his hands around my waist, lifting me off with ease until he's carrying me in his arms, a show for his people no doubt. His body feels strong against mine, his chest wide and his steps purposeful. He's hidden behind his cape once more, and it makes it easier to pretend that he's just a man, and that this is just a moment of pretense between newlyweds.

Cheers erupt around us, and my cheeks heat until they're blazing. I'm stiff in his embrace, yet I force myself to smile as Felix gently carries me toward the entrance, my body pressed against his.

This is what I'd imagined it'd be like with Nathaniel. He'd carry me, and all of Althea would celebrate us. It'd be the start of a new chapter, one where he and I would officially be a family of our own. Instead, I'm in the arms of the most feared man in the world, forcing a smile onto my face for his people.

Felix takes his time walking toward the palace, and I take the opportunity not just to study his people but also to study the exterior of the palace. It isn't white, as I initially assumed. It's covered in snow.

Felix's entire body appears to relax as we enter the palace, and his shoulders sag, almost as though in relief. He holds me a little tighter as he carries me to the staircase, and I squirm. "You can put me down now," I whisper, but he shakes his head, his hood swaying a little.

"Let the staff have a show. They deserve it."

I glance at the people around us, each of them smiling with happiness and hope. It's the hope that surprises me. Their gazes are filled with longing and expectation, and I need to find out why. Silence engulfs us as we reach the top floor, which is devoid of members of staff. "This is my floor," he tells me. "Ours."

Ours. The thought of that doesn't scare me as much as it did yesterday, but I'm still worried. I can't help but think of Nathaniel and everything I wanted to share with him. Instead, I'm being carried into what appears to be Felix's bedroom, the room surprisingly similar to the one in the tent.

"What is on your mind?" he asks as he puts me down, and I look up in surprise, instantly feeling guilty. "I have not seen you make that expression before."

He's been watching me that closely? "Oh, it's nothing. I was just thinking of home," I admit.

He looks at me as he pushes back his hood and undoes his cloak, then lets it fall to the floor. My eyes widen when it rises back up all by itself, flying over to a hook by the entrance. "The boy," he says, his voice soft despite the edge to it.

I freeze and try my best to face him, and not to let my fear show. He knows about Nathaniel? Felix takes a step closer to me, and I take a step back, until I'm pressed against one of the bedposts. He places his gloved finger underneath my chin and tips my head up, forcing me to face him.

Earlier today I thought his eyes made him look somewhat human. In this moment, they just highlight how inhuman the rest of him looks. The veins on his skin are thick, dark, and throbbing, as though they have a life of their own, making it impossible to determine what his face truly looks like underneath.

"I will not permit you to so much as think about that boy. If you dare pine after him or hang on to any hopes of ever being with him, I'll kill him myself and I *will* make you watch. Leave the past where it belongs, Arabella."

I shudder and try to move away from him, pressing myself against the wood harder. He tightens his grip on my chin, his eyes roaming over my face as though he's trying to make sure I heard him.

"They were right," I whisper. "You are a monster."

He takes a step back, and I can just about make out a warped smile on his face. "I never pretended to be anything else."

CHAPTER TEN

Arabella

I stare out the window, feeling more lost than ever as I lean back against the windowsill, the room as eerily quiet as it has been since Felix left me here. The palace is warm, but it looks bleak, cold and dark outside, the scenery a perfect replica of my feelings. The small areas that are illuminated by torches show that there's nothing but snow and ice out there. Even if I wanted to, I doubt I could find my way home. Is this what the rest of my days will look like? Will I die here, trapped in a prison of ice? If I tried to run, where would I even go? Even if I could survive the journey, there's no way I could get into Althea undetected, and my chances of freeing Nathaniel are slim to none. Besides, I suspect that Felix would hunt me down.

It's hard to say how long I've been here, since the sun never rose as I'd expected it to, but it feels like I've slept two full nights. Both times, I woke to the smell of a warm meal and a freshly drawn lavender-scented bath, but I have yet to see any attendants. Thankfully, I haven't seen my husband, either.

I sigh softly as I rise to my feet, my gaze roaming over the room. The many artifacts and clothes indicate this is Felix's bedroom, so it doesn't appear as though this is a glorified prison cell assigned especially to me, but even so, I don't dare leave.

Exhaustion washes over me, my eyelids becoming heavier as I move to stand in front of the fireplace. The darkness feels unnatural, and I can't help but wish for the sun to rise soon, even if it's just so I can see farther away and check out my surroundings.

I'm snapped out of my thoughts when magic shimmers gold in front of me for a few moments and then a cup and a teapot appear, hovering in midair. I watch as tea is poured into the cup, my hand pressed against my chest. I'm frozen in place as the teacup tilts from left to right, almost as though telling me to take it.

I glance around the room, but there's no one here who could have done this. My hands shake as I grab the cup for fear it'll fall, the familiar smell of lavender washing over me. I don't dare drink it lest it be poisoned, but the cup flies out of my hands, pressing against my lips softly, insisting that I take a sip. It pauses its movements when a knock sounds, and I turn toward the door nervously as it swings open. Elaine steps into the room, still in the same riding outfit she was in when we departed Althea. She must have just arrived.

She hesitates when she sees the teacup and the pot hovering in midair, her eyes wide. "It appears the palace has taken a liking to you," she says, her voice filled with a sense of wonder. "Fear not—it's harmless. The palace provides for the emperor and many, though not all, of the palace's other inhabitants, often arranging food and drinks as it pleases. When the palace wants to feed you, it's almost impossible to say no. I was informed that our attendants were not able to get to your room—it's rare, but occasionally the palace becomes overly protective. Apparently, it aimed to ensure all threats are kept away while providing for you itself."

My stomach tightens at the implication. That explains why I haven't seen any attendants. Because there never were any. The food I've eaten... they were my favorite meals, and I never even questioned it.

"The emperor sent me over to extend his apologies for his absence," Elaine explains, snapping me out of my thoughts. "Just before we left Althea, an avalanche buried one of our cities and cut off an important trade route. Our soldiers were deployed immediately, but the second he heard about it, the emperor set off to personally help. He should be back in a matter of days, weather permitting."

Panic takes root deep inside my stomach, and I take a calming breath. An avalanche? "Are there any survivors?" I ask, my voice trembling. I can't help but feel like this is my fault—it's my curse, my misfortune. If what Elaine is saying is true, that avalanche must have happened the moment the Shadow Emperor married me, and if he finds out I'm to blame, he'll kill me to protect his people.

"Please do not worry, Your Excellency," Elaine says, a kind smile on her face. "Considering much of Eldiria's terrain, our people are always prepared for the worst. The emperor has gifted those who live in areas at risk with magic crystals that our sorcerers have embedded protection spells in. So no one has been killed, but they're trapped, and no one is able to get them out quicker than the emperor. He'll return soon, victorious."

She steps back and nods toward the door. "While we await his safe return, I wondered if you might like a tour of the palace," she adds, a hesitant smile on her face. "I sincerely apologize for not having been here to help you familiarize yourself with your new home, Empress. I've failed you by not traveling faster when I realized the emperor had left you here alone."

Did she come straight here when she returned? "It can wait," I tell her, my voice soft, but she shakes her head and gestures toward the door, a determined look in her eyes. It's clear she means well, but all I can think of when I see her is that if not for her, Nathaniel and I might have escaped. I'm certain it was her voice I heard. "Very well. I would love a tour," I say hesitantly, pasting on the smile I reserve for members of my father's court.

Elaine nods, a hint of relief in her eyes as she steps aside and stands by the door. I take a deep breath as I walk over to her, wishing

I could retaliate against her for what she did to Nathaniel and me. I wish I could make her feel even a hint of the torment she has brought me. Instead, I smile at her as she leads me down the long corridor toward the grand staircase.

"This entire floor is the emperor's, and now yours, too. I'm one floor below you." Candles on the wall flicker on as we walk toward them, and I jump in surprise. I rest my hand on my chest and stare at one of the candles, taking in the slight buzzing of magic around it.

"Ah," Elaine murmurs. "The entire palace is enchanted. It has been for over two hundred years, ever since the day Theon's mother passed away."

"Two hundred years?" I repeat softly. "How old is the emperor?"

Elaine smiles and tilts her head toward the staircase. "I suppose he looks as though he's around thirty years of age, and to me he is. In reality, he's just over two hundred years old. Time moves differently in the palace. I've been here for just over a decade now, but it is as though only two years have passed." How is that possible? Is that why she looks so young, and why I've been reading about her for a decade when it appears she hasn't aged at all from the first time she was mentioned alongside Felix?

Elaine bites down on her lip as though she's misspoken and rushes down the stairs. "This is the audience room. It's where you'll usually find your husband, and where he receives correspondents and holds meetings. It's the only room in the palace accessible to anyone who does not live here. If they attempt to roam the palace, they'll find themselves going around in circles, always ending up in this room."

"Is that the case for me, too? Are there places I physically cannot go because of an enchantment?"

She looks surprised at my question, and then she shakes her head. "No, Your Excellency. No such restrictions were placed upon you. Nothing is inaccessible to you, but I would recommend that you stay away from the east wing. It's in desperate need of repairs, and it would be hazardous for you to enter."

I nod and follow along, taking note of the different rooms in the palace, the way doors open and close by themselves. Everything in this palace is so far from everything I've ever known that it leaves me feeling disoriented. I've always been taught to fear magic, yet here it is used without reservation.

"The imperial kitchen," Elaine says, pausing in yet another doorway. "This kitchen is used exclusively for members of the court." I look into the room to find plates washing themselves and a broom moving around, the entire room buzzing with magic. "The palace provides anything the emperor and his inner circle might need, while the staff primarily focuses on the soldiers and craftsmen who live on palace grounds. We're uncertain what the root of the magic is, but we are grateful for it."

We pause by two large dark mahogany doors, delicately carved with florals that almost seem real. "I suspect you might like this room," Elaine says just as the doors swing open.

I gasp as we walk into the largest library I have ever seen, my broken heart finding some relief at the sight of the thousands of books surrounding me. Thousands of tales I could lose myself in to escape the reality I'm forced to face. I smile as I run my fingers over the leather-bound spines, each of them well cared for and many of them ancient.

"That's the first time I've seen you smile," Elaine says, her voice soft.

I turn toward her, startled. I suppose she's right. I've had no reason to smile since she and Felix walked into my life.

"Our emperor is rough around the edges, but he's a good ruler, and his heart is in the right place," she says, a pleading look in her eyes.

I stare at her, wondering how she could possibly believe that.

There can be no goodness in a man like him. A good man would not conquer half the world, and what for? To please his ego? To satiate his boredom?

"Felix... can he read my mind?"

Elaine's eyes widen and her lips tilt up at the edges, revealing a small smile that transforms her face. She's a beautiful woman, but even a hint of a smile makes her look ethereal.

"Felix?" she repeats, smiling. "No one calls him that."

I pause, my hand still on one of the books on the shelves that I was about to pull out. He gave me a part of himself that no one else has? Why?

"No, he cannot read your mind, Your Excellency. He's just good at reading people."

I pull away from the bookcase and turn to face her. "Do you know why he married me?"

She inhales deeply and looks away. "He was hoping to tell you this himself, but considering the circumstances, I hope he won't mind if I tell you some of what I know. You deserve the truth."

I nod, fear running down my spine. I suspected there was a reason behind his decision to marry me when he could've had Serena, and I have this sinking feeling that whatever Elaine is about to say will only make my already dreadful circumstances worse.

"You were shown to us in a prophecy, Your Excellency. You are meant to break a curse that Eldiria has been under for two hundred years. You're meant to set Eldiria free."

I try my best to keep the utter horror her words instill from showing. They must not know that I'm cursed myself, and that bringing me here is likely to increase the misfortune they must already be facing. If they find out I can't even save myself, let alone an entire empire, my life is forfeit.

"The emperor was cursed to live his life in the shadows, taking his kingdom with him," Elaine continues. "He once told me that Eldiria used to be a beautiful place, filled with rolling green hills, but by the time the emperor celebrated his twentieth birthday, winter had come and never left, and the sun disappeared forever. All of Eldiria's crops started to die, and there currently are no fertile grounds left in our empire. We constantly battle to keep our people fed. Our rivers have run dry, and the forest closes us in, making trade near impossible. It's not possible to hack our way through it, either, because each morning the trees are back where they were. As if that weren't enough... the people are becoming infertile, too. There hasn't been a single child in a decade. We're an empire at the brink of extinction."

I stare at her in disbelief. How is this unknown to the rest of the world? This must be why he keeps conquering different parts of the world. If trade is made too difficult by the forests, he must enforce that trade. How did I know nothing of this? Throughout the years, I've read every piece of literature I could find on curses and magic, but none ever mentioned the Shadow Emperor's curse. Almost as though she can see the question written all over my face, Elaine smiles knowingly. "The curse cannot be spoken of to people who are unaware of it, unless they are within the palace's walls. I have tried my very best to pinpoint the cause of this, and the most I can find is an energy signature similar to the one in the palace."

"How did it happen?" I ask. Who could possibly be powerful enough to cast a curse that lasts centuries?

"This is as much as I can tell you," Elaine says, regret in her eyes. "I must leave your questions for the emperor to answer. I apologize, Your Excellency."

She hesitates and looks down at her feet. When she looks up at me again, her eyes are filled with genuine remorse. "Not just for not being able to provide you with the information you seek, but also for stopping you in the caves. I have no acceptable excuse, Your Excellency.

I did it out of hope for my people, out of desperation... but I understand more than anyone what it means to give up someone you love."

My expression hardens, and I look away. I won't give her my forgiveness. "You did what was expected of you," I say instead.

Elaine nods, both of us quiet as she walks me back to Felix's floor. My mind is in turmoil as I try to process everything I just learned. The Shadow Emperor thinks I'm someone capable of breaking a curse, and that is exactly the role I'll have to play if I want to stay alive. I'll have to pretend to be stronger than I am, braver than I've ever been before. If I am to survive, I must pretend I'm capable of what they expect of me.

CHAPTER ELEVEN

Arabella

I place my hand on the door handle and hesitate, knowing deep down that I'm about to do something Felix likely doesn't want me to do. My chest expands as I take a deep breath and quietly walk out of the room, Elaine's words still ringing through my mind.

Her tone was off when she told me to stay away from the east wing, and if there's one thing I've learned as Althea's forgotten princess, it's that the right information wielded at the right time can deliver a bigger blow than the mightiest of weapons. I'm far from powerful, so I'll have to try my best to outsmart the Shadow Emperor if I want to stay alive.

The corridors are empty as I slowly make my way toward the entrance of the east wing, and the temperature continues to drop as I walk. The air becomes heavy, and judging by the worn carpets and the damaged walls, it's clear this part of the palace hasn't been maintained.

The moment I walk through the large arch that separates the heart of the palace from the east wing, the torches all extinguish, leaving me temporarily blinded as I try my best to adjust to the darkness. My heart races, and for a moment, I hesitate. Was Elaine right?

Something feels wrong here, yet I can't suppress the feeling that there's something in the east wing I need to see.

I carefully take a small step forward, my path illuminated by the slivers of moonlight entering from the cracks in the ceiling, only for every door I walk past to slam shut, as though I'm being kept out by the palace itself, when it was so welcoming during my tour yesterday.

I pause by a torn portrait, a beautiful and elaborate dagger still embedded in it, the emerald on the hilt shimmering. My hands tremble as I pull it out, magic buzzing all around it, a shimmery gold sheen enveloping it. Unlike the cuffs and other magical artifacts my father has used against me throughout the years, this doesn't feel malicious. I'm barely thinking straight as I hide it in the deep pockets of my dress, praying it won't cut straight through the fabric and hurt me. I'd been considering stealing a dinner knife so I'd have something to defend myself with should the need ever arise, but this is much better.

My gaze roams over the two curled parts of the portrait, and once more, I follow my instincts as I push the two pieces of the canvas flush against each other, my brows rising at the sight of the completed portrait. I'm mesmerized for a moment as I stare at those familiar turquoise eyes, the golden specks sparkling. *Felix.* I take in his unmarred face, devoid of the black veins that try to obscure it, and for a few moments, I just stare. Is that what he looks like underneath? His jaw is chiseled and strong, his lips full without being overly so. He looks like a living god, and I suspect the painting is hugely dramatized to appease the subject's ego.

I step back, unable to shake my conflicted feelings. I'm uncertain what I was supposed to find here, but I know it wasn't this, nor was it the dagger. There's something else, and I can feel it calling me, like a low buzzing that runs all over my skin, urging me to come find it.

I shiver as I walk farther into the east wing, the temperature growing even colder, frost appearing at the edges of the torn paintings that line the wall. Black tendrils of something dark cling to the walls, entirely in contrast with the golden magic that surrounded my new weapon. It feels evil, even more so than the weapons my father used to punish me. My teeth begin to clatter as I make my way up a surprisingly well-maintained tower, certain I hear voices in the distance.

It's almost as though I'm being led forward by an invisible force as I put one foot in front of the other, a woman's voice becoming more and more audible with each step I take. My breathing becomes more shallow as fear sets in, the cold air turning it into little puffs of smoke. My intuition overrules every hint of panic, making me forge ahead, until I'm standing in the only open doorway I've come across, all the way at the very top of the tower.

I inhale sharply when I notice Felix standing in the corner of the room, his long black cape blowing in the icy wind. He's still in his travel cape, so he must have just arrived and headed straight to the east wing. Felix appears to be standing in front of a mirror that's just out of view for me, and I take another cautious step forward, my heart beating so loudly that I fear he can hear it.

My eyes widen as the mirror comes into view, and for a second, I am certain I see a woman in it—pale skin with unseeing eyes and blood-red lips, but then I blink, and she is gone.

Felix's eyes find mine in the mirror, and he whirls around, an expression I can't quite describe on his face. "What are you doing here?" he shouts as he steps toward me.

I stumble back, reality finally catching up to me. I knew there was a chance I'd get caught, but I was so certain he hadn't returned yet. "I...I—" I stammer, the look in his eyes filling me with pure terror.

He takes off his cape and throws it over my shoulders in one smooth move before cupping my cheeks with warm hands. "You're shaking, Arabella. You're freezing." He sounds furious as he leans in and picks me up the way he did when we arrived at the palace. "Are you completely out of your mind?" he chastises as he begins to walk back the way I came. "Has no one warned you how dangerous it is to come here? You could've frozen to death without even realizing what's happening."

His cape feels warm, and I instinctively press my face against his neck, needing his warmth more than I even realized. "I was just wandering around and got lost," I lie, wishing I could ask the questions on my mind. The more I think about it, the more certain I am that I saw a woman in that mirror, and it's clear Felix didn't want me to find out about her. Is she what I was supposed to see?

"Don't ever come here again," he warns as he carries me down the stairs and into our room. "It isn't safe."

I nod reluctantly and push away from him a little, expecting him to lower me to the floor, but instead, he sits down on the bed with me in his lap, holding me tightly, his head on top of mine.

"This wouldn't have happened if I'd been there to show you around myself," he says, his tone filled with regret. "If all goes well, I won't have to leave for another few weeks, so with a bit of luck, we'll be able to make up for lost time."

Though his words are undoubtedly meant as reassurance, they do nothing but fill me with fear and apprehension. If he's back, then that makes tonight the first night we'll spend together as husband and wife. It's our wedding night.

CHAPTER TWELVE

Arabella

My heart hammers in my chest as my fingers curl around the dagger I found in the east wing. It looks ancient, and something about it feels magical. It's thin and small, yet it looks powerful.

Powerful enough to kill a monster.

I bite down on my lip as I carry it to Felix's bed, hiding it between the headboard and the mattress with trembling hands, unsure whether I'll even have the courage to use it. All I've been able to think about since Felix left me in the bedroom is the curse he expects me to break, and each time, I come to the same answer. The only way the prophecy is true is if I'm meant to kill him. In the little time I've had, I've pored through as many books as I could find in his library, but all I was able to learn is that curses are supposed to end when the one who was cursed dies.

My time here is limited, and I'd rather die fighting him and end this early, instead of suffering at his hands endlessly, until whatever is left of my soul is ripped apart. I'll lose my own life in the process, but it's only a matter of time before he figures out I'll only bring him further misfortune and kills me himself. At least this way, I die for a worthy cause.

I jump when I hear a sound in the room and turn around, scared to get caught before I even make an attempt at his life. My eyes widen when I see a nightgown hovering in midair. It moves back and forth, as though it's indicating for me to follow.

I hesitate before taking a cautious step forward. The magic in this palace is unlike anything I've ever experienced before, and though it doesn't feel harmful, I'm still wary. All my life, I've been told that magic is a double-edged sword, that all it does is harm, and I'm scared it might be true.

The nightgown floats toward a steaming bath, the scent of lavender filling the room. "You love lavender, don't you, Palace?" I remark, my voice barely above a whisper.

The nightgown appears to nod, and I smile ruefully as I stare at the steaming bath, a chill running down my arms. I'm still freezing, and the bath the palace has drawn for me looks irresistible. Despite my heavy heart, I find myself smiling as I undress, giving in to the palace's demands. I suppose this is its odd way of readying me for our first night together. "I won't sleep with him," I murmur. "This is all futile, but I suppose it's a good ruse. He'll never see it coming if I appear willing."

All that meets me is silence as the water moves over my body, washing me without me having to lift a single hand. For a moment, I allow myself to lean back, my eyes falling closed. If not for the Shadow Emperor, Nathaniel might already have asked for my hand by now. We would be betrothed and allowed to spend some time together, preparing for our wedding. How will he react when he receives the news of my passing? I hope he'll know I was his till the very end.

A soft gasp escapes my lips when I hear the sound of the door opening, and my heart begins to race. I wrap my arms around my chest and sink deeper into the tub, but it's not enough to keep Felix's attention off me. I expected him to stay away for several hours more since he left the room due to an emergency meeting, but perhaps I'm mistaken about the time. The constant darkness has been disorienting.

"This is quite the surprise," he says, his voice gravelly. Not even the moving veins across his face can hide his blatant appreciation, or his building desire. It emboldens me, gives me the courage I've been seeking.

"Mere hours ago, you rightfully reminded me that it is our wedding night," I tell him, my voice devoid of the tremble I'd expected. "I am a princess, Your Excellency. If there is one thing I am most accustomed to, it is fulfilling my duties."

"It appears you are exceedingly forgetful, Arabella, for you are no princess. Not anymore." He crosses his arms, his eyes roaming over my face as though he's trying to see through my façade. I'd expected his gaze to dip down in an attempt to catch a glimpse of what is now rightfully his, but he has yet to do so. "You are my empress."

His eyes sparkle possessively, and my heart skips a beat, an unfamiliar feeling rushing through me. No one has ever willingly and enthusiastically laid claim to me like that—I've never truly belonged anywhere. Yet this man that I so despise seems somewhat proud to call me his. My heart begins to hammer in my chest as I square my shoulders and straighten my spine, allowing my chest to rise above the water. "Perhaps you'd like to join your empress?" My voice trembles this time, uncertainty taking root as I take a deep breath in an attempt to steel my nerves.

Our eyes lock as his hands move to his cape, and he unties it, letting it fall off his shoulders and onto the floor. Felix walks toward me as he unbuttons his shirt, and I tense, my eyes flitting to the bed, where I hid my dagger.

"What's wrong, wife?" he says, his voice velvety smooth, a hint of amusement in it. *Wife*. It feels like a mockery to be called that, yet I don't doubt his sincerity.

"N-Nothing," I stammer, reminding myself to be brave.

My breath hitches as his shirt hits the floor. I've never seen a man in such a state of undress, and I never thought I'd ever see anyone but Nathaniel like that. The veins that run over his face mar the rest of him, too, moving furiously as though to obscure his body, yet they can't. Even through the darkness, he looks strong.

His hands move to his trousers, and I bite down on my lip as I take in the deep V right above, his abs clearly visible. He smiles at me bemusedly just before I squeeze my eyes closed, and moments later, I hear his trousers drop to the floor. The water ripples as he enters the tub and I inhale sharply, uncertainty settling deep inside my chest. Water sloshes over the edge of the tub, and I jump when I feel his legs brush against mine.

"Open your eyes," he orders. I obey, trying my best to hide my emotions. I keep my gaze trained on his face, not daring to let it dip lower. "Regretting your invitation, Empress?"

Indignation courses through me, and I narrow my eyes as I try my best to keep them on his face. "I am merely nervous, Your Excellency. Though I do not regret my invitation, I've now found myself uncertain what to do next."

He smiles in a way that makes me think I've caught him off guard. "Do you wish for me to show you?" he asks, his tone filled with longing, his chest rising and falling rapidly.

The question surprises me. I'd expected him to take the lead from this point forward, but it's clear he's intent on seeing how far I'll take this. "Yes," I say without thinking, acting on my impulses instead.

My eyes widen when shadows surround me, pushing me toward him slowly. I press my hands against his chest, exposing myself as I look at the water for a hint of his shadows, yet finding nothing. I've never seen anything like it, and a small part of me can't help but marvel at the sight of something I've only ever heard rumors about.

His eyes roam over me as I sit on my knees between his legs, my breasts exposed above the water and my hands on his body. His skin is warm, and somehow that, too, surprises me. I was certain he'd be as cold as the rest of his country.

"So long as there's a shadow in a room, it's under my control," he whispers as though he recognizes my need for answers, his voice a soft caress.

"H-How?" I ask, my voice filled with wonder. He's an alchemist, and he shouldn't be able to control shadows in the way he does. It felt like he had his hands on me as he pulled me closer, and natural shadows shouldn't be able to do that. It goes against the law of equal exchange, which dictates that something cannot come from nothing. Yet when he uses his shadows, it doesn't feel like Elaine's magic. It's different somehow; it doesn't feel like an exchange of any kind. I usually see a shimmer of some sort when magic is used, but there was nothing this time.

He smiles and gently tucks my hair behind my ear. "You're curious about me," he murmurs, a hint of relief in his voice. "It's a power I was born with. My father was an alchemist, but my mother was a powerful sorceress born with the innate ability to manipulate shadows. My magical powers are near nonexistent compared with my alchemy, but my command over shadows is innate. However, that is not what I meant to show you."

I try my best not to tense when he grabs my wrist and moves my hand over his shoulder, and then back down his chest, soap slowly appearing underneath my hands. He's using my hand to wash himself with, and I raise a brow, uncertain whether I'm impressed with his powers or indignant he's having me act like his handmaid.

Felix lets go of my wrist and stares at me in surprise when I begin to rub his shoulder with my thumb, and I ignore the way his eyes roam over my breasts. A thousand feelings I can't make sense of rush through me. The idea of him was far more terrifying than the reality he's presenting me with, and I don't quite understand why.

I force a smile and place my trembling hands on his chest, massaging in the soap reluctantly as I plot his demise. Even if I fail to kill him, he'll end my life swiftly so long as I point a blade at him, won't he? Felix raises his hand to my face and brushes the back of his fingers over my cheek, his touch oddly gentle. "I wonder what goes on in that wicked mind of yours," he murmurs.

A hint of panic rushes to the surface before I remind myself that Elaine said he can't read my mind. I grin at him and tilt my face. "You wouldn't believe me even if I told you," I whisper.

He's silent for a moment, and then he laughs, startling me, his teeth perfectly straight and white. My hands still as I begin to wonder what he looks like underneath all those thick, moving veins. "They appeared when I was twenty," he tells me, his voice soft. "The veins. It is hereditary, it appears."

I nod, surprised he volunteered information about himself, although perhaps I shouldn't be. He is, after all, my husband. It should be natural for us to make some sort of attempt to get to know each other, but it doesn't quite feel that way.

My nerves get the best of me as I slide my hands down his chest, his body strong underneath my fingers and so very different from mine. His breath hitches when my hands dip lower, disappearing under the water as I slide them over his abs. His breathing accelerates, and my heart starts to race for reasons I can't comprehend. My nerves have a different edge to them, and curiosity overtakes my fear as I look into his eyes. He's the most powerful alchemist in the world, yet right here, right now, it feels like he's just a man—one who is utterly enthralled by me in a way no one has ever been before.

I watch as his chest rises and falls rapidly, his gaze burning. He looks so very human in this moment, despite the darkness slithering on his skin. The way he's looking at me...that's *desire*. I bite down on my lip when my hands reach his thighs, and he grits his teeth as though *he's* the one being tortured.

His eyes are lowered as he reaches into the water, his hand wrapping around my waist. "Let me take you to bed, beloved."

CHAPTER THIRTEEN

Arabella

I'm trembling as I put on the nightgown that's hovering by the bed, feeling oddly conflicted. Something about the bath we took together made me lose my resolve, made me wonder if perhaps I'm mistaken and he isn't as much of a threat to me as I've convinced myself he is.

I bite down on my lip harshly as I get into bed and reach for the dagger, acutely aware of how close he is. I lie still and grip the dagger with all my strength when I hear the sound of him rising from the water, followed by footsteps. My heart is hammering in my chest as he approaches me, and I squeeze my eyes closed, trying my hardest to gather my courage.

When I found the dagger, I'd been so certain that it was a sign, a solution to a seemingly unsolvable problem. Yet now that it's time to use it, I'm second-guessing myself. The Shadow Emperor, *my husband*, doesn't seem quite as evil as I've always thought him to be, and I'm scared I'm making a mistake.

The sound of the covers being lifted fills my ears, and the bed dips as he lies down next to me. It's now or never. If I don't do this now, I'll lose much more than just my life. I won't let him take my innocence. I won't give him what I wanted Nathaniel to have. I tighten my grip on the dagger's hilt, my blood rushing through my ears as I steel myself.

"Arabella," he says, his voice soft.

I turn toward him and raise my dagger, my eyes roaming over his body for a split second as hesitation hits me. Then I look into his eyes as I bring my arm down with as much force as I can muster, burying the blade deep into his heart.

He grunts in pain, his eyes widening a fraction. Black blood rapidly covers both of us, and regret washes over me. "I'm sorry," I whisper, pushing the blade in deeper. He's the one they call a monster, yet it is I who acts like one. "I had no other choice."

His hand wraps over the hand I'm holding the dagger with, and he keeps it there as his gaze settles on the blood that's coating my hands now. He raises a brow, clear confusion blending with pain, and time seems to still as I wait for him to respond, to retaliate.

I thought he'd have ended my life by now in punishment for my actions, but he merely stares at me, a small smile on his face. "I wondered if you'd do it," he murmurs, his voice laced with pain. "I didn't think you'd have the courage." He tightens his grip around my hand and pulls the dagger out, blood rapidly coating my nightgown before the bleeding simply *stops*.

My hand slips out from underneath his as he throws the dagger to the side, letting it clatter onto the floor loudly. His eyes find mine, and I scramble back, fear gripping me. Shadows start to move around me, keeping me captive as Felix sits up and holds his hand up, a damp cloth materializing out of thin air. He watches me as he wipes his chest, revealing perfectly unmarred skin. It's almost as though I didn't stab him at all, not a single trace of the damage I inflicted present. He's a true monster after all. I should've known it wouldn't be easy to kill him...and now I'll pay the price for attempting to.

"I told you I'm called the Shadow Emperor for a reason, my love.

There's nothing you can hide from me. I knew you placed that dagger against the headboard the second you did it. I've been wondering whether you're merely a meek princess from a tiny irrelevant country, or whether you have it in you to be my empress. I suppose I have my answer now."

He leans in and places his hands at the collar of my nightgown, tearing it right down the middle with ease, and I clutch at the sheets. I can see how aroused he still is, and based on the size of him, I have no doubt I'll be in even more pain than I would have been had I cooperated with him. There is no way that something like that could fit inside me without ripping me apart.

The shadows tug at me, pushing me onto my back. My hands are forcibly lifted above my head, pushing my chest out and exposing me lewdly, my hair strewn over the pillows. I whimper, but I don't dare protest. Not after the stunt I just pulled.

Felix leans over me, his gaze heated. He holds his hand up, and another cloth appears. My entire body tenses when he reaches for me. I try to pull away, but I'm unable to move.

"My blood is poisonous, sweetheart. The longer it's on your skin, the more harm it'll do, though I'm starting to suspect you're immune. It should've burned the moment it touched you, but your skin is unblemished."

His touch is gentle as he wipes my neck, removing the sticky black blood that sprayed all over me. He takes his time with me, and much to my surprise, there's no anger in his eyes. He isn't trying to hurt me, not in the slightest. If anything, he merely looks morose. "I'll be honest, Empress. I hoped you could do what I have failed to do and end my life, but it wasn't meant to be."

I tense when the cloth in his hands brushes over my nipple, the sensation foreign somehow. It feels more sensitive than it usually would, and heat rushes to my cheeks, making me avert my gaze.

"I can clean myself," I whisper, scared to speak up after what I just did.

"Can you promise me that you won't lunge for the dagger all over again if I let you go?"

I nod.

"Hmm, but then again, you also vowed to spend your life with me when we got married, yet here we are."

"I only promised to be with you until death do us part," I say through gritted teeth. "I was just expediting the *death* part."

Felix pauses, and then he bursts out laughing, the sound surprisingly melodic. I suppose it is not out of character for a demon to have his charms.

My eyes widen when he lifts my legs and spreads them indecently, seating himself between them, placing my legs on either side of his hips. Felix grabs the edges of my nightgown and continues to rip it apart until I'm lying in his bed completely bare, shadows tugging at my ankles and wrist, pinning me down for him.

"My love," he says, his eyes roaming over my body. "If someday, you manage to kill me, I'll die a happy man. You must be cautious, however. As far as I am aware, killing me is impossible. I've tried, and I've never been able to figure out why I cannot die. Perhaps the curse won't let me since it would die with me." He sighs and looks away for a moment, his expression becoming forlorn. "My blood is exceptionally poisonous, so don't spill it unnecessarily."

I blink in surprise. What does he mean, *I've tried*? He's tried taking his own life? I can't quite comprehend someone doing that, but my heart aches at the mere thought of it.

Felix glances back at me, his gaze relaxed. A new clean cloth materializes in his hands, and he continues to wipe down my breasts, his movements slow and sensual. The way he's got me exposed for him makes me feel vulnerable, but it does something else to me, too. The nerves I feel are foreign, laced with an emotion I can't quite place. I bite down on my lip when I recognize it as arousal, and Felix smiles as though he knows exactly how he's making me feel as he slowly caresses my body with the cloth in his hands.

"Now, tell me why you attempted to kill me. Was it because I pushed you too far in the tub? Or were you instructed to kill me?"

My heart starts to race at the thought of suspicion falling to my kingdom. My people could suffer endlessly because of my actions today. "It has nothing to do with Althea," I profess. "I just...I wanted to...I didn't want you to touch me."

His movements still, and the way he looks at me changes. "You wanted to save yourself for that boy, huh?"

I part my lips to answer, but the truth echoes in the silence between us. Felix inhales sharply and lowers his forehead to my stomach, like he can't bring himself to look at me.

"You're mine, Arabella," he whispers against my skin, his voice tormented. "You're *my* wife. Not only did you attempt to kill me on what I consider to be our wedding night—you also tried to keep something that's mine from me so you could give it to another man. What do you think would be suitable punishment?"

"You aren't going to kill me?" I ask, my voice trembling.

He raises his head, and the look in his eyes brings forth guilt and sorrow unlike anything I've felt before. I'd expected him to be mad, but the way he's looking at me can only be described as deeply hurt. Because of me. "You'd choose death over being my empress?"

Felix cups my face, a humorless smile on his face. "I will not kill you, nor will I release you from this bond, Empress. For as long as you breathe, you are *mine*, and you *will* learn your place. You belong with me, Arabella. By my side is where you will spend your days. Try to fight it, and punishment is all that awaits you."

He leans in and presses a soft kiss against my neck, and I gasp in surprise. His harsh words are entirely in contrast with his soft touches, and it begins to dawn on me then. Perhaps he isn't the monster—I am.

I inhale sharply as a new sensation washes over me when his teeth graze over my collarbone, leaving me wanting more. My heart starts to race and heat rushes through my body, stealing away my every thought. "I'll make it so that you can never be with him again," he warns me, our eyes meeting for a moment. "I will bind you to me in more ways than one."

He takes his time pressing featherlight kisses in a trail all the way down to my chest, each building the desire I hadn't expected to feel. "Felix," I plead, my voice unrecognizable. I've never sounded so... *lustful*.

"Admit you want more, Arabella."

"Is this my punishment?" I ask, my voice huskier than I'd intended.

Felix's eyes flash, and that same lust I saw in the bathtub lights up his eyes once more. "It would be most suitable, would it not? It is, after all, our wedding night." I bite down on my lip as his shadows glide over my body until it feels as though several hands are touching me, some twisting my nipples, others stroking my neck and thighs, overstimulating every sensitive part of me. A soft moan escapes my lips unwittingly, and Felix's eyes fall closed for a moment, his chest rising and falling rapidly. "Tell me, wife. Do you accept your punishment?"

I nod sharply, and his tongue flicks over my nipple in response, making me cry out instinctively. I need more of what he's doing to me, but I don't dare admit to it. Instead I involuntarily arch my spine, and he chuckles, seemingly pleased. The sound shouldn't bring me so much relief, but it does. I've never felt remorse like I felt when he looked at me as if I'd betrayed him, as if I'd broken the heart I'd been convinced he didn't have.

Our eyes lock as his shadows gather around me. "Felix!" I whisper when I'm pulled to the edge of the bed, my legs spread wide as he kneels between them on the floor.

He grabs my thighs and lets his eyes roam over my body, his gaze lingering, almost as though he's committing the sight of me to memory. "I want my name to be the only thing on your lips tonight, beloved." Felix presses a kiss right between my legs, stealing my breath. "Think only of me. Let me give you what no one else can," he pleads, right before he leans in and tastes me.

My desire rapidly becomes uncontainable, and sounds I've never made before leave my throat. If this is punishment, I'm sorely tempted to make several more attempts at his life. Felix drags his tongue right over the spot that keeps me at the edge and smiles. "*Beg*, Empress. You want my tongue on your clit, do you not?"

My pleasure builds each time he flicks his tongue, all rational thought escaping my mind. "*Please*," I whisper eventually, delirious.

His laughter rings through the room before he places his hands on my thighs, gripping tightly as he gives me what I'm begging him for. His tongue pushes me over the edge, and wave after wave of pleasure washes over me, my inner muscles contracting painfully.

"*Fates*," I groan.

"*Felix*," he corrects me. "The only one you'll call for is *me*."

My legs tremble, and Felix gently kisses my thighs as I try my hardest to regain control over my body.

"Next time, I won't be so gentle with you," he warns me as he takes me into his arms. The sheets rapidly fly off the bed, changing themselves instantly before he lays me back down. "Let this be a lesson."

CHAPTER FOURTEEN

Felix

I watch my wife as she browses through the books in the library, a smile spreading across her beautiful face when she pulls out a leather-bound tome. She takes a seat at one of the tables and flicks through the pages, her eyes lit up in delight. I underestimated her. I thought I'd married a meek woman I could easily conquer, but nothing could be further from the truth.

It shouldn't surprise me that the book that excites her so is one on toxic poisons and potions. I bite back a smile as I walk toward her. Perhaps I shouldn't have taken things quite so far last night. I have earned her ire, and while that should fill me with remorse, it instead fuels my desire.

Unlike my people, I do not believe true love is what will break this curse. However, I am no longer opposed to trying. Making Arabella of Althea fall for me is the biggest challenge I have ever faced, but I will bring her to her knees.

She looks up at the sound of my footsteps and slams her book closed, the smile melting off her face. I watch as her cheeks heat, a hint of shyness in her gaze.

"Plotting my demise once more, I see." I tip my head toward her book, and her eyes widen as a blush spreads across her cheeks. Her face is so expressive that it's instantly clear she was only reading the book out of interest, but I can't help but tease her.

"You said I shouldn't spill your blood," she tells me, shrugging. Arabella holds the book up and grins. "This way, I won't."

I sit down opposite her and place the wooden box I brought with me between us. "My love," I murmur. "If you want me to touch you, just say the words. There is no need to seek out punishment in such a convoluted manner."

Her lips fall open in shock. "I...I w-would *never*," she stammers.

I take the book from her and open it in the place she bookmarked. "Nightshade," I read, chuckling. "*Atropa belladonna*, no less."

Does she have any idea how swiftly I'd have killed anyone else in her position? Yet when she looks at me that way, all I want to do is take her right on top of this table. Leaving her all alone in bed last night was torture, but I knew she wasn't ready for more, and sleeping next to her when I wanted her so desperately felt impossible.

I gather my shadow and push it underneath the table, making her feel like my fingers are wrapping around her ankles. She gasps, and I smile at her as I interlace my fingers, placing them clearly visible on the table while my shadow spreads her legs.

"Beloved," I tell her. "My feelings are awfully hurt. Belladonna won't be sufficient to harm me. That would merely irritate me. I would've expected hemlock, at the very least. Do you truly think so little of me? Perhaps I should show you the true strength of my body, so you might not underestimate me again."

Her eyes are wide, and she sucks down on her lower lip for a moment when shadowy hands slip underneath her dress, trailing up her calves, stroking her inner thighs.

"H-Hemlock you would've tasted," she says, her cheeks bright red. I thought she looked beautiful last night, but seeing her sitting opposite me with curiosity and desire in her eyes...*Fates*.

Does she know that everything my shadow feels, *I feel*? Her skin is a delight, and so is the way she trembles against my fingers, her eyes moving from my hands on the table to my eyes.

"But belladonna," she adds, her voice shaking, "is sweet. I could've slipped it in your wine and you'd never have known."

I smile at her and lean in, lifting my fist to my temple so I can rest my head against it. "I daresay the plans you're concocting count as attempted murder, and I need not remind you of the punishment for that, do I?"

I snap my fingers, and her undergarments disappear, leaving her bare underneath her dress. She gasps, her eyes wide. "Felix!"

I smirk at her, loving the way my name sounds on her lips. I'd merely come to the library to give her a present, yet I cannot resist her allure. She makes it so easy to tease her.

"Were you imagining the way I'd punish you after you poison me, wife?"

She's breathing hard, and though she shakes her head, I recognize the lust in her eyes. *"Never."*

Perhaps the man she thinks she's in love with is not as much of a threat as I thought he was. She might believe she's heartbroken, but she isn't. She's furious that her freedom has been ripped away, but she isn't mourning a relationship that was forcibly ended. Not truly.

"Felix," she warns me. "I did not make an attempt at your life."

"No, but you were planning to."

"That is merely an assumption you were making. Is that the kind of ruler you are? You judge your subjects before giving them a chance to make their case?"

"No, beloved. But as it turns out, I am that kind of *husband*." Her eyes flash with anger, and I can't help but chuckle. "You are mine," I tell her. "You are my wife, Arabella. I was lenient yesterday, but it appears I must satisfy your desires lest you scheme against me. If I keep you satiated, will my life be safe?"

"You are immortal," she reminds me.

The way she speaks to me is exhilarating, and I can't help but want to tease her more. Except this time, I want her to beg for it. I draw a shaky breath when my thumb lightly caresses her, and I find her wet. "Tell me you want more," I whisper, my voice pleading. I don't understand what kind of hold she has over me. I've never wanted a woman the way I want her, nor have I ever felt so out of control.

Her expression changes, and she bites down on her lip. "I won't," she tells me, her eyes flashing defiantly, but she fails to hide that near-hidden plea written all over her face. She looks into my eyes as she shifts her hips just a touch, so my fingers are pressing against her harder.

"Very well," I murmur, pulling my fingers away. I watch as the word *no* forms on her lips, yet she won't let it slip out of her mouth. "Beg me for it, Arabella, just like you did last night. Say *please*, and I will drop down to my knees underneath this table and give you what you want."

She crosses her arms and looks away. "I would never. If anything, I'm grateful for your leniency."

I chuckle, unable to help myself. Does she realize how badly I want to take her? I want my cock buried deep inside her, moans tearing through her throat. What has she done to me? I never expected to desire her, or to find being around her so intoxicating. She was never meant to be more than a means to an end.

I watch her closely as I push the box I brought with me toward her. "A gift."

She frowns as she opens it, her eyes widening at the sight of the slender dagger. "Since you seemed to have taken a liking to the blade you used last night, I thought you should have one of your own. It's silver, in case that is on your list of murderous plans." I tip my head toward the hilt. "The stones are the same color as my eyes, so you may think of me each time you draw your blade."

Her lips fall open in shock, and I burst out laughing. I'm meant to court her, yet I cannot resist taunting her.

"You won't be laughing when I stab you in the back."

I lean back in my seat. "Won't I, beloved? For you to stab me in my back you'd have to be awfully close, and each time you voluntarily come to me, all I carry is a smile."

She looks disarmed, and my heart does an odd thing. It appears to skip a beat. *Arabella of Althea.* She was meant to be a demure princess, yet it seems I have met my equal at last.

CHAPTER FIFTEEN

Arabella

I clutch my fur coat tightly as I make my way through the dark courtyard toward the sounds of sparring just behind it. The palace provided me with riding pants and thick fur-lined boots, and I couldn't be more grateful for them on this freezing morning. The icy wind whips against my cheeks, and any sane person would have turned back toward the warmth and safety of the palace. Instead I walk into a seemingly abandoned tower and make my way up the spiral staircase toward a lookout point I found several days ago. Every day, I've come here, quietly observing the courtyard and all other parts of the palace I can look into. I've spent every waking second gathering information about my surroundings and the inhabitants of the palace, but I have yet to learn anything unusual.

I've barely seen Felix in the week since that afternoon in the library, either, and every night since, I've fallen asleep alone. It should've been a relief, but every night, countless new questions float through my mind. It's clear he's immortal, and if killing him was my purpose, I would've succeeded.

I'm certain the only reason he didn't end my life was because he thinks I'm still of use to him—because he thinks I'll break his curse some other way. If I want to stay alive, I need more information about my immediate surroundings, Eldiria as a whole, and the curse—and I'll need to make sure he never finds out about my own penchant for misfortune.

I pause when I near the top and peer out of a small window, my eyes widening as the rows and rows of soldiers come into view. This is the first time I've seen them all train together. Normally, that part of the palace's courtyard looks empty but for the shimmery gold all around it. I've been wondering if perhaps it was an enchantment of some sort that disguised what was underneath, but each time I tried to walk in that direction, I'd end up getting lost.

I raise a brow as I watch carefully. This is not at all how Althea's soldiers train—far from it. These soldiers are all viciously fighting one another, real blades drawn and magic being used freely. I stare in disbelief as one soldier casts a spell, while another directs it back before it hits him, causing burns to appear all over the caster's arms. He screams for a split second, then Elaine rushes up, the air sizzling light blue around her. Moments later, his wounds are healed, and he looks down as he's obviously reprimanded by her.

It's no wonder this is the strongest army in existence. They train as though their lives depend on it, and considering what I've learned so far, that might very well be the case. My gaze roams over the hundreds of people until I find Felix standing right in the middle of all the chaos, at least a dozen soldiers attempting to take him on all at once. For once, he's shed the black uniform he normally wears, his torso bare, icicles in his dark hair.

My cheeks heat as I watch him move, unable to shake the memory of our wedding night. I'd be lying if I said he didn't make me feel pleasure unlike anything I've ever known before, and I'm surprised he didn't demand anything from me in return. I was taught that pleasing my husband in bed would be one of my primary duties as a wife, but Felix didn't seem to expect that from me, nor did he consummate our marriage when it is both his right and duty to do so. He is not what I expected, and I fear him all the more for it. If there's anything I've learned growing up in Althea, it's that I'm safer when I can predict behavior and consequences.

I take a deep breath as I try my best to assess just how many soldiers there are and what their powers might be. It's valuable information to have, even if only to sell in return for a safe voyage someday. I begin to mentally catalog everything I see, but every few seconds, my gaze is drawn back to Felix. He seems to be in his element, and it's clear that not even a dozen warrior wizards can take him on. Their magic seems to glide off him, and I can't quite figure out how he's doing it. It's a shield of some sort, that much I'm sure of. Is he able to use his alchemy powers against any magic thrown his way, much like the way another soldier just threw back a spell? I've never even read of such strong command over alchemy powers, but then again, he must've had at least a century to master it. Felix isn't just immortal, he's close to all-powerful.

It makes it even stranger that he didn't consummate our marriage when he clearly wanted to. I was so certain that a man as powerful as he is would be used to taking whatever he wants with no care for anyone else's feelings, but I'm starting to wonder if I was wrong. He didn't retaliate when I quite literally stabbed him in the heart, and even when he did lose his composure, it wasn't because of what I'd done—it was because I'd been thinking of Nathaniel on our wedding night. In the library, too, he seemed to merely be teasing me when he could've demanded my body without offering me any kind of pleasure or comfort in return.

I draw a shaky breath as I try to tear my eyes off him, uncomfortable with the confusion he's left me with. He doesn't seem to be the evil man the history books portray him as, and in the week I've spent sneaking around, I've learned that his staff all seem to revere him. I know all too well what it's like to be misunderstood and judged unfairly because of a curse I had no hand in. The parallels between us leave me feeling off kilter, and the conviction I arrived here with is faltering. Perhaps it's hubris, but the thought of being able to break his curse fills me with a sense of hope and purpose—something I've never felt before. It seems impossible, but a small part of me wishes to believe it's true. Perhaps then, my cursed existence would be worth living.

"There are six hundred soldiers on the training grounds, of which four hundred and thirty-nine are sorcerers or sorceresses."

I whirl around at the sound of Felix's voice and lose my footing, pure terror crashing through me as I begin to fall down the stairs, only for his arm to wrap around my waist. He pulls me against him and holds me tightly, our eyes locking.

Heat rushes to my cheeks when I realize his torso is still bare, and I press against his chest in an attempt to create some distance between us. He merely grins and keeps holding me against him. "Tell me, Empress. That's what you were trying to figure out, isn't it? You've come here every day, so I figured I'd best ask Elaine to drop her protective enchantments, allowing you to see what you've been seeking."

My lips part to refute his question, but that knowing look in his eyes lodges the words in my throat. "Sorceresses?" I repeat instead. "Do you allow women other than Elaine to join your army?"

He turns us around so I'm pressed against the stone wall and places his left forearm beside my head, his free hand cupping my face gently. I gasp when warmth flows from his palm and through my body, relaxing my taut muscles. I hadn't realized just how cold I was until he took the chill away.

A soft sigh escapes my lips when the warmth reaches the tips of my toes, and Felix's eyes flash. His thumb brushes over the edge of my mouth, and an unfamiliar feeling rushes down my spine. "Yes," he says, his tone different from before. His thumb brushes over my bottom lip, and he leans in a fraction, his gaze on my mouth and his breathing uneven. "It's not uncommon for our male soldiers to have more brute strength, but our female soldiers are often far more cunning. They're better strategists, and they often accomplish missions far more efficiently than their male counterparts can. Eldiria is lucky to have two hundred and eight sorceresses among our soldiers."

"You don't consider women inferior to men?"

He chuckles, the sound oddly mesmerizing. It's odd to hear him make such gentle sounds, to see that twinkle in his eyes, when every other part of him looks so monstrous. "Only a foolish man would ever underestimate a woman's formidable strength, Arabella. Only a foolish ruler would weaken his own empire for fear of a sorceress's magic when nurturing those who are often forgotten and forsaken forges the deadliest blade."

I exhale shakily as I search his eyes, a mixture of relief and hope settling deep in my chest. His words mended a part of my heart I didn't realize was broken, and it just adds to my confusion. "Do you not fear that I will use my knowledge about your army against you?"

He gently brushes the back of his hand over my cheek, his eyes never leaving mine as he presses his body flush against mine. "I do not," he replies, his voice soft. "For my people are now yours, and I know you will not forsake them as others have."

"I tried to slay you on our wedding night," I remind him, my voice different now, unrecognizable.

He laughs, and my heart seems to respond to the sound, its beating accelerating just a touch. His proximity shouldn't confuse me so, and I should be pushing him away, yet I find myself rising to my tiptoes. "Yet somehow, I am certain you will never raise a blade to my people." His gaze roams over my face, and his smile transforms into something that can only be described as mischievous. "Besides, I thoroughly enjoyed punishing you for the mess you made. If anything, I welcome you to try it once more."

"I—"

"Have dinner with me tonight, Empress," he says, cutting me off and taking a step back. "It's clear you have questions that only I can answer, and I do not want to be at war with you. I understand that you don't wish to be here, but I've waited for you far longer than you could possibly know, Arabella. Hear me out tonight, I beg of you."

CHAPTER SIXTEEN

Arabella

I glare at the note that flies around my room, folding itself into the shape of a butterfly as it goes around in circles, occasionally pausing and unfurling in front of me, but never quite long enough to let me catch it and tear it to pieces. I've read the message a dozen times now, yet the palace insists on keeping it hovering around. It would not surprise me if Felix had a hand in this.

"I see you're enjoying yourself," I mutter into the empty room, feeling somewhat out of my mind when the butterfly appears to nod. I have yet to get used to the amount of magic entwined into daily life at this palace, and it hasn't ceased to amaze me. The note unfolds itself, and I sigh when Felix's handwriting comes into view.

> *Meet me in the courtyard when the bells ring six times. Dress warmly for our dinner tonight.*
>
> *Yours,*
> *Felix*

"At last," I murmur when the note flies onto Felix's desk and stays there. My relief is short-lived, though; before long, my wardrobe doors open, and three gorgeous travel dresses appear. The palace seems to have a clear favorite, because a black riding dress reminiscent of Felix's uniform moves forward, turning this way and that way, as though to show off its best features. Just like Felix's uniform, the Eldirian emblem is actively being embroidered on it, over and over again. It's a gorgeous piece, and it's obvious it's meant to complement his.

"I don't think I'll be needing that. A simple dress will do just fine," I say as I march over to the wardrobe, only for every piece of clothing to disappear until all I'm left with is the black riding dress. "Much like your master, you seem to make a habit of providing the illusion of choice," I snap. The dress seems to shrug, its sleeves moving, and I glare at it as I snatch it out of the air.

The dress molds to my skin perfectly, and I take a deep breath as I look into the mirror, barely recognizing myself. I'm used to wearing light colors befitting a princess, but even I can't deny that the jet-black outfit paired with my sleek, long dark hair makes me feel both beautiful and powerful.

A thick dark cape similar to Felix's appears around my shoulders, and I stare at my reflection. "Where exactly is he taking me tonight for you to dress me this way?" I ponder. Until I saw tonight's outfit, I'd assumed we'd be having dinner at the palace, but it's clear that isn't the case.

The thought of leaving these palace walls and exploring more of Eldiria, and its possible escape routes, fills me with equal parts excitement and hope. I'd been so certain Felix would keep me confined in the palace, the way my father always had.

"You look beautiful."

I whirl around in surprise and raise a hand to my chest, only to find Felix leaning back against the wall in the corner. "How long have you been standing there? Did you...did you watch me get changed like some sort of...*pervert*?"

His eyes widen, and then he bursts out laughing as he pushes off the wall. "You never cease to amuse and surprise me," he says, pausing in front of me. His touch is gentle as he brushes my hair out of my face. "No one in my vast empire would ever dare speak to me the way you do, Empress." He rocks back on his heels and shakes his head. "I have yet to decide what is sharper—your blade or your words."

"Perhaps you'd like a reminder of the former," I threaten, peeved he snuck up on me. "I would be happy to oblige."

He grins, his perfect teeth making an appearance. It's odd how I've begun to recognize his expressions, even through the moving veins that attempt to obscure them. It's his eyes—they refuse to be silenced. "If you wish to feel my mouth on your skin, you only need ask, wife."

My lips part in surprise, and heat rushes to my face, my response earning me another chuckle from Felix. He places his index finger underneath my chin and pushes my lips closed as I do my level best to glare at him. "Much to my regret, I arrived too late to be treated to the sight I have been dreaming of since I tasted you. I'd love for you to remedy that."

"You're such a...*pig*!"

Felix stares at me blankly for a moment. "What is a pig?" he asks, his eyes narrowing slightly, something akin to amusement flickering in his gorgeous eyes.

I raise a brow in confusion. "Do you...do you not have pigs in Eldiria?" I ask, instantly feeling bad. I'd forgotten Elaine's words about the curse resulting in crops and livestock dying. "Th-They're pink, and often a bit fat, and they e-eat everything."

"You think I'm fat?" he asks, his voice soft as he reaches for my hand and slides it over his uniform, his abs strong underneath my hand, even through the fabric. "Perhaps I should extend our army's two-hour daily sparring session."

I stare at him in disbelief and shake my head. "You mustn't," I plead. If word got out that I was the reason behind extended brutal training sessions, I have no doubt I'd earn his soldiers' unending ire. It'd thwart my plans to get on their good side before I even had a chance to approach any of them.

Felix laughs again and buries a hand in my hair, his eyes sparkling. "I am merely jesting, Empress," he says, his voice soft. "Of course I'm familiar with pigs."

I pull my hand off him and look away, stunned. I didn't think the Shadow Emperor was capable of making jokes and laughing the way he does. The more I'm around him, the more the concept of who I thought he was falls apart, and the same can be said of me. He brings out something I never knew existed—something fearless and authentically me. I don't recall a time where I've felt comfortable speaking my mind without fear of retaliation, yet somehow, I am certain he will not harm me. It's an instinctive feeling, nestled deep in my chest, and I've never felt anything quite like it before. It's implicit trust, and I'm certain it's misplaced.

Felix places his hands on my cape, and it instantly transforms into a much simpler one, leaving me intrigued as to where we're going.

CHAPTER SEVENTEEN

Felix

I transmute a cloak from the wardrobe into a simple one, and it appears around my shoulders moments later. Arabella stares at it, but it isn't the fabric she's staring at, it's the air surrounding it. I've suspected this for a while now, but I believe she's able to see the energetic trail that alchemy and magic leave behind. More than once, I've seen her stare at the air just after I've transmuted something, and she's done the same whenever Elaine casts a spell, but I have a feeling she isn't aware that it's a rare ability. Sometimes it's hard to remember that she grew up in a country that punishes what it does not understand, to its own detriment.

"We'll be going into town disguised as a regular couple," I explain, reminding myself that patience is what I need. It's not my strong suit, but with Arabella, I must have it. My people need her, and I cannot force her to help them. I'd hoped she was capable of killing me, that the prophecy related to her wielding a weapon, but since it appears not, the answer must lie in her powers.

I offer her my arm, and she hesitates before taking it. "Under normal circumstances, it would be possible to walk to the nearest town," I tell her. "But it is too cold to do so, so there is a carriage waiting for us."

She nods, her eyes gleaming as though she's soaking up every bit of information I'm giving her. My wife is terribly easy to read, and she doesn't even realize it. "Trying to walk would mean certain death," I warn. "It is too cold, and though the palace is relatively safe, there are magical perils outside of it, courtesy of the curse."

Her expression falls a touch, and I bite back a smile as I lead her down the stairs, acutely aware of her proximity. I don't recall the last time a woman held my arm the way she does now. I've slept with women, but there's never been any kind of true intimacy. It's novel, and I'm surprised to find I don't despise her touch.

She falls into step with me as we exit the palace through the servants' back door, and I wonder what she sees as she takes in my kingdom. To some, the snow is beautiful, but others see it for the curse it is. I know I should speak to her as we walk toward the carriage, but I can't think of anything to say. Every time I speak, I seem to push her further away. I've always gotten far through brute force, but perhaps that was not the right decision when it comes to Arabella. Perhaps I should have taken Elaine's advice and courted her. If there had been time, and the boy she ran away with was not a problem, I might have considered it, however foreign the concept might be to me.

"Careful," I warn her as rose plants slither through the snow, their thorns out for blood. One of the plants approaches us, no doubt hoping to slither its way around our legs to draw our blood, and I grit my teeth as I transmute the air around us in an effort to keep it away.

Roses were my mother's favorite flowers, and from the day I was born, they have haunted me, appearing in the palace like harbingers of doom. I'm so consumed by the hatred I feel that I fail to notice that Arabella is shaking. I pause and glance down at her to find her eyes filled with fear. No doubt this is the first time she's experienced anything like this.

"Arabella," I whisper, turning to face her. I brush her hair out of her face, my heart sinking when I see the fear in her eyes. This is the same woman who viciously stabbed me in the heart on our wedding night, yet the magic around us scares her.

"These rosebushes feed on people's life-force. Their roots extend to the core of our lands, feeding the curse. You must be cautious around them, but never fear when I am with you. I will always keep you safe, wife."

She looks into my eyes, and the cautious trust she gazes at me with does something unexpected to me. It fills me with tenderness, something I've never felt before. "The roses in the courtyard," she begins, her voice trembling as I hold the carriage door open for her. It's been enchanted to look common and avoid attention, but it's luxurious on the inside.

"No," I tell her, offering my hand as she gets into the carriage. "Those roses are different. It's unclear why, but every time a sorcerer or sorceress in the palace is lost to the curse, a new rose blooms on the courtyard walls, almost instantly freezing over. Though their thorns are sharp, those roses aren't sentient like the ones we just saw, and they won't harm you."

She nods and stares out the window, trying her best to see through the glass and failing. "I remember when these fields used to be filled with flowers." My voice is soft, filled with regret. "Rolling green hills, stunning flower fields with winding rivers flowing through them. Eldiria used to be the most beautiful place I've ever seen."

She looks into my eyes, and for once, she looks disarmed, compassionate even. I gaze down and wrap my arm around the back of the seat, my arm just about touching hers as I transmute my own body heat to warm her, frost running up my spine. My wife sighs happily as she looks out the window, and she leans into me just a touch. It would've been imperceptible to anyone but me, and the implication gives me hope. She no longer fears me as much as she did on our wedding day.

"We're here," I murmur, jumping out before reaching for her.

Her eyes widen when I wrap my arms around her waist and lift her out of the carriage, trying my best to remember not to use alchemy on her. She tenses when I wrap my arm around her shoulder, and I lean in. "We're pretending to be an ordinary couple, remember?"

She sighs as I lead her through the alleys toward the town center. Arabella is visibly shocked when she sees the elderly managing the stalls, many of them looking weary, and far too many of them dressed in too few layers.

"The curse's effects keep getting worse," I tell her. "There hasn't been a child in well over a decade now. It's surprising how quickly liveliness turns to longing, playfulness turns to wishfulness. There's no laughter, no playing, no children running in our kingdom. The curse keeps us trapped here, with few resources to sustain ourselves."

Arabella inhales shakily, almost as though the curse didn't seem real to her until now. I pause as we walk past a row of beggars and transform some of the gold hidden in the embroidery of our cloaks into coins to give to them.

"Homes regularly collapse. Each time someone attains a small sense of happiness, it's ripped away from us. Misfortune follows us all. The stalls here are all wooden so they can be rebuilt with ease, but they do not provide warmth."

I can tell that she's struggling to comprehend what I'm telling her. It's hard to, when you have never suffered the effects of a curse so cruel. "My people are going hungry, and so many of them have lost their homes. No amount of money can rebuild this country when every attempt leads to repeated destruction. Just as the woods can't be cut down, some homes cannot be rebuilt, and some lives cannot be saved. Those who possess magic suffer worse. There aren't many of them left. Many of the ones who remain have joined our army."

Arabella turns toward me, concern laced with curiosity in her eyes. I think it might be the first time she's looked at me without her guard up. "What happens to those who possess magic?"

I grimace and look away, my mind drifting to Raphael, my closest friend—perhaps my only true friend. Elaine's continued allegiance isn't to me. Not truly. Her loyalty has always been with him.

"Their power is leached out of them over time, and they must constantly fight to stay in control. The curse makes them go mad with pain, whispers into their ear to surrender. Eventually, most give up, their magic bleeding into the ground, strengthening the curse. The curse takes from them until nothing but a rose remains. Their bodies vanish, and a new rose blooms in the palace."

She looks as heartbroken as I feel, and some of the guilt that courses through me is put to rest. Arabella must have realized why I've brought her here—to show her the suffering of my people, to show her that it isn't just me she'd be helping if she breaks this curse. It feels manipulative, but I'm desperate, and so are my people.

"Some pretty earrings for you, my lady?"

I turn toward the jeweler and nod at Arabella, who approaches his stall. She takes the earrings from him and holds them up, attempting to see better in the dark. They look like green sapphires to me.

"Only eight hundred silvers," he tells her. "But for a pretty maiden such as yourself, I'll make it seven hundred and eighty."

Arabella gasps and hands him back the earrings in a rush. "That's too expensive!" she says, and I stare at her in surprise. She's a Princess of Althea. I didn't expect her to have a notion of what anything costs at all. Most princesses I've met have never paid for anything themselves. What kind of life has she lived?

Howard's smile drops, and he cradles the earrings gently. "You must be traveling through via the trade routes," he says, his voice weary. "Everything here is more expensive, my lady. After all, we risk our lives every time we go out to import goods. The ice is nothing. It's the woods. They don't want to let us leave, and each time we try, we risk never making it back home."

She looks shaken, no doubt remembering the way the forests opened up for us. Coming back is easy; leaving is a different matter.

"I'm looking for a ring for my wife, Howard," I tell him, and he freezes, his eyes sliding toward me. I'm barely recognizable in the cloak that covers my face. It's identical to the ones we all wear to keep us warm, but he's familiar with my voice.

When he looks back at Arabella, his eyes are filled with awe. He straightens, and then he bows to her. "Your Excellency," he says to her, "forgive me my ignorance. I heard rumors, but I didn't dare dream it could be true. The end of this curse is in sight for us at last."

I wrap my arm around Arabella's shoulder, and she leans into me, surprising me. She seems shaken. I suppose hearing others speak of the curse so freely makes it all more real for her. "A ring, Howard," I remind him.

He nods and takes out a velvet box for us, filled with exquisite rings. I stare at Arabella while she stares at the rings. Her eyes fall to a thin band with a small diamond. Not at all what I'd expect her to choose. I expected her to go for the biggest diamond Howard has, and I'd happily have given it to her.

I reach for the ring and grab her hand. "I have to get you some gloves, too," I murmur as I slide the ring onto her finger. It's too big, so I resize it for her as it lies around her finger until a small ball of residual gold hovers in the air. I push it toward Howard, and he nods. "We'll take it."

I hand him a bag of gold coins, but his focus is entirely on Arabella. He's looking at her like the beacon of hope she is.

"Come," I tell her, "let's get you some gloves before we head to dinner."

She nods, and this time when she looks at me, there's no venom in her beautiful eyes.

CHAPTER
EIGHTEEN

Arabella

I'm silent as Felix leads me to a private room inside a small restaurant at the top of a tower. Thanks to the torches by the stalls, I'm actually able to see most of the marketplace, and it feels refreshing to have a view of some sort instead of just the endless pitch darkness, and to see so many people.

Thankfully, we weren't ambushed by more supernatural wonders that I can barely comprehend as we explored the surprisingly bustling town. How something as beautiful as a rosebush can be that terrifying astounds me. Eldiria is not what I expected. Everything here is deceptive—including my husband. He might be the cruel emperor that tore me away from everything I've ever known, but I've also come to see the man whose heart bleeds as he watches his people suffer.

His eyes drop to the fireplace by our table, and the fire begins to blaze hotter just as I take off my brand-new gloves. It almost feels wrong to sit here, knowing that so many of the people I can see from the window would do anything to feel this kind of warmth.

"Are you still cold?" Felix asks, concerned. His cloak disappears from his shoulders and reappears around mine, his gaze roaming over my face. How much of himself has he already given to his people? All I've thought of since we got married was all I lost. I never realized that he's lost so much more than I have.

I'm probably far from the kind of woman he would've wanted to marry, yet he's trapped in this situation as much as I am. Perhaps more so. I was so absorbed in my own pain and loss that I inflicted upon him what I suffered from for years, never taking a moment to assess whether the rumors about him were true or not. I've been thinking of ways to deceive him, to trick him into believing I can break this curse when I'm powerless, useless—all so I could safeguard my own life at the expense of so many others.

"I can't help you," I whisper, the truth escaping from my lips before I realize what I'm doing. "I wish I could, but I can't."

He stares at the fire, quiet for a moment before he speaks. "I believe you can, Arabella. Long before you were born, a seer sought refuge at my palace, offering a prophecy that could save us in return for protection from the curse. She had seen different versions of the future, and there was one in which she not only survived but saw the curse broken, too. I offered her a binding spell that kept her safe, and she gave me her prophecy as well as a promise to show me the woman in the prophecy when the time was right. I'd begun to lose hope until a few months ago, when she showed me *you*."

I cannot deceive him after everything I just saw. I cannot give his people hope where there is none. My decision might put my life at risk, but all I'm doing is expediting the inevitable. "I want to believe that, Felix. I do. But I know myself better than anyone else. I cannot help you."

He tears his gaze away from the fire and looks at me with an expression I've never seen him carry before. It's desperation. "Are you willing to try? I beg of you, Arabella. Help me save my people, and I will give you anything you want in return. *Anything*. If it is in my power, it's yours."

I look into his eyes, startled by the conviction I see. "I'm willing to try," I say, my voice soft. "On two conditions."

He nods, indicating for me to continue. My heart races as I gather my words, praying I won't be punished for this.

"I want you to ensure Nathaniel Orathis's safety and well-being, meaning that he is free from any punishment and reinstated in his former occupation." Since Althea is now one of Eldiria's vassals, he can easily make that happen. My father cannot deny him.

Felix's eyes flash dangerously as he pulls a hand through his thick, dark hair. For a moment I wonder if he'll punish me for thinking of Nathaniel, and an odd sense of longing rushes through me.

He leans in over the table to brush my hair out of my face, the back of his fingers trailing over my cheek. His eyes are filled with such intense longing and loneliness that a hint of shame tugs at my conscience. I'm his wife, yet here I am, pleading for the safety of the man I'd rather be with instead. "Consider it done," he whispers, his hand falling away. "Continue."

I swallow hard and look down at the ring he bought me. "Second, I want you to let me go. I don't believe it possible, but if we manage to set your people free, then I want you to set me free, too."

He turns away to stare out the window, my heartbeat the only thing I hear in the silence that surrounds us. "Very well," he says eventually, and I exhale in relief. "I'd like to work on undoing the curse's effects. If we can find a way to make our grounds fertile again, then I'll consider our deal done."

I nod, reading between the lines. "Undoing its effects? You don't believe we can break this curse outright?"

Felix smiles, his expression forlorn. "I've tried for nearly two hundred years. If there was a way to truly break the curse, I would have found it. My people seem to think that the answer lies in true love, but I don't believe that to be the case. I am, however, willing to try anything, no matter how ridiculous. If I am to grant you these two conditions, I must insist that we try everything we can to break this curse, and with a bit of luck, we might mitigate its effects through one of our attempts."

"True love?" I ask, confused.

"There were two main components to the curse, and based on my research on curses, if we could undo just one of them, the curse might come undone," Felix explains. "The first part was about the kingdom being cast in shadows, which has resulted in eternal winter and infertile grounds. The second part, however, was about a true union. I was cursed never to be loved, never to be chosen."

I bite down on my lip, a shiver running down my spine. "I...what do you need me to do?"

Felix's eyes roam over my face, his expression unreadable. "You must give our marriage an honest chance. My people aren't wrong to assume love could break the curse. Based on all the research I have done, it is possible for that to be the solution. It isn't likely, but it's possible. On the other hand, it could mean that we merely need to unite our bodies physically."

Give our marriage a chance? "You want me to—" I whisper.

Felix shakes his head. "I won't force you, Arabella. I won't take you against your will, but I'd like you to give this a chance. I can make you feel pleasure unlike anything you've ever felt before. In due time, perhaps it truly will lead to love. We must try."

I recoil from him and wrap my arms around myself. The mere thought of ever being with him makes me feel like I'm betraying Nathaniel and ruining every chance of ever being with him. "I can't," I whisper, even though a small part of me *wants* to.

Felix's expression hardens. "Then I'll see to it that the boy hangs."

"Don't!" I swallow hard, panic awakening something fiery within me, something that I've felt before, just before I'm involved in one of the many incidents that resulted in me being called cursed.

"Then what will it be? His future is in your hands."

I clench my hands and nod, my shoulders drooping in defeat. "If you guarantee Nathaniel's safety, I'm willing to give you a chance, Felix... whatever that entails."

Relief flashes through his eyes, and he nods. "Very well. However, I'm not used to sharing anything, Arabella. If you commit to giving us a chance, I will not have you thinking of him. Until the day I let you go, every single part of you is mine. Do you understand?"

I stare at him, at the thick slithering veins that completely obscure his face, his dark hair, and the fire in his eyes. My heart is filled with regret as I nod. "I understand," I whisper.

Felix looks into my eyes, seemingly satisfied with what he finds, and he leans back. "The other part of the curse might be easier to unravel. I suspect the key lies in the magic you hold within. You were prophesied because you're special somehow. What is it you can do?"

I flinch, panic seizing me instantly as memories fill my mind. Every punishment I've been through, the pain in my back, my sister's tears.

"Arabella," he says, snapping me out of my thoughts. "Magic is not banned here. It's celebrated. You will never be punished for being powerful. Never. I swear it."

I nod, knowing that it's true, yet I struggle to put my faith in him.

"Will you tell me what type of magic you have? I promise that no harm will come to you. You are my wife, Arabella. No one would dare touch you."

He speaks to me with kindness I didn't expect of him, and my panic deflates. He's right. I'm married to the Shadow Emperor himself. He's the most famous alchemist ever to have lived. Right by his side is the safest place I can be.

"This is why I don't think I can help you," I admit, my voice so soft it's barely above a whisper. "I don't have any powers, Felix. My mother was a sorceress, and I've always hoped I inherited some of her magic, but I didn't."

He reaches for my hand over the table and squeezes gently. "I know for a fact that you do have powers, Arabella. I've seen the way your eyes linger when spells or alchemy are performed. I know you can see energy trails, and that is a rare talent."

I stare at him in disbelief. "It's not normal to see magic?"

He grins and shakes his head. "It's an indication of immense power, beloved. We'll figure this out, okay? Together."

CHAPTER NINETEEN

Felix

"Natural disasters have tripled in the last fortnight," Elaine tells me as we walk toward the atrium together, her brow creased in concern. "It's never been this bad, Theon. With each passing day, I grow more worried. It is almost as though the curse knows you've married the empress, and I'm unsure if the resulting rise in incidents is a good sign or the opposite."

I think back to my conversation with Arabella last week and shake my head. "I'm not sure, either," I admit. Arabella and I have been working together to research the curse and any potential powers she has, but we're both coming up empty. "I've consulted Pythia, and she insists that it's Arabella who'll break the curse, though I'm still unsure how."

My mind drifts to the way my wife looked when I explained the true union aspect of the curse, essentially insinuating that we should sleep together even if it's just to rule it out. She looked apprehensive and unwilling, to say the least.

I've been giving her some space, ensuring I don't come to bed until I'm certain she's asleep so as to not overwhelm her or push her away, but each night, it becomes a little harder to stay away. I've never craved intimacy, yet falling asleep next to her has been surprisingly soothing. Every morning, I wake with her in my arms, caught in a web of limbs and long hair. She holds me a little tighter when I attempt to pull away, her lips pressed against my neck, my name a soft sleepy whisper that inevitably makes me stay in bed longer than I should. My empress is enchanting me with one single word, one that's reserved solely for her. My name.

"It feels intentional," Elaine says as we walk over to the training grounds. "The incidents are taking place at opposite ends of the empire, almost as though to spread our army thin. I'm concerned for the empress's safety."

I shake my head in reassurance. "She's safe here at the palace so long as she doesn't enter the east wing—you know that as well as I do. If she leaves at all, it'll be with me."

Elaine nods, but I see the concern written all over her face. We've never had a real chance at breaking the curse, and I know she's scared our one and only opportunity will slip between our fingers.

Elaine continues to update me on the state of our empire's affairs, but all I can focus on is the vision in black ahead of me. Something dark and primal rushes through me each time I see Arabella in clothes that are clearly designed to complement mine, even though I know it's the palace providing them for her, and not something she's chosen of her own accord.

I watch as Arabella studies the roses climbing on the palace walls, her eyes filled with sorrow. She's been different in recent days—kinder, more patient. She's even smiled at me a handful of times as we pored over books together to find ways to draw her magic out, and I was shocked to find she instantly became even more breathtaking. When she smiles, her eyes soften and twinkle beautifully, and her head falls back just a touch as she looks at me.

"You're smiling at the sight of her," Elaine says, sounding elated.

"I'm not," I lie.

She grins and steps back. "You should go to her. It looks like she might have some questions about the roses. No one knows more about them than you do."

I throw her a good-natured glare before I walk over to my wife. Arabella looks up, our eyes locking, and then she does that thing again—she smiles at me. There's no longer any hostility in her eyes, and though it isn't a huge change, it feels like it is.

"Felix," she calls, her voice so melodic and sweet that I can't help but smile back at her. "Felix!" she calls again, panicked this time as she throws her hands up. I look up just as shards of ice dislodge from one of the palace's towers, large icicles headed directly for me, only for them to remain suspended mere inches above my head. "Thank the Fates," my wife says, her hand on her chest. "Thank the Fates you caught that."

I raise a brow and shake my head. "That wasn't me, Arabella."

"Wh-What?" she stammers, confusion flickering through her eyes. Moments later, the ice comes crashing down, and I grimace as it cuts my skin, blood splattering everywhere before my body has a chance to mend itself. "Felix!" Arabella screams, pure horror ringing through her voice as she runs up to me.

I grab her arms and force myself to smile through the pain. Just because my skin heals itself doesn't mean I don't first feel every bit of pain I otherwise would've felt. "I'm okay," I reassure her. "I'm okay, Arabella. Make sure you don't touch my blood—not under any circumstances. I'm uncertain why it didn't burn you last time, but I'd rather not risk it."

"I'm sorry," she repeats, over and over, tears streaming down her face. "This is all m-my fault. I'm s-sorry, Felix. I didn't... I should've t-told you the t-truth."

"What truth?" I ask, my tone gentle as I transmute my blood off my skin and the snow, and far away from her.

She looks at me with so much remorse in her beautiful eyes that all I want to do is pull her close. "I-I'm c-cursed, Felix." She begins to sob and buries her face in her hands. "Misfortune f-follows me everywhere I go. Fires. Floods. Tornadoes. Earthquakes. That avalanche...I'm certain it's my fault, and th-this, too..."

I cup her face gently, my mind whirling. "Look at me," I plead. "Please, Arabella."

Her eyes flutter open, and I step closer, my heart hammering in my chest. If what she's saying is true, it all finally makes sense, and cautious hope rushes through me. "You aren't cursed, beloved. For a curse to be strong enough to cause natural disasters, it'd have to be decades in the making. I've studied curses extensively for well over a century, and those rumors about magic turning against its users? They aren't true. That is why those in our safe havens have not incurred misfortune of any kind—because there is no such curse." She looks at me as if she wants to believe me but can't. "Think back carefully to the way the icicles didn't hit me right away. I think I know what you wield, Arabella, and you were right. It isn't magic."

"I'm n-not cursed?" she asks.

"No," I reassure her, smiling. "You are not nearly old enough for any curse tied to you specifically to have grown that strong, and there is no curse of magical bloodlines. You aren't cursed, Arabella. Quite the opposite. You have no idea what you just did, do you?"

She shakes her head, and I stare at her in awe. Even with her lashes frozen thanks to her tears, she's breathtaking. "You wielded air, Empress."

CHAPTER TWENTY

Arabella

I sit up in bed and glance at the clock Elaine gifted me a few days ago, when I complained about the eternal darkness and my inability to keep track of how much time passes the way I would in Althea. It's early in the morning, and Felix has yet to return to the palace. He left shortly after we discovered I might have air wielding powers, due to yet another avalanche, and I'm growing concerned. When he takes Sirocco, he's often back by nightfall, but he's been away for three nights so far.

Three nights have never felt so long. I've been unwilling to admit it to myself, but I've grown accustomed to waking at night to find him holding me tightly, the rising and falling of his strong chest bringing me a sense of comfort I've never known before.

Every night, I find myself pretending to be asleep when I hear the slightest sound in the corridor, in the hope he'll walk in and join me in bed. He thinks I'm unaware of his attempts to give me space, and with each night I spend alone in our bed, I wish more fervently that I'd just admitted how safe I feel in his arms. Perhaps then, he wouldn't have stayed away so long.

I bite down on my lip and try to refocus on my book, only for my thoughts to keep returning to Felix. I've scoured through his library in search of books about elemental powers, only to find little to nothing. As it turns out, elemental powers of any kind are incredibly rare, and the last known wielder lived over a thousand years ago.

I sigh as I lean back against my pillow. Felix must have been wrong. There is no way someone like me possesses such a rare and powerful power, and if I did, surely I'd have known? If I'm that powerful, why did my powers never save me when my father hurt me?

I've even tried to levitate objects, the way Felix claims I levitated the icicles, but that, too, was to no avail. The more I try it, the sillier I feel. I'm as powerless as I've always been, and the hope I'd begun to feel has started to douse.

I startle when the bedroom door opens and at last Felix walks in, our eyes locking for a moment. My heart skips a beat at the sight of him, and I sit up instinctively, only barely able to suppress my desire to walk up to him.

"You're still awake," he says, hanging his head for a moment. His clothes are soiled with filth and blood, and defeat fills the air between us. He takes a deep breath as he walks past the bed toward the bathtub, which has already started to fill itself, and I blush when I hear the sounds of his clothes hitting the floor.

"How did it go?" I ask carefully, feeling oddly shy. I feel like I've waited an eternity for him to return safely, yet now that he's here, I'm at a loss for words. Every moment of intimacy we've shared has been under the cover of night, little stolen moments I've pretended I'm unaware of.

I bite down on my lip when I hear him sink into the water. "We lost a lot of people this time, both soldiers and civilians. I've never seen anything like it. Elaine was right. It's like the curse knows I found you, like it knows we're closer than ever to ridding ourselves of it."

I don't have the heart to tell him that I think he's wrong, that I don't have any powers after all. It's clear he needs hope and reassuring words, and I want nothing more than to give him that, but I'd be lying if I did. "I'm glad you're home safe and sound," I tell him instead, meaning the words. "I was worried about you."

He rises from the water, and my heart begins to beat a little faster as I gently close my book. Felix walks to the bed wearing nothing but a pair of black shorts, and I look down at my hands to keep from staring. I know the feel of his body by heart, and once or twice, I've let my hands wander at night. Even so, looking at him outright feels scandalous.

The bed dips when he joins me, and I glance over, unable to help myself. "You're hurt," I murmur, aghast. I rise to my knees and reach for him without thinking, surprised to see fresh raised scars on his skin that even the moving veins can't hide. The bleeding has stopped, but it's clear these wounds aren't disappearing the way they usually would.

I trace over them with the tip of my finger, and Felix grabs my wrist. He presses my palm flat against his chest, and I look into his eyes to find him gazing at me with an expression I've never seen before—not even the night I stabbed him and he punished me for it. His eyes are filled with vulnerability and longing.

"The wounds don't heal as fast when they're inflicted by the curse. This time it tried to bury me in an avalanche. The wounds are from sharp ice. Much like the rosebushes we encountered, the ice seemed sentient, too." A shudder runs down my spine, and I gently trace over the rapidly forming scar tissue with the edge of my thumb. "They'll be gone by tomorrow morning, but they don't disappear instantly. I've wondered if I'd die if I let it hurt me enough, but it always stops just before I die. It's clearly aware that it'll die with me. I wish I could just put an end to this already. I'm tired of watching my people suffer, knowing I'm the one to blame. If I'd just let the woods cage us in like they try to, maybe my people and I would've perished together, and that'd have been the end of it."

"There's no use pondering the what-ifs. If it's true that I was prophesied, the curse wouldn't have let you go even if you had taken different steps. We'll figure this out," I tell him, repeating the words he told me back to him.

"Perhaps so," he says, reaching for my hair. He gently pushes it behind my ear, his gaze roaming over the lace nightgown the palace provided me with tonight. "I'm just so tired, Arabella. Tired of this endless fight, of the curse's effects on my body and mind, and the..."

"The what?" I urge.

My breath hitches when he reaches for the thin strap on my shoulder, his gaze heated. My chest begins to rise and fall more rapidly, and Felix draws a shaky breath. "The unending loneliness," he whispers, his hand falling away.

I reach for his hand and put it back on my shoulder hesitantly. "But you aren't alone anymore," I murmur, my heart beating a rhythm I'm unfamiliar with. Something hot and heavy settles deep in my stomach as he looks at me, hope warring with desire in his enchanting eyes.

"Just because I'm no longer alone doesn't mean I'm any less lonely," he says, his voice breaking. "You're my wife, but you'll never be mine. You wouldn't be here if given a choice."

"I *am* yours," I whisper as I use his hand to push the strap off my shoulder. "I promised to help you, so let me. You asked me to give our marriage an honest chance, didn't you? This is me trying."

His gaze darkens, and he swallows hard as his eyes trail down my body, only to linger on the way the fabric of my nightgown clings to my chest, my strap hanging off my shoulder. "I need you to tell me in clear words what it is you're trying."

I bite down on my lip harshly, my nerves getting the best of me. "I think we should consummate our marriage."

CHAPTER TWENTY-ONE

Felix

I stare up at my wife, her eyes brimming with uncertainty, like she can't quite believe what she just said, either. "Our marriage isn't valid until we consummate it," she reminds me, her voice trembling. "Maybe that's what the *true union* part of the curse relates to."

"You don't want this," I whisper, my eyes falling closed. Her hand is still pressed against my chest, and I struggle to let go of her wrist. She has no idea what she's saying, what she's asking for. I want her with a passion burning fiercer than the hottest of fires, but this isn't what I wanted it to be like between us. I'd planned to tease her and draw out parts of her she's always kept hidden, until she truly desires me.

"I do," she tells me, quiet confidence written all over her face. "While you were away, I tried to find out more about the curse and any potential powers I might have that could help, but the more I think about it, the more I feel like we have to try the obvious first."

I sigh as I reach for her and cup her face. I suppose this technically is a duty we both ought to fulfill, and perhaps I'm foolish for wanting it to be more.

Arabella places her hand over mine. "Don't make me get my brand-new dagger," she warns, her eyes twinkling mischievously.

I can't help but chuckle, and I wonder if she realizes that I hadn't laughed in years until she walked into my life, yet now it comes to me so easily. "Maybe you should," I whisper. "Make me lose control in that way only you can."

"How do I make you lose control?" she asks, her voice soft. Arabella drags our joined hands down slowly, letting me explore her soft skin, until she reaches her collarbone. "Like this?"

I groan and grab her waist, flipping us both over so I'm on top of her. "Yes," I all but growl. "Like that."

Arabella gasps when I part her legs with my knee, and I watch her carefully, looking for the smallest hint that she might not want this. "Felix," she whispers, her breathing accelerating a touch as she caresses my temple with the tip of her fingers, our eyes locked. She hasn't recoiled from me in some time, nor does she struggle to maintain eye contact the way so many others do. Every once in a while, it's as if she really sees me, and those moments are addicting, maddening.

I sigh as I lean in, my nose brushing against hers. "I could never resist you," I whisper against her mouth. "I've never known a yearning so all-encompassing, until you."

Her hand slides into my hair just as I bridge the distance between our mouths to taste her. She kisses me back instantly, her spine arching slightly as she pushes herself against me, her grip tightening on my hair. I'd wondered if it'd been a charade, if it'd all fall apart the moment I touched her, but this passion is genuine, and it's intoxicating.

She's panting as I drag my lips to her ear, her body restless underneath mine. "I've dreamed of this more times than I should admit," I whisper into her ear before kissing her just below it. "I wondered how you'd sound if you were to whisper my name as though your body drips with a need only I can satisfy."

I snap my fingers, and our clothes disappear just as the sheets cover us, and the mere feel of her bare body against mine nearly sends me over the edge. I groan as my teeth graze over the soft curve of her shoulder, and I bite down softly, wishing to mark her yet knowing that I need to be gentle with her tonight.

I push myself up on my forearms to look at her, my heart instantly beating faster at the sight of her. I draw a shaky breath as I take in the way her long dark hair is spread over my pillows and drag my eyes down, cataloging her collarbone and the curve of her chest. Somehow, she looks even more beautiful than she did on our wedding night, and I suspect it has everything to do with the way she looks at me.

Our eyes remain locked as I slowly lower my mouth to her nipple, and a thrill runs down my spine when her lips part just as my tongue caresses the rapidly hardening bud. She arches her back, and I chuckle as I give in to her silent pleas, taking delight in the way she squirms underneath me, the way she moans.

Arabella tightens her grip on my hair when I move lower, leaving a trail of kisses down her stomach. "Felix," she whimpers uncertainly when I spread her legs and lift them over my shoulders.

"Let me," I plead, my whisper caressing her skin as I kiss her inner thigh. "I'm desperate for another taste."

She relaxes slightly, only for her head to fall back when my tongue parts her folds. She moans my name as I circle her clit with my tongue, and I groan against her skin, my cock throbbing painfully at the sound of her. Her nails scrape over my scalp as I take my time to torture her, bringing her to the edge and keeping her there, only to gently push two fingers in and stimulate her further with teasing come-hither motions.

Her legs begin to tremble, and I grin as I indulge myself, lapping her up until she's panting my name over and over. She's the sweetest poison. Each little sigh, each touch just corrupts me further, until all reason is lost and I'm left at her mercy. Arabella does not realize the hold she has over me, for if she did, she'd keep me trapped between her legs, hers to command as she pleases.

"Please," she begs. "Please, Felix."

I tighten my grip on her thighs and give her what she wants, driven to near delirium by her moans. Her muscles tighten, and I groan in delight when she tightens her legs around me. There's nothing more beautiful than watching the way she loses control—because of *me*.

I lay my head on her stomach as she comes down from her high, my heart overflowing with satisfaction as I make the sheets disappear, sweat coating both of our bodies. I could have sworn the room got hotter as she came, and I can't help but wonder if her air powers might have fueled the fire subconsciously.

"That was... I..."

Her breathlessness only further fills my chest with delight, and I grin as I move up, until my cock is lined up perfectly. "That was *what?*" I inquire as I push against her, not quite entering her just yet.

Arabella looks up at me from lowered lashes, her eyes brimming with desire. She's a vision, with a rosy blush that extends down to her chest, her entire body on display for me. "It was perfect," she whispers, almost as though she didn't want me to hear her answer.

I draw a shaky breath, unable to make sense of the way my heart reacts to her words. "Tell me you can take a little more."

She nods, her gaze filled with certainty. I grin as I call my shadow to me so she'll feel my tongue against her swollen clit even as I push into her a fraction. Arabella moans and bites down on her lip, her hips tilting in a silent demand for more, and I obey dutifully, ensuring she continues to feel languid soft strokes as I cup her face.

"You have no idea how long I've waited for this," I whisper, pushing in a little deeper. "How many nights I've slept beside you, fantasizing about doing *this* one day."

Her breath hitches when I push halfway into her, and she whimpers a little. "It's too much," she tells me, her hand wrapping around the back of my neck.

I hold still and lean in to press a soft kiss to her cheek. "You're doing so well," I promise her. She's soaking wet, and I know she can take me. "You're taking my cock like it was made for you." I didn't think it possible, but she flushes a deeper shade of red, and I stare at her in wonder. "Can you take a little more for me, beloved?"

Arabella nods, and I take a deep breath before pushing fully into her, tearing a pained moan from her beautiful throat. "I'm sorry," I whisper, kissing her neck. Remorse rushes through me as I hold still and drop my forehead to her shoulder. I'd hoped it wouldn't hurt at all, given how wet she is, and if I'd known, I'd have taken it even slower.

"I'm okay, Felix," my wife tells me as she caresses my back with the tip of her fingers, her touch soothing, reassuring. "It only hurt for a moment."

I push myself up on my forearms and look into her eyes, finding nothing but reassurance. She cups my face, our eyes locking, and something about this moment seems to stretch indefinitely, searing itself into my memories. A thousand years could pass, and I'd still remember this moment with her. I'm certain of it.

"How is this?" I whisper, rocking back and forth gently.

A soft, needy sound escapes her lips, and she turns her face away, almost as though she's embarrassed of her own desire. I chuckle and nip at her exposed neck. "Don't hide from me like that," I murmur, my strokes becoming a little deeper, a little faster. "Show me that I'm pleasing you, Arabella, I beg of you."

She looks back at me, her gaze roaming over my face hungrily as the feeling of my tongue lapping at her intensifies in line with my thrusts, and though she tries to bite them back, the most beautiful moans leave her lips.

"Yes," I groan when her pants come a little faster just as my own movements begin to become more erratic. "Show me, beloved. Let me watch you fall apart for me."

I can't help but moan when her muscles contract around me, and just like that, she involuntarily takes me over the edge with her, wave after wave of overflowing desire unlike anything I've ever known taking control of me. "Arabella," I moan as I collapse on top of her, my mind filled with nothing but her.

She hugs me tightly, and I sigh happily as I kiss her neck again and again, my complete satiation in contrast with the knowledge that I'll never get enough of her.

CHAPTER TWENTY-TWO

Arabella

I begin to stir and turn over in search of Felix, only to find him standing by the foot of the bed, packing a bag. "Arabella," he murmurs, his gaze roaming over me affectionately. "You're awake."

I sit up and clutch the bedsheets, covering myself as I try my best to meet Felix's eyes, thoughts of last night rushing through my mind.

"I'm sorry, beloved," he says, sighing. "A hurricane destroyed one of the empire's most important horse breeder's stables." Felix continues to pack. "I wish I didn't have to go, but I must. They provide most of our army's horses, and I have to minimize the damage."

"I'll come with you," I tell him, trying to ignore the tenderness between my legs. "If you truly are right, and I can wield elements, then it's best for me to practice outdoors until I'm certain I can control my powers. What if I accidentally create a tornado? Besides, I don't think anyone but you could teach me."

Felix nods, his gaze pensive. "We'll be away for at least a fortnight, and it won't be comfortable."

I nod as I slip out of bed and wrap myself in our bedsheets. "I understand. How much time do I have to pack?"

He looks down at his feet for a moment, as though he isn't sure bringing me with him is the right choice. "I have to attend a strategy meeting before we head out, so that gives you about an hour. Pack enough of your things for a fortnight, but do not worry should you forget anything. So long as you remember exactly where you left an item, I can retrieve it for you."

I nod and throw him a reassuring smile, and he sighs as he turns to walk out of the room, giving me some privacy to get ready and pack. I'd been worried that things would be awkward between us this morning, but thankfully, that isn't the case. Even so, the thought of being alone with him for a fortnight fills me with a new kind of nerves.

I pack as quickly as I can, but by the time I make my way down, my mind is still filled with memories of everything he did and whispered to me last night, and I have no doubt my cheeks are rosy. I'd initiated the consummation because it felt like the right thing to do, but by the end of the night, he had me begging for more. What happened between us didn't feel like a mere formality, but it should have.

"Your Excellency," Elaine says, smiling as I approach the palace's large gates. "I hope you have a most pleasant trip together."

I try my hardest to smile back at her without giving away how flustered I feel this morning, but the way she grins tells me I'm failing.

"Ready?" Felix asks. I nod, and he takes my bag from me before touching my cape and transforming it into the same plain one we wore several evenings ago.

"Will I ever be able to do that?" I ask, unable to hide my wonder.

"It is unlikely," Felix murmurs, his fingers wrapping around my hood to pull it up. "As far as I'm aware, I'm the only alchemist still alive. Elemental wielding and alchemy are very different powers. Elemental wielding allows you to call the elements to you and bend them to your will, and if the few records I was able to find on it are correct, it requires no exchange as alchemy does. To change your cape, I have to exchange one type of fabric for another and perform several transmutations in rapid succession, but that isn't possible with elemental powers. You could, however, call air to you at will and create a tornado, for example, but at most I might be able to make things float by transmuting air and moving it from one area to another. Depending on what you're trying to do, my powers are a lot more limited than an elemental wielder's would be."

Felix pauses once we reach Sirocco, and my nerves overtake me when I realize I'll be riding with him once again. Being in close proximity to him makes me nervous in a way it didn't before. I keep thinking of the way he made me feel in bed, the way he touched me, and how incredible it felt. I know he can't read my thoughts, but I have a feeling he can tell what I'm thinking of.

Felix wraps his hands around my waist, startling me as he lifts me on top of Sirocco. He pauses, our eyes locking for a moment, before he pulls away and sits down behind me, our bodies connected.

Within seconds, Sirocco starts to move at such a high speed that I'd be terrified if I wasn't so hyperfocused on Felix behind me. He's got his arm wrapped around me, and the way his forearm touches the underside of my breasts has my cheeks flaming and my heart racing. He isn't keeping as much distance as he did the last time we rode together.

My back is pressed against his chest, my bottom between his legs. I didn't find our position quite this intimate last time, but now it's all I can think about. I'm startled when Felix leans in, his lips brushing over my ear. "Sit still, Arabella. You're making this very difficult for me, just like you did last time."

I turn to look at him, startled once more by his proximity. My lips nearly brush over his, but he doesn't move back. He just looks down at me with an expression that instantly reminds me of the way he teased me last night.

"One more hour," he says, his voice hoarse. "Try not to torture me any more than you already do. Keeping up Elaine's enchantment is getting more and more difficult the farther away we get from the palace. My magic is very weak compared with hers."

I look into his eyes, mesmerized by the beautiful gold specks in them. "What enchantment?" I ask.

Felix smiles, but there's something sinister in that smile, something dangerous. "The one that keeps you from feeling what kind of effect you have on me, wife. Since we agreed to give our marriage a chance, I won't hide such things from you any longer, but I also don't intend to shock you mere minutes into our journey."

I turn away in a rush, staring ahead in an effort to hide how flustered I am. He's...aroused? The thought of that has my cheeks heating. I can't help but think of the things his tongue did to me, desire rushing through me involuntarily.

I'm so flustered by the time Sirocco comes to a standstill that I'm not certain I can face Felix. Instead, I turn toward the woman rushing toward us, her cheeks rosy. Her smile drops slightly when she notices me, as though she expected Felix to come alone.

Felix jumps off and turns toward me, his hands wrapping around my waist like they did before. He takes his time lifting me off, his hands lingering longer than they need to.

"Alison," he says, turning toward the woman once my feet hit the floor. "Meet my wife, Arabella."

Alison stares at me, her expression betraying her shock. This is the first time Felix has introduced me to someone who wasn't instantly happy to meet me. Alison seems far from it. If anything, she looks crestfallen.

She curtsies, and I take her in. Long blond hair, bright-blue eyes. She's beautiful, and I can't help but wonder if that's the kind of woman he's normally interested in, someone whose features greatly differ from mine. I'm not entirely clueless. I recognize the jealousy I see in her eyes, and I have a feeling it's warranted.

"It's an honor to meet you, Empress," she says, her voice trembling. "Your Excellency," she adds, turning toward Felix. "The stable has collapsed, and we lost some of our horses."

Felix nods and grabs my hand, causing Alison to tense, but Felix doesn't appear to notice. Normally I'd shake him off, but instead, I find myself tightening my grip on him.

"Alison and her family are the best horse breeders and trainers the empire has to offer. We might not have crops, but we have some of the most talented people. Their horses are one of the main reasons we're able to make it through the woods."

I nod in understanding. They've had to become creative and hone their skills to earn a living. Unlike most other countries, there is no farming here, and even trade is risky. What I've come to love most about Eldiria is its people. They never cease to impress me. I've spent weeks quietly observing the hundreds of people working in the palace, and all the soldiers that train so diligently, and I've never seen more hardworking people.

"I'll make my way there myself," Felix tells her. "You head back inside."

Alison's expression tells me she prefers to stay, but she doesn't defy Felix. With one last lingering look at him, she turns away and heads toward the tall building in the distance.

I struggle to hide my shock when we arrive at what once used to be their stable. Even Felix looks grim. There's wood lying everywhere, and no part of the miles-long stable is still standing. I see the way Felix's shoulders drop and instinctively place my hand on his arm. He turns to look at me and smiles humorlessly.

"This one won't be easy, but it's fixable. It'll just take a bit longer than I expected. Just watch and see if you can feel or see my alchemy, all right?"

I nod, and much to my surprise, Felix takes his cape off. He turns toward me and wraps it around my shoulders, enveloping me in his warmth and scent. It startles me, and he smiles. The way he smiles at me is different now. Intimate, almost. Last night has transformed us both.

"I thought you never took your cape off outside the palace," I murmur.

He nods. "There's no one around for miles. I'll put it back on before we go inside."

He turns away, and just as he lifts the first piece of wood into the air, snow starts to fall. Felix looks up at the air, a crestfallen expression on his face. It breaks my heart to see both him and his people work as hard as they do, only to be knocked down again and again.

For hours, Felix works tirelessly, putting the stable back in place piece by piece. All the while, I watch him, and it's clear that though he makes it look easy, it's anything but. Sweat has drenched his uniform and a frown has etched its way into his face. Just as he asked me to, I try my best to focus on how his alchemy works, but it's hard to make sense of the energy trails I'm seeing and feeling.

Felix turns to me when it begins to snow harder. "You should head inside, Arabella. The snow is becoming too much. I don't want you to get cold."

I shake my head. "I'm fine," I tell him. "These two cloaks are keeping me perfectly warm. I'm okay. I'll stay here with you."

He looks into my eyes, a longing in them that I've never seen before. I've never seen Felix look this forlorn. At the palace, the curse is something everyone seems to have learned to live with. But I think cases such as these reopen the wounds for him. I never thought I'd have any sympathy for him, and I didn't think I'd ever want to understand him... but now I find myself wishing I could share his burdens. Guilt eats at me when I think back to the way I treated him, the way I stabbed him and lamented his existence—as though I could do more harm to him than he already faces on a daily basis.

He takes a step closer, his hand trembling as he raises it to my face. My eyes fall closed when his ice-cold hand wraps around my cheek, and I place my own hand on top of his. "Go," he says. "She won't let me help my people. She won't make this easy. I don't want you to have to watch this. I don't know what I was thinking, bringing you on this trip with me."

She? I frown, tempted to ask him who it is he's referring to, yet well aware that isn't what he needs right now. Felix always seemed indestructible to me, but as he stands before me, I recognize the broken soul that resembles my own. "I'll go," I whisper. "If you come with me."

He shakes his head and starts to reply, but I place my hand on his arm and look up at him. "Come inside, Felix. This doesn't need to be finished in one night. It's snowing, and it's getting colder and colder."

"You're worried," he says, sounding surprised. "About *me.*"

I nod. It's hard for me to come to terms with. I never thought I'd care about him at all, but it hurts my heart to see him so defeated. "I'm your wife," I say without thinking. "It's my right."

He smiles then and nods. "Very well, *wife*. Let's head back inside."

CHAPTER TWENTY-THREE

Felix

Alison jumps up from her seat when Arabella and I enter the mansion, her gaze lingering on me far longer than is appropriate. If Arabella notices, she certainly doesn't let on.

I glance at my wife, surprised at the mild annoyance I feel at her indifference. As my wife, it should be indignation she feels, not indifference. I managed to force her to give our marriage a chance, but I can't enforce feelings. Chances that this is how we break the curse are slim to none, but I could never live with myself if I didn't truly give it my all.

I'm uncertain what I'd prefer... the cooperative Arabella beside me, or the version of her that'd happily slit my throat in my sleep. Her behavior is everything I could have wished for, yet I find myself tempted to provoke her so she'll give me an excuse to punish her.

"You must be cold," Alison says, approaching me with a blanket in her arms. "I already sent my parents to bed. I hope you don't mind."

Arabella takes a step away, her expression unreadable.

"I'll retire early tonight, too. The stable isn't done yet, and there's still a lot to do tomorrow. I'll speak to your father in the morning—I suspect the repairs will take longer than anticipated. I'll need to make use of his office to handle some matters this delay causes."

Alison nods, her gaze lingering on me in a way that would have aroused me a mere few months ago. Now it repulses me. I reach for Arabella's hand and entwine our fingers, startling her.

"Let's go to bed."

When Arabella looks up at me, it isn't indifference I see. It's anger. Strangely enough, the fire in her eyes has the edges of my lips tipping up into a reluctant smile. Perhaps she's not quite as unaffected as I thought she was.

Her fingers are stiff in mine, her touch reluctant as I lead her up the stairs. She hesitates in the doorway of the room I usually use, her eyes pausing on the bed.

I watch as she grits her teeth and can't help but wonder what it is that's making her frown so. She walks toward the window and leans against the wall, a quiet storm brewing within her as she looks out the window, even though there isn't much to see.

I close the door behind me, strangely on edge. No one has ever made me feel this way before. I can't even quite name the emotion I'm experiencing. It's entirely novel.

"You took me to your mistress's house?" she asks, her voice so deceptively soft that she nearly manages to hide the anger laced in it.

"She isn't my mistress, Arabella."

She turns to face me and crosses her arms over her chest. Standing there in the moonlight, with her long dark hair flowing down her body, she's never looked more beautiful.

"Have you slept with her?"

My heart rate accelerates, another new experience. My heart rarely races outside of battle, yet that's all it does around her. I swallow hard and nod as I face my wife.

"You told me that every part of me belongs to you. You ordered me not to even think of the man I thought I'd marry. Are you telling me that those terms aren't mutual?"

I lean back against the closed door, reveling in this experience. "I have lived a long life before you, Arabella."

She falls quiet, her eyes filled with the same venom she used to direct my way before we came to an agreement.

"You're jealous," I murmur.

She lifts her head and clenches her jaw for a moment before speaking. "I'm not jealous, Felix. I feel disrespected. You're asking me to sleep in a bed you've bedded another woman in, in the house a former mistress lives in. I don't expect much from you, but I expected basic courtesy. My expectations were clearly misplaced."

I glance at the bed and shake my head. "It's been years since I actually took a woman to *bed*, Arabella. I hate that kind of intimacy. I've not slept with anyone in this bed, though I won't deny that something happened between Alison and me about a year prior to our marriage. I agree that her behavior is inappropriate, and I should not have allowed that. I am, however, not guilty of your other accusations."

The frost in her eyes melts just slightly, and I sigh in relief. It's strange to have someone defy or question me the way Arabella does. I'm so used to being feared, to people obeying my every whim, that I hardly know how to handle Arabella.

"If that is true, then why do you insist on me sleeping in your bed?"

"You are my wife," I say simply. "Besides, my responsibilities are numerous, and throughout the years, yours will increase too. Sharing a bed is the best way for us to maximize our time together."

She looks away, her jaw clenched. "I won't be here for years."

I have no doubt that she's once again thinking of that boy. If I could force every thought of him out of her, I would.

"Perhaps so, but you're here now."

I raise my hand and lift her into the air, moving her toward me until she's standing in front of me, her eyes blazing. She gasps and swings her legs in the air for a moment, as though she's trying to regain her balance, before crossing her arms and staring at me through narrowed eyes.

"Arabella, I appreciate that you're at last treating me like your husband. I do, but love, I'm tired, and I'm cold."

I'm surprised I have as much patience as I do. Had she been anyone else, I'd have done some extensive damage in an effort to silence her complaints. Yet with Arabella, I strangely don't feel that desire.

Her expression softens, and she nods. "I apologize," she says. "I shouldn't have said anything."

I lift my hand to her face and cup her cheek, my hand ice-cold compared with her skin, but she doesn't push me away. "Don't apologize for doing what any wife would. This is exactly what I asked of you. I don't know if we'll break the curse this way, Arabella, though I'm certainly intent on trying. This is a step forward from the veiled hatred I worried I'd have to get used to. Small steps are all we need, until eventually, we find ourselves doing the impossible."

She nods and takes a step away. "You should take a warm bath," she murmurs. "You truly are freezing."

I nod and turn to walk away, for once filled with hope. I still remember the way she looked when I first saw her in the Mirror of Pythia. Her eyes were filled with hope. I wondered then if she'd infect me with it, too.

She did.

CHAPTER
TWENTY-FOUR

Arabella

My heart races as I lie down in the small bed I'll be sharing with Felix. Somehow, it feels different here. In our bedroom at the palace, there's always so much distance between us, and not just physically. The distance between us is notably absent here, but perhaps there is more to it.

Was Felix right? Am I truly jealous of the past he shares with Alison? The mere thought of him touching her the way he touched me fills me with rage. Knowing that she's more intimately acquainted with his body than I am fills me with a desire for pure violence. Is it simply possessiveness that any wife feels toward her husband, or something more?

"Arabella."

I look up to find Felix standing in the doorway, a loosely tied robe covering his body. His eyes flash with a mixture of humor and intrigue as he walks toward the bed.

"Wife, are you once more plotting my death? Might I request that you refrain from attempting to murder me in my sleep tonight? I am rather tired, beloved." He smiles at me as he gets into bed, turning toward me as he lies down next to me.

"I...I wasn't."

He props himself up on his side and smirks at me. "Then why is it that your beautiful honey eyes are filled with murderous intent?"

My eyes roam over his chest, taking in the robe that barely covers him. Images of him with Alison flash through my mind, and I grit my teeth. When he told me that he's never shared a bed with her, what exactly did he mean? Is he insinuating that their encounters were so passionate that they never made it to a bed? "What murderous intent?" I snap. I turn my back to him, my mood inexplicably sullen.

Felix moves closer and wraps his arm around my waist, enveloping me in his embrace from behind. "You need not worry about her, Arabella. Many women have come and gone, but you will always be my empress, my *wife*."

His words are sweet, but we both know I'm just a means to an end for him. "When we first arrived, you said *she* wouldn't let you save your people," I murmur eventually. "Who is *she*? Who were you referring to?"

Felix tightens his grip on me and pulls me flush against him, his nose settling against the back of my neck. "My mother," he tells me, his voice filled with torment. "It was my mother that cursed us."

My eyes widen as deep-rooted shock settles in my chest. "What kind of mother would ever curse their own child?"

"One that didn't want to have a child," he murmurs, his body relaxed against mine. He's never held me this way before, and I'd like to think that my presence offers him at least a touch of solace.

A curse so cruel cast by his own mother... it makes me think that perhaps, I may not have had it so bad with my own father. I'm uncertain whether I can even truly understand the depth of his pain. I've hated him from the moment he first stepped foot in Althea, but the more time I spend with him, the more I find myself wondering whether he deserves my hatred at all.

"If anyone understands the damage a parent can cause, it is you, isn't it, beloved? You should know that you have me now, for as long as you want me. My country is yours. My people are yours."

My eyes fall closed and I inhale shakily. Even now, he's concerned about *me*. I turn toward him, and he wraps his arms around me, holding me tightly and offering me the consolation I'm silently asking for. What has his life been like? I know more than anyone what it feels like to be the one outsider in a crowd, to feel lonely in a place you call home... and I can't imagine spending over a century feeling that way. The curse must have taken so much from him, and the guilt that weighs down on him must be heavy.

"Will you tell me about your mother?"

He looks into my eyes for a moment before nodding hesitantly.

"Her name was Myralis," he whispers, as though he doesn't dare say her name out loud. "She was rumored to have been the most beautiful woman across the seven seas, and my father insisted on having her. What he did to her is similar to what I did to you. He proposed marriage by arriving with an army that could easily overthrow her small kingdom. Not only am I cursed, I'm born of a monster. No matter how I rebel, I ended up walking in his footsteps."

"So she married him to save her kingdom."

He nods. "He took her away that very day, not even giving her a chance to break her engagement. You see, my mother was about to marry the man she loved, and my father arrived mere days before the wedding. He forced her to marry him on the very day she would have married the love of her life, and she never forgave him for it."

Felix pulls away from me and runs a hand through his hair, his expression telling me that he's as aware as I am that history is repeating itself. There's regret in his expression, and it makes me wonder how he truly feels about our marriage.

"You can make someone marry you, but you can't make them love you. My father learned that the hard way. She died shortly after giving birth to me, and she cursed me with her very last breath.

My father told me that she'd been trying to curse the only thing she thought he would ever truly love, which only proved that she didn't know him at all. My father never loved anyone but himself. He barely paid me any mind as a child and left me in the care of palace attendants, but in the years before he died, he'd call me to his quarters nearly every day. Each time, he'd tell me a little about my mother. At first, he'd only ever talk about how much she hated me, and how desperately she'd wished to get rid of me before I was even born. Often, he'd ponder if she'd been happier if I'd never existed, and if he'd have won her over if not for me. It wasn't until he was closer to death that he began to tell me about the way he forced her into marriage, and everything he'd done to her. It's as if he thought telling me the truth would offer him atonement of some sort. It's sickening to know that as much as I've tried not to, I've become just like him."

He looks so tormented that I wish I could take away some of his sorrows. If I could share them with him, I would. I blamed him for taking away my future, but his was forsaken from the moment he drew his first breath. His entire life has been in the curse's clutches, and his marriage was no different. Does a small part of him resent me?

"You're wrong, Felix," I tell him. "Our circumstances aren't the same. Your mother was trapped for life...but you? You're letting me go when this is all over. You requested assistance, not acquiescence."

He nods at me, his expression hardening. "Someday, we'll both be free," he says, his tone carrying a hint of exhaustion.

I never considered that our marriage coming to an end would result in *his* freedom, too. What would he do with it? When he's no longer bound by this curse, who will he choose to spend his days with?

CHAPTER TWENTY-FIVE

Arabella

"Close your eyes," Felix tells me, and I oblige. "Do you feel the air moving around you?"

I inhale deeply, trying my best to focus on what he's telling me. He's spent an hour trying to explain how he uses his alchemy powers to transmute air, but it isn't helping, and I haven't been able to access my powers. I'm starting to wonder if I truly have any powers at all, or whether the people in Althea were right, and I was simply cursed.

I've taken far more time away from Felix's duties than I expected. The stable is only half built, and we've spent days practicing.

I try my best to calm my mind, to truly *feel*, the way I'm certain I've been able to occasionally the last few days. "Yes," I whisper, eventually. It's subtle, but I can feel the buzzing in the air, almost as if the air around us is tangible.

Felix moves behind me and grabs my hand, extending my arm until we're both reaching up toward the sky, our fingers entwined. "Do you feel the way the air moves along your skin as you move?"

He's standing right behind me, his lips brushing against my ear with every word, and I let my eyes close again. "Yes," I murmur, unable to calm my heart. His body feels strong against mine, our positions intimate. Perhaps this is the reason I struggle to focus.

"Feel the way the snow falls, the way it disrupts the air. Look." I open my eyes to find snow piled on top of us, as though a translucent shimmery golden shelf is holding it. "Do you feel the concentration of air below the snow I'm holding up?"

I gasp when I feel it and turn to face him. "I do!"

He smiles at me, his eyes twinkling with amusement, and I can't help but blush. "Hold your hand out."

I lift my hand, palm facing upward. Snow rapidly coats my glove, and I frown in annoyance.

"Just stand still, love. Feel the air that hovers around you. Focus on it. Try to imagine a layer of air between your hand and the snow, then inhale deeply and pull more of that air toward you, building an additional layer on top of the one you already have."

I close my eyes in an attempt to focus, doing as Felix asks me to. Even thinking of magic makes me feel panicked. It reminds me of the punishments my father used to dole out, but that's something I must get past. I inhale shakily, my heart filled with fear as I try my hardest to visualize air pushing up the snow, as though it's an invisible tray. It feels different this time, almost like the air I'm trying to move isn't trying to resist my intentions; rather, it accepts it and allows me to guide it. Something sparks deep in my chest, almost like a feeling of acceptance, and I smile involuntarily.

"Open your eyes, beloved."

I do as Felix asks, shocked to find the snow that was on my glove hovering slightly above it. It's nothing like what Felix did, but it worked. I grin, my concentration broken as I turn to face him. "Did you see that?" I ask, unable to keep my excitement restrained. I've never felt anything like this before, where the flow of magic and I are fully in sync. "I did it!" I truly do have powers. I've had them all along—I just didn't know it.

Felix nods, a big smile on his face. His eyes are twinkling, and I pause in surprise. Standing here in the snow, staring at me with such pride in his eyes... it does something to me. It elicits feelings I've never felt before, ones I can't quite name.

"Let's try one of these ice balls now," I say, taking a step back from him. He's far too close. Felix is different here. I didn't notice the difference until now, but he's far more relaxed. His brow isn't furrowed, and he doesn't look quite as haunted. He looks like he's just a man, not the emperor of a kingdom that desperately needs him. As he stands before me, he looks like he could just be my husband.

I bite down on my lip, instantly racked with guilt. He might be my husband in name, but it's Nathaniel I'm going back to, and it's becoming harder to remember that. I tear my gaze away and bend down, grabbing a handful of fresh snow.

"Arabella."

The way he says my name has me looking up at him, the snow falling through my fingers. The intensity in his eyes makes my heart beat a little faster, and I struggle to look away from his inquisitive gaze.

"What were you just thinking about?"

I open my lips to answer, but no words come out. Instead, shame and guilt fill me. I'd been thinking of Nathaniel, and the look in Felix's eyes tells me he knows it.

He raises his hand, and I gasp when I'm lifted into the air. He keeps me at face level to him, his expression one I struggle to read. "Answer me."

"Nothing," I rush to say. "I was just thinking about the technique you taught me, and whether I can lift anything heavier."

He looks into my eyes and takes a step closer, his body pressing against mine as he leans in. "Don't lie to me, Arabella," he whispers. He cups the back of my head before weaving his hand into my hair, his grip tight but not painful. Felix tilts my head, exposing my neck. I gasp when his lips brush against my skin, a strange sense of excitement rushing down my spine.

He kisses my neck, his touch soft despite the edge in his voice. "Remember our agreement. You're *my* wife. Until the day I let you go, I will not permit you to think of another. I've let you get away with it once or twice in an effort to maintain the peace between us, but I've had enough. I *will* eradicate every stray thought if I must. I'll overwrite every memory until I'm all you can think of."

He lifts me up higher and presses a kiss to my throat, his touch hot amid the cold air around us. Felix wraps his arms around my waist, and I swallow hard as I push against his chest, the desire I'm feeling only fueling my anger.

"This is the only way you'll have me, Felix. Bound and suspended in midair, with no way to resist you or walk away."

He freezes, the movement barely perceptible. "So you keep telling me, with both words and actions," he says, his voice soft.

He drops me to the floor and I gasp as I try to balance myself. Felix turns and walks away, never once looking back at me. I stare after him, instantly regretting the words I spewed in anger, words I don't even think I meant.

CHAPTER TWENTY-SIX

Felix

"I'm sorry, Felix."

I finish placing the last piece of wood back on the barn before turning toward Arabella. She stands in front of me, her cloak covered in snow. Her cheeks are rosy, and the expression she carries portrays genuine remorse.

"I made you a promise, and I failed to keep it. You were right—I was thinking of Nathaniel. I can't simply stop doing that, Felix. I'm trying, I swear it, but I'm only human. He's the man I thought I'd marry, someone I spent years falling for. I can't just turn that off, but I swear to you that I'm trying."

I take in her sincerity and nod. When I asked her for that promise, I didn't truly believe there was a chance we could make things work between us, but as she stands before me she lights a spark of hope deep inside my barren heart.

"Apology accepted," I tell her simply. I don't dare admit it, but I dislike arguing with her. Besides, I know better than to expect her to ever truly want or choose me.

Arabella breathes a sigh of relief and moves closer to me, her eyes roaming over the finished stable. It took so much of my energy that I fear we'll have to cut our trip short. I must return to the palace soon.

"It looks great," she murmurs. "I can't believe you rebuilt this in so very little time."

I shake my head. "It took far longer than I expected."

Arabella takes another step closer, surprising me. I don't recall her ever taking the initiative to stand by my side in this way. "You must be cold," she says, her eyes roaming over my no-doubt-frozen hair. "I was told that this area has hot springs. From what I understand, they're large outdoor natural pools. That might help. Why don't we head there? I don't think it's very far."

The thought of the warm water brings a smile to my face. "We can't stay long," I tell her. "I have to head back to the palace soon. My magic is depleted, and I feel on edge. Being at the palace will stabilize me."

Arabella nods and grabs the edge of my sleeve. She's not quite grabbing my hand, but she's certainly much closer than she's ever voluntarily been before. "We can head back now, if you want?"

I lean in and brush her hair out of her face. "No, let's go to the springs. They're one of the few wonders Eldiria has left."

I offer her my arm, and she takes it without an ounce of reluctance. I wonder if she realizes that she no longer looks at me with disgust and hatred.

The snow is falling heavily as we walk toward the woods, and she's quiet as I lead her through the trees, to a secluded area. Arabella gasps when she sees the steam from afar, the full moon illuminating it beautifully. This is one of the few remaining treasures in our empire, and I wish I could show her how it once looked. Eldiria has always been a beautiful country filled with lush greenery and natural wonders. Even if we do manage to break the curse, I don't think it'll be possible to restore what was lost.

"You go first," I tell her. "I'll turn my back, if that makes you feel more comfortable."

Her eyes widen when she realizes what us bathing together entails, and I see her mentally debating whether or not she should run. "Go," I tell her. "I'm getting cold, and I won't go if you won't join me."

She nods. "Turn around," she whispers, and I oblige. I don't remember my heart ever racing before I married her, but that's all it does around her. I've waited for her all my life. Now that she's here... it all feels so surreal. I guess in a way, it isn't real. The only reason she's agreed to help me is because she wants to go back home to another man. Home for her will never be with me.

I hear her walk through the woods, and then she gasps. I smirk to myself, wishing I could witness her experiencing this hot spring for the very first time. I still remember the first time I ever dipped my toes in one.

Once I'm sure she's had enough time to submerge herself in the water, I turn and grab her clothes, bringing them closer to the water. I pause at the edge, my breath catching. She's leaning back against the stone wall, her shoulders barely above the water and a rosy blush on her cheeks. She looks beautiful.

Arabella watches me as I unbutton the black uniform I'm wearing, and I love the way her breathing accelerates. I expected her to turn away, but her eyes follow my every move. She bites down on her lip when my hands settle on my trousers, and then her eyes catch mine. She seems to realize what she's doing and swiftly turns around, making me chuckle.

Things are changing between us. I'm not sure what caused it, but I'm grateful for it. Every once in a while, she looks at me like she can really see me—the man behind the myth.

I'm strangely nervous as I enter the water. She makes me feel so many emotions I thought were lost forever. Before her, I'd been clinging to the last shreds of my humanity. I'd been numb, never truly experiencing life. It kills me to know that these moments with her won't last forever. I'll only have her for as long as this curse is in place. Right until the end, this curse will see to it that I suffer.

I walk up to her and place my hand on her shoulder. Arabella tenses, and for a moment I'm certain she'll push me away, but then she turns around and looks up at me. I know I'll always remember this moment. It's just me and her in these heated waters, heavy snow falling all around us. When all is said and done, this is the moment that'll accompany me at the end. She's the only person that's ever been truly mine. She's the closest thing to a family that I'll ever have.

"You look tired," she says, and I nod.

"Using my powers outside of the palace is far more draining, and this particular case wasn't as simple as I initially thought."

She surprises me by placing her hands on my shoulders, her eyes fixated on my collarbone as she massages my sore muscles. No woman has ever done that for me before. She's so close that I could pull her flush against me. I wonder how she'd react if I did that. Fates, just a single step closer and she'd feel how she affects me.

Arabella looks up at me, her breathing irregular. "I didn't mean it," she says eventually, her voice soft.

"What is it you're referring to?"

"When I said that the only way you'd have me was if you bound and forced me... I didn't mean it. I shouldn't have said that."

The edges of my lips turn up into a smile, and I reach for her, wrapping my hands around her waist. A soft gasp escapes her lips, delighting me. "Is that so?"

She nods, her cheeks crimson under the moon that illuminates her body. The water is too dark to see her body fully, but the mere hint of it has me painfully hard.

"Prove it," I whisper.

Arabella's eyes widen slightly, and then she pulls herself closer to me, pressing her body against mine. Her arms wrap around my neck, and I groan. Feeling her breasts pressed against me like that, my cock up against her stomach... I long to lift her into my arms and bury myself deep inside her wet heat, but I must resist. "This is a dangerous game you're playing, wife. Do not underestimate how much I desire you."

"You told me to prove it," she whispers, her voice trembling.

I thread my hand through her hair and use my powers to lift her up higher, her breasts rising above the water, until she's at face level with me.

"Then do so."

Arabella's hand trembles as she reaches for me. She cups my face gently, her thumb brushing over my bottom lip. She leans in and presses a soft kiss to my cheek, startling me. I've never been treated with such tenderness before.

"How is that?"

I smile at her and grab her chin, tipping her face toward mine. "It's not enough."

Then I lean in and brush my lips over hers, gently, carefully, giving her a chance to pull away. Arabella tenses for a moment, but then she presses her lips harder against mine, trying to kiss me back awkwardly. I smile before taking her bottom lip between my teeth, teasing her before I force her lips open, kissing her the way I did the night before we came here.

She moans, her body moving against mine as I take her mouth roughly, my cock slipping between her legs as I deepen our kiss. The water begins to feel hotter—or perhaps she is simply making my body overheat with desire. It would be so easy to push inside of her. It would take mere seconds to take what belongs to me, yet I won't. I want her to voluntarily give herself to me, the way she did last time.

Arabella's hands slip into my hair as I rub my cock against her, teasing her. Could I bring her to the brink of an orgasm just like this? I call my shadow to me and let it run over her body, making her feel as though my fingers are brushing over her pussy.

"Felix," she moans. "Wait. Wait." My heart twists painfully, and I pause, my breathing ragged as she drops her forehead against mine. I've never known this longing, this desire to have her want me.

Her hand wraps into my hair, and I groan in delighted surprise when she kisses me, taking away the sense of rejection I'd felt. Arabella hugs me tightly, her legs wrapped around me, and I lean back as I envelop her in my embrace, taking as much as she's willing to give me. I can't recall the last time my heart raced the way it does now. I doubt I've ever felt quite this alive. She's destined to save my people... but I suspect she's already saved me. She saved me from my miserable existence and gave me something to live for, and she doesn't even realize it.

The two of us stare up at the moon, sharing a moment I never thought we'd have together. There was a time, not too long ago, when the silence between us felt painful. When did it become comforting instead?

CHAPTER TWENTY-SEVEN

Felix

"How was the trip?" Elaine asks with barely contained excitement. She's been hovering around my desk for an hour now. I wondered how long it'd take her to ask the question.

"It was fine."

I clench my jaw and continue to sign the mountain of paperwork she's placed in front of me, authorizing the purchase of more weaponry and salary payouts for our soldiers. Our empire looks like it's thriving, but we're only barely keeping our people fed and our outer territories from finding out how bad things are. Thanks to our safe havens, there are countless sorcerers and sorceresses helping us grow crops and develop weapons that are transported to Eldiria regularly, but if not for them and our well-maintained trade routes, many of our people would have starved.

I glance at the letter on the corner of my desk for the hundredth time this morning, my heart heavy. I asked Elaine to put any letters from Althea on the edge of my desk, so I could use my alchemy powers to teleport them to me while on our trip, but I purposely left them. Arabella was different throughout our trip. She let me in, and for the first time since I learned about the curse, I truly believed that perhaps love could break it after all.

This envelope will set us back. I know what it contains. Proof of the release and reinstatement of Nathaniel Orathis, just as I ordered. I was foolish. In an attempt to placate Arabella, I also requested a letter from her sister. All it'll do is reinforce Arabella's desire to go home, but I cannot withhold it from her, either.

"*Fine*? Was the trip unsuccessful?"

I drop my quill and look up at her with a sigh. She'll never leave me if I don't tell her what she wants to know. "That depends on how you define *success*," I remark dryly.

"The empress," she says, her voice a hint of reverence in it. "Are things not going well with her?"

I look back at the papers in front of me, unsure how to answer. "Things are going well," I tell her. "She has air wielding powers. Her control is weak, but she's strong-minded. I have no doubt her powers will grow rapidly, and she'll subjugate them with ease."

Elaine leans against my desk and stares at me. "That's good," she murmurs, her voice lacking her previous enthusiasm. "But how does she feel about you? Have you made any progress?"

Elaine is one of the majority who believe that love is what will set us free. Despite her reverence for logic and her strategic mind, she refuses to listen to reason. I suppose I'd be the same if I were her. The epic love she shared with Raphael sustains her to this day, long after he's gone. I can see how a love like hers could make the impossible happen.

I remember how they were together, constantly radiating with happiness, the two of them inseparable. Though she might never have said the words, I know the only reason she doesn't give in to the curse is because she hopes breaking the curse will bring him back.

I hand her the papers I've signed and get started on another stack, trying my best to ignore her burning gaze. "No progress, then," she says as she crosses her arms over each other, her disappointment palpable. "What did you do?"

I sit up and run a hand through my hair. "What makes you assume I *did* anything?"

How do I explain to Elaine that Arabella has no intention of staying here with me? The more I remind myself of that fact, the more my heart aches. *You're letting me go when this is all over. You requested assistance, not acquiescence*, she said. We grew closer throughout the trip, but in the end, it's futile. This letter will reinforce her desire to guard her heart, if she hasn't already. Perhaps that's why she didn't let things go further between us in the springs—because she's fulfilled her duty by consummating our marriage, and anything beyond that is an unwanted chore.

"You're one of the best men I know, and in time, the empress will see that. Please be patient with her, be gentle. Don't scare her away just to protect yourself."

Her eyes are blazing with sincerity, and I struggle to form a reply. Before I have a chance to say anything at all, a soft knock interrupts us.

The door opens without my prior consent, and I rise to my feet with a frown on my face, only to freeze in place when Arabella walks in with a tea tray in hand.

She pauses mid-step, her eyes drifting from me to Elaine, an expression I've never seen before in her eyes. I didn't expect her to seek me out—she never has before.

Elaine grabs the papers I've signed and smiles tightly before bowing her head politely. "I'll see to it that these are actioned," she tells me before rushing away.

The room falls into silence when Elaine closes the door behind her, and I look back down at my papers, feeling conflicted. I need to give Arabella the letter on my desk. I should have done it when we got back yesterday—I can't postpone it any longer.

Arabella places her tray on my desk and I glance at it, avoiding her gaze. I don't want to look into those honey eyes of hers that will never look at me the way she no doubt looks at that boy.

"You've been so busy since we got back," she says. "Take a break."

I look up at her, unable to resist temptation. She's beautiful today in that red dress. Her dark hair is flowing down her body, and her lips look cherry red, but it's her eyes that have me mesmerized.

"A letter came from Althea," I tell her, my voice soft.

Her eyes widen, longing and hope fighting for dominance in her expression, and it hits me hard. The mere thought of that boy puts a look in her eyes that inspires jealousy within me, and I'm tempted to set the letter ablaze.

Instead I hand it to her.

Arabella's hands tremble as she picks up my letter opener, and I watch her intently as she reads its contents.

She lifts her hand to her chest and exhales in relief, tears gathering in her eyes. "Oh, thank the Fates," she whispers.

"It isn't them you should be thanking. If you'd like me to, I'd be happy to send a reply to your sister."

She looks up at me then, her eyes widening. "Thank you, Felix," she says, her gaze downcast, as though she's trying to hide that her thoughts are on him once more. No matter what I do or say, I can't force him out of her mind. I might be able to conquer countries, but I cannot do the same to my wife. If she thought she'd get away with it, she'd probably run back to him this very instant.

"That's quite all right," I tell her. "Arabella?"

She clutches the letters against her chest and looks up at me, a smile on her face. Has she ever smiled for me like that? That boy isn't even here, and he's earning her smiles with such ease.

"You apologized to me at the springs, but it should have been me. I promised you I'd be patient with you, and I wasn't. I shouldn't have bound you with my powers and kissed your neck against your wishes that day in the snow. I lost my temper, and my behavior was unacceptable."

She relaxes her stance and looks at me, her gaze searching. "I'm your wife," she says, her voice barely above a whisper. "Touching me is within your rights."

I look into her eyes, wondering if things could have been different if she and I met under different circumstances. My mother never did learn to love my father, and Arabella seems to be following in her footsteps. Will she end up cursing me, too? Did forcing her to marry me put my people at risk more than they already were?

"I have no interest in exercising my *rights*," I tell her, meaning every word. I want her to come willingly. Not out of obligation, but because she wants me.

Arabella looks surprised, her body turning rigid at my words. She stares at me, a hint of anger in her eyes. "I see. I suppose I should be grateful for that."

I take a sip of the tea she brought me, at a loss for words. I let my eyes roam over her body and try my hardest to suppress the rage I feel at the thought of her with that boy. "You ran with him," I murmur thoughtlessly, my soft tone hiding the uncontrollable rage I feel. "Just the two of you... it must not have been the only time you found yourself alone with him."

She tenses then, a brief flash of panic in her eyes before she manages to hide it. "It was. Of course it was. I was the Crown Princess of Althea. I was monitored constantly." She looks to the left, as she does every time she hides something from me or attempts to lie.

"Did he touch you, Arabella?"

She takes a step back, her eyes wide with fear. She might not say it, but I see it in the way she looks at me. To her, I'm the monster that tore her away from her family and the boy she loves. I'm the monster that keeps her captive.

"No," she whispers, her gaze downcast. "You *know* I was untouched when we—please don't hurt him, Felix. I beg of you. I swear I'm trying my hardest to harness my powers. I'm doing all I can. *Please.*"

She would beg for him, huh? The Crown Princess of Althea would sacrifice her pride for the son of a duke. Her desperation to keep him safe is palpable, and it's scathing.

"I won't," I tell her. "I won't hurt him." There's no point. Even if I did kill him, he would forever become the person she pines after. Killing him won't help me. But then again, nothing can. Not in this regard.

"Thank you," she whispers, and I look away, unsure what it is about this exchange that's eliciting feelings I didn't think I had. I'm *jealous*.

"Repay me by continuing to do your best to help my people. Meet me in the courtyard tomorrow, and we'll resume your training."

Arabella nods, seemingly hesitating.

"Is that all?" I ask. Until now I wanted her in my presence for as long as she'd allow it, yet in this moment all I want is to return to a time before I met her. I wish I could return to a time before I knew what hope felt like.

CHAPTER TWENTY-EIGHT

Arabella

Felix bends down and picks up a handful of snow, seemingly unaffected when yesterday's conversation is still running through my mind. He's been different, distant.

"Do you think you can make this ball of ice float? It's heavier than anything else we've tried before, but I'm certain you can do it."

I bite down on my lip and shake my head. "I'm not sure, but I can try."

Felix nods and throws the ball in the air, where it stays. "As you know, I have never taught this to anyone," he admits. "I was never taught myself. It was intuitive for me, and I suspect it would have been for you, too, had you not been forced to keep your powers suppressed. Give yourself time and grace, Arabella."

He seems unaffected today, but I can't help but feel like he's been avoiding me since we got back. Elaine attempted to excuse his behavior by telling me that he's been reviewing the reports that arrived in our absence. She explained that each time Felix conquers a territory, he leaves its ruler in their seat, offering protection and resources from other territories in return for taxes and trade. Every day, Felix handles a different country's requests and reports. He's been so busy that the only time I've seen him was in his office. Yet there's this niggling feeling deep within my heart that tells me he's avoiding me. It's odd, because it goes directly against what we agreed upon. It's stranger still since I thought we got closer throughout the trip.

I sigh and bend down, making myself a ball of ice of my own. I squeeze my two gloved hands together. Once I have a ball of ice in my hands, I stare at it, trying my hardest to make it float the way I did with the snow, but nothing happens. I sigh in defeat, and Felix walks up to me. He places his hand on my shoulder and smiles. "Don't give up so quickly, Arabella. I could feel energy simmering around you. You're doing something, though it might not show."

I nod and try to focus on the ice in my hand, acutely aware of Felix's hand on me. At least he's no longer actively avoiding me. Nothing happens, and my frustration just mounts. He chuckles and throws me a sweet smile that makes my heart skip a beat and my stomach flutter. Heat unlike anything I've ever felt before rushes through my body, and an instant later, the ice suddenly melts, water leaking out of my hands.

Felix stares at my hands in disbelief. "You...you *melted* the snow."

The way he looks at me has my heart constricting with fear. He's looking at me the way the jeweler did, with hope in his eyes.

"Felix," I whisper, shocked. "I have no idea how I did that."

He takes a step closer to me and cups my cheeks, his eyes on mine. "That's okay, Arabella. So long as you have the ability, you'll master it. I'll be there to help you along the way. Do you know what this means? If we could get the ground to warm, we might be able to grow crops in Eldiria, rather than relying on our trade routes. We might be able to feed our people without having to risk death to gather supplies."

I nod, a small part of me hoping he could be right. If only I could truly make that kind of difference.

"What was it that you were thinking of when the ice melted?"

I tense, my cheeks heating rapidly. I want to lie, but I can't. Not when there's so much at stake. I look at him, certain my cheeks are bright red, and force the word out. "You," I whisper. "I was thinking of you having your hand on my shoulder. It distracted me."

Felix looks startled for a moment, and then the look in his eyes turns into something deeper, something that makes my heart beat a little faster. "If this is what happens when I touch your shoulder, then that explains why the temperature in our room increased so much when I took you to bed, and why the hot spring seemed to become hotter that night."

I blush fiercely at the memory of both nights. Part of me thought it'd happen again now that we're back, but he's been avoiding me, and each night, I've fallen asleep all alone.

Felix bends down and makes me another ball of ice. "Try it again," he says, his voice laced with excitement.

I smile and take it from him, trying my hardest to focus on it, but nothing happens. He watches me closely, and dread fills my stomach, but my failure doesn't seem to faze him. He smiles and grabs my free hand, pulling my glove off slowly, startling me.

I look into his eyes, my heart racing. What is he doing? Felix turns my hand over and raises my palm to his lips. His eyes are on mine as he presses a kiss to it. I swallow hard, a thousand different feelings rushing through me, along with a kind of heat that seems to both burn inside and outside my body. This...what is this? I've never quite felt like this before.

"Look," he whispers, tipping his head toward my other hand. I glance over, finding only water on my leather glove. "The ice is gone."

I nod, confused in so many ways. It's clear that my emotions control my powers, but I shouldn't be feeling anything at all for Felix. I can't, can I? This isn't just lust. It's more.

"Shall we try it again?" he asks, snapping me out of my thoughts.

I pull my hand out of his and hold it to my chest. "No," I whisper, taking a step back.

I turn and rush away, my heart racing and my thoughts uncontrollable. What is happening to me? Just yesterday, I was so relieved to hear Nathaniel had been set free and that things were going well at home. When I read Serena's letter, telling me how much she missed me, I vowed to myself that I'd make it back to them as soon as I possibly could. That's what I promised her in my reply. So why is it that each time Felix touches me, he makes me want to stay?

CHAPTER
TWENTY-NINE

Arabella

I stare at my sister's letter, re-reading my favorite paragraphs over and over again.

Nathaniel and I both miss you terribly. I'm worried, Arabella. We are both worried for you. I wish you could come back home. If I could take your place, I would.

Home. Going home is what I should be focused on, yet not even my sister's letter keeps my mind off Felix. I keep thinking of the way he touched me at the hot spring, the desperation in his eyes, and the connection I felt. He made me feel desire more intense than anything I've ever felt before, and it felt like more than lust.

I place my sister's letter down and pick up an empty piece of parchment when I feel the magic swirl within me, eager to rise to the surface. No matter how hard I try, my thoughts continue to return to Felix. I find myself wanting to touch him again, and I want him to look at me the way he did that night in the hot spring, under the full moon.

The piece of paper in my hands catches fire and I gasp, panicking for a moment, before I realize that the fire doesn't hurt me. I stare at it, mesmerized. It's burning the paper, but it's not hurting me.

Felix could be right. If I can harness fire, I could melt the snow that never seems to stop falling. Could I truly warm the ground sufficiently for crops to grow? If I can manage it, I'd be able to save so many lives.

Perhaps that's what I should focus on. That is how we'll break the curse. That's how I'll make my way back home. I sigh as I stare at the ashes in my hand, unsure how to call upon the right elements. Fire could be destructive if I can't control it. Large parts of this palace are made of wood. I could do some unthinkable damage.

"That smells interesting."

I whirl around at the sound of Felix's voice, my cheeks heating. He's leaning against the doorway, looking striking in his jet-black uniform. The look in his eyes has my heart racing, and I take a step back.

"Felix," I say, the high pitch of my voice betraying my nerves. He smiles knowingly and pushes away from the wall, stepping toward me instead.

"First you run away, and now you attempt to set our palace on fire. Should I be worried? Is this another convoluted attempt at my life?"

"I...I was just practicing."

"You were trying to set something ablaze inside our bedroom? Darling, all you need to do to accomplish that is let me touch you."

I can't help but smile shyly, relieved his mood seems lighter today than it has been in some time. He hasn't been the same since we returned, but when he kissed my palm in the atrium, I caught a glimpse of the man I've begun to miss, the one that's standing in front of me now.

Felix reaches for my hand and brushes away the remaining ashes on my hand, drawing circles on my palm with his thumb. "What were you thinking of to call upon the fire?" He looks at me pleadingly, almost as though he fears my answer.

My eyes roam over his body, pausing on his breeches before I catch myself and tear my gaze away, my cheeks flaming. "Nothing," I whisper. "Nothing at all."

Felix steps closer to me, and I move back, bumping into the dresser behind me. He smiles and wraps his hands around my waist, lifting me on top of it with ease. "Is that so?"

I nod, though I know I've never once managed to lie to him without him seeing straight through me. Felix's eyes twinkle in amusement, and I wonder if he realizes how handsome he looks when he smirks like that. The more time we spend together, the easier it gets to catch glimpses of his expressions through the moving veins that try to obscure it.

I swallow hard when he takes a step closer to me and parts my legs to stand between them. He's so close, our position similar to that night in the springs yet entirely different all at once. "Hold this," he says, handing me another sheet of parchment. "Let's see if I can help you practice."

I take it with trembling hands, and Felix smirks as he reaches for me, his hand threading through my hair. He tilts my head to the side, exposing my neck before he leans in, and a soft gasp escapes my lips when he kisses my neck softly.

My heart races so loudly I fear he might hear it. I try to close my legs in an effort to contain my desire, but instead, the movement pulls Felix closer to me, my legs wrapping around him. Before I have a chance to undo my mistake, Felix's fingers wrap around my thigh, hooking my leg up higher.

Heat begins to simmer within and around me, and he pulls away, but instead of looking at me, his gaze lands on my hand. He smiles when ashes and lingering sparks are all he finds. "Again," he orders, handing me another piece of parchment.

I take it from him, my heart racing and my body filled with desire. I clutch the parchment tightly when he smiles at me and leans in, his fingers wrapping around my chin. He holds my face in place as he moves closer, placing his lips at the edge of my jaw. He presses soft kisses to my skin, one after another, moving closer to the edge of my lips with each one.

Just as he reaches the corner of my mouth, he pulls back. Once again, his eyes settle on my hand, and he smirks as he blows away the ashes.

"Again."

I'm certain my cheeks are crimson as he hands me another piece of parchment. I'm trembling with need as I take it from him, wanting more of what he's doing to me.

Felix smirks as he reaches around me, his hand wrapping around the back of my head. I hold my breath when he tilts his head, once again pressing a kiss to the edge of my lips.

My body moves of its own volition as I arch my back, the movement making my lips brush over his. Felix chuckles, the sound reverberating through my body as he finally kisses me, his lips fully capturing mine.

The kiss is different today. It's more intense. His tongue brushes over my lips, and I instinctively open up for him, losing myself in the feelings he arouses in me. The way he moves his body against mine, making no attempt to hide his desire, only heightens my own longing. Felix's fingers tighten around my thigh, his touch turning rough, as though he's as ruled by desire as I am.

Just as I raise my hand to place it around him, he pulls away, his forehead resting against mine.

"That settles that, then. You didn't burn me. The only thing to catch fire was the parchment. You have more control than you realize, Arabella."

He pulls away, his eyes lingering on my lips. Felix smiles at me before he turns, leaving me staring at his back as he leaves the room, my body still heated from our kiss.

CHAPTER THIRTY

Felix

I haven't stopped thinking about the way Arabella kissed me back—the way she seemed to want more. There was something in her eyes, something I can't identify yet can't ignore.

In all the years I've roamed this earth, there isn't much I've truly considered mine. Even the palace I live in belongs to the kingdom, not to me. As is the case for most of my belongings. As a ruler, I don't consider any of the things that surround me my own. Nothing and no one... until her. There's something about Arabella that I find hard to resist.

I'm hesitant as I walk into my bedroom. Ever since we got back, I've ensured she's fast asleep before I join her in bed, my treacherous mind continuously reminding me that she stopped me in the springs, and that she's leaving eventually. I know that it's never been me she wanted, but tonight I can't bring myself to stay away.

I walk in to find Arabella standing by the mirror in the corner, her hands on the ties of her corset. She seems startled to see me, and I smile shakily. I recognized the desire in those beautiful honey eyes of hers this afternoon, and I know she wishes she didn't feel it. I can tell she's conflicted—she has been since she read that letter from Eldiria.

I lean back against the door, her eyes meeting mine in the mirror. Her fingers fall away from her corset, her breathing accelerating just slightly. Her cheeks are rosy, and she's looking at me the same way she did this afternoon.

I raise my hand, using my powers to pull the tie on her corset loose. Arabella gasps, her eyes widening, and I bite back a smile as I continue to undo her corset. Watching her expressions brings me such intense enjoyment. She seems to believe that she hides her feelings well, but those eyes... I love her eyes.

Her corset comes loose, falling to the floor before she has a chance to grasp it and keep it in place. She clutches her chemise, trying her best to cover her breasts, and I smirk as I move on to her skirt. That, too, has endless ties and knots.

How women wear these things is beyond me. It takes me a minute to undo the dreaded thing, and then it, too, falls to the floor, leaving her standing in a loose-fitting chemise. I want that off as well, but I'd better not push my luck. I have no doubt the dagger I gave her is somewhere on her person, and I don't want it pointed at me.

"I thought you weren't planning on touching me. You had *no interest* in exercising your *rights*, didn't you?"

Her cheeks are crimson, and I see it now. She's angry I said I wouldn't exercise my rights. My beautiful wife might not realize it, but she wants me more than she lets on, more than she'd admit to herself.

"I *didn't* touch you."

"I felt your hands!"

I hold them up, a faux innocent look on my face. "But they're right here."

Every once in a while, she lets her temper run free. It's in these moments that she acts the way I imagine a wife would. I love that fire in her eyes, the bite in her voice. I love when she treats me without fear, as though I'm her equal. There isn't anyone in this world that'd dare do some of the things she unknowingly does.

I turn and walk away before I'm tempted to tease her further. I have no doubt that my wife is a lethal little creature, and I'd better not push her too far. I'd love another opportunity to punish her again, but I can do without the bloodshed.

"Come," I say against better judgment. "Help me bathe."

"Wh-What?"

"Help me bathe," I repeat, letting my cloak drop to the floor as I walk toward the bathroom. "Or would you rather the female attendants help me?" Arabella starts to nod, so I add, "Or perhaps I should call for Elaine."

She stills, and I turn back to look at her. I watch as she grits her teeth, a hint of possessiveness crossing her eyes. She might not have any feelings for me, but she considers me *hers*. It's not much, but it's more than I could have hoped for.

I start to undress, leaving her to decide whether or not she's coming after me. I've just about gotten my uniform unbuttoned when I hear her footsteps behind me, and I can't help but smile. It's strange. No woman has ever made me feel this way, so why her? Why does she have such a hold over me?

"Help me undress," I tell her, turning to face her. I might have told her that I won't exercise my rights, but I have every intention of tempting her into touching *me*.

She glares at me, but her cheeks are crimson and her eyes are roaming over my exposed chest and abs. She takes a step closer, her hands trembling as she grabs the lapels of my uniform and pushes it down my shoulder.

I watch her closely, wondering what she's thinking. Does she find my body repulsive? Most people do, yet somehow I find myself wishing she's different. My jacket falls to the floor and she moves her hand lower, placing it on the waistband of my trousers. Fates.

Her touch is affecting me more than I expected. I'd only intended to antagonize her a bit, but it looks like it's me that's suffering now.

"Go check the bath's temperature," I tell her instead. She pulls her hands away and I let my eyes fall closed, praying for composure. Would this have been easier if she weren't so beautiful? If that chemise weren't sheer in the candlelight?

"The temperature is fine," she tells me as I finish undressing, unable to hide my desire from her. Her eyes widen as she watches me step into the tub, and I sigh in relief once I'm hidden from her. Is this what the priests refer to as karma? Is this instant punishment for trying to entice my wife?

"Come here," I tell her, not willing to admit defeat.

She kneels beside me, her breathing uneven and her face a deep crimson. It only makes her more beautiful. It makes me wonder what she'll look like underneath me.

I hand her the bar of soap, and she takes it with shaking hands. I expected her to refuse and walk out, but there's more curiosity in her eyes than anything else. If I'm not mistaken, there's a hint of desire too. It's faint, but it's there. For *me*.

I thought she'd run the bar of soap over my skin, but instead she lathers it in her hands before putting it down. I'm tense as she places her hands on my shoulders, taking her time to massage in the soap.

"You've done this before?" The mere thought of her touching another man has me seeing red.

"Not for anyone but you, but I'm quite familiar with the concept of bathing."

I bite back a smile, hiding the fact that I tremendously enjoy her wit. I doubt she realizes that no one else would dare joke around with me. I thought I'd find being married a nuisance, but it fills a void I didn't realize existed.

"Join me," I murmur.

Her hands pause their movement, and I turn toward her, wrapping my hands around her waist and lifting her in before she has a chance to decline. She gasps when her body is submerged in the water, her white chemise rapidly becoming see-through.

"Felix!" she shouts, and I force myself not to smile at the outrage on her face.

"It's easier for you to clean me when you're in here with me," I tell her, keeping my face carefully blank. She stares at me, as though she's trying to ascertain if I'm being truthful, and I feel bad instantly. This is new to her. It's not just me, and marriage, but this entire environment. She takes away the loneliness I've always felt, but in return I'm only giving her misery and discomfort.

"I apologize," I tell her, my mood souring. The time we spent away made the lines between us blur, and I've allowed myself to think of this marriage as real when it's anything but. "You needn't do this."

She rises to her knees between my legs and shakes her head. "You're my husband," she whispers. "I want to be the one who does this for you. I don't believe you're quite the monster you think you are, despite the viciousness that continues to leave your lips."

Her words disarm me, and I lean back to watch her. She places her hands on my chest, palms flat, her wet chemise clinging to and outlining her magnificent body. I can't remember the last time I desired a woman as much as I do my wife.

I wrap my hands around her wrists, keeping them in place. "I..." I'm not sure what I'm even trying to say.

I'm not like most men, Arabella.
I'll hurt you.
Run, while you still can.
Don't let me in.

I let my eyes roam over her face, her body. She's perfect. I didn't realize it when I first saw her in the Mirror of Pythia, but she's the most beautiful woman I've ever seen. Her long dark hair and those honeycomb eyes. Those lips that I want another taste of. She's beautiful, but it isn't just her looks. It's the energy she exudes. I've never met anyone quite so pure. It makes me want to corrupt her. Own her. Defile her.

I lean in, and her eyes fall closed, her breathing a little more rapid. Her chest rises and falls, her hard nipples on display for me.

I had no intention of trying to break this curse through love. It sounds ridiculous to me—it always has. But with Arabella, I find myself hoping for the impossible.

My lips brush over the edge of hers, softly, gently, as though I am not sure of what I'm doing. A soft sigh escapes her lips, and much to my surprise, she doesn't pull away. "I take it back," I whisper against her lips. "I take back what I said. I'm exercising my rights."

I close the distance between us, my lips softly brushing over hers. She leans into me, and I capture her lips, my movements soft and slow, almost as though this moment might break.

Arabella's arms move around my neck, and I lift her by her waist until she's seated on top of me, straddling me. I bury one hand in her hair and kiss her deeper, harder, eliciting soft moans from her.

She moves on top of me and I groan, needing more. It's as if the sound snaps her out of her daze, because she freezes and pushes away from me.

The look in her eyes can only be described as torn, and I sit back in defeat as she rises in a rush, running off before I even have a chance to stop her.

I run a hand over my face as the bathroom door closes behind her, lust and regret mingling into yet another foreign feeling.

I rise to my feet to follow her, but by the time I reach our bedroom, she's gone, our bed empty.

CHAPTER
THIRTY-ONE

Felix

My darling wife has managed to evade me for three days now, and for the first time in decades, I don't fully understand someone's motives. She keeps giving me hope that she might want me, too, but more than once, she's run the moment I make a move.

I raise a brow and lean back against the windowsill as I watch her walk into the atrium, a large stack of firewood in her arms. What is she up to now? True to her word, she's been working on harnessing her powers day and night.

I watch as she drops the pieces in the snow, keeping a single one in her hands. She closes her eyes and stands in silence, as though she's willing the wood to catch fire.

"Your Excellency," one of my advisers says. I turn toward him, annoyed at the interruption. "They have gold. I think we should consider them as a possible target for conquest."

I stare at the map and nod. I'm tired of conquering and consequently having to manage so many territories, just to keep alive my people and the countless magic users who continue to be persecuted. Even then, I can't save them all.

I glance back at the window to find Arabella still standing in the middle of the atrium, the snow piled so high that only half of her is visible. I might not be able to save my people, but *she* can. When she first appeared in the Mirror of Pythia, I was uncertain about her. Now I can see it clearly. Her powers will save us.

I always knew that it wouldn't be love. It was a ridiculous notion, yet somehow I find myself disappointed. The right thing to do would be to step away and focus on helping her with her magic, yet I can't resist her.

"Take over," I tell Elaine, and she smiles. She's witnessed the change in us, and I suspect she's happier about it than Arabella ever will be. I know why Arabella is holding back. She's still clinging to the life she left behind, and the man she wants to return to.

I'm restless as I descend the stairs, the distance between my audience room and the palace's atrium seeming greater than ever. I don't recall the last time I rushed through these corridors, yet I find myself impatient to get to her.

I breathe a sigh of relief when I see her standing in the middle of the atrium. Snow is falling heavily around her, yet she stands still, trying her hardest to focus. Something about my wife tugs at my heartstrings.

I walk up to her and solidify the air above her, sheltering her from the snow. She looks up, and then she turns around. She's ethereal, and she was absolutely worth waiting for. When her eyes land on mine, my heart starts to race, as it always seems to around her.

"Felix," she whispers, her cheeks rapidly turning rosy.

"There's nowhere for you to run today, beautiful."

"I'm not running," she denies.

I smile and place my hands on her shoulders, turning her around so she's facing away from me. "Are you sure?" I ask, leaning in until my chest is pressed against her back. I wrap my arms around her, hugging her from behind.

"Of course I'm sure," she says, but she fails to hide the tremor in her voice.

I smile and tighten my grip on her. "You don't seem to be having much luck with the firewood," I murmur, my lips brushing over her ear. Arabella shivers, and I chuckle.

"Let me help you. Close your eyes, my love."

Part of me expected her to defy me, but she closes her eyes without complaint.

"Let me tell you what happens when *I* close my eyes. I see you, Arabella, sitting opposite me in our bath, the water rendering your chemise transparent. The fabric sticks to your skin, your dark nipples hardened and clearly visible. In my mind, I lean in, capturing your lips first before making my way to your neck."

I move my lips then, placing them right below her ear. "In my thoughts, I kiss you, just like this." I press a soft kiss against her neck, enjoying the way it makes her shiver. "Then I make my way down, kissing your collarbone, until I reach the top of your breast. That chemise of yours? I rip it to shreds, until you're fully exposed, your body mine to take."

She trembles against me, her breathing fast-paced. I might not have her heart, but I will have her body. I'll take that first, until she surrenders and gives me all of her. I want her every thought, her every desire. I want her love. But first, I'll need to seduce my wife. Perhaps it isn't right, but I've never been an honorable man.

"Then I finally get a taste of your body. My lips close around your nipple, and I listen to the way you moan for me as I suck down on it." She gasps, and I smirk as I turn my hand inward, keeping her in my embrace while I cup her breast fully, my thumb brushing over her nipple.

"I kiss my way down, pressing a kiss to your stomach. After that, I lift you up into the air—"

Before I can finish my sentence, the firewood in her hands bursts into flames, and she drops it, letting it sizzle out. She turns in my embrace, her arms finding their way around me, and I smile down at her.

"You did it."

She nods. "Did you see that? I was so startled that I dropped it, but I really did it!"

I smile, her excitement infectious. "Thoughts, my love. You can fuel your magic with your thoughts. Desire appears to be a conduit for your fire."

I wrap my arms around her waist, keeping her close so she has no chance to slip out of my embrace. It's been a few days since I had her this close, and I won't let this moment fade.

"Try it again," I tell her. "There are pieces of firewood on the ground. Channel your thoughts, and set them ablaze."

Arabella hesitates. "I'm worried, Felix. What if I set something else on fire?"

"You won't. Each time I kissed you, it was only the parchment that burned. You could easily have set me on fire, but you did not. Today, once again, it was only the firewood that went up in flames. So long as you have a target in mind, your magic will find its way. You must trust that it will."

Arabella nods and slides her arms down to clutch the lapels on my uniform. Her eyes fall closed, and I watch as her cheeks turn rosy, the tips of her lips turned up into a slight smile. I wish I knew what she's thinking about. I tense when I realize that it might not be me. When she closes her eyes, it might well be that boy she sees.

Could she be standing in my embrace while thinking of another? My anger rises as I watch the snow behind her melt, a large flame coming into view. This is what I hoped for, yet the victory is tainted.

Arabella opens her eyes and smiles, but her joy doesn't last long.

Her smile melts away as she looks at me, and I resist the urge to ask the question I need an answer to.

"I can't hold back anymore," I tell her.

Arabella bites down on her lip, her gaze filled with fire. "What does that mean?" she whispers.

"It means I'm going to ensure that every time you close your eyes, I'm all you can see. I'm going to explore your body, learn every little thing that makes you moan, until you have so many memories that you don't need to fantasize to call upon your fire. I'm going to invade your every thought, until my name is what you whisper in your sleep."

I'm going to erase every thought you have of that boy, and replace it with thoughts of me.

I'm going to make you feel so good you'll never want another.

I'll take your body, repeatedly, until you give me your heart.

"I'm going to make you mine."

CHAPTER
THIRTY-TWO

Arabella

I'm beyond nervous as my fingers trace over the lace at the edges of my dress's sleeves. All day, all I've been able to think about is Felix's words. The look in his eyes as he told me that he'd make me his... the things he said to me. Part of me suspects that he's doing this because he knows it'll help me hone the powers his empire needs most, but another part of me is hoping that it's more than that.

When did I stop seeing Felix as a monster? When did I start to consider him my husband in more than name? Was it during our trip, when he showed me vulnerability I'm certain he's never shown another? Or perhaps it was when he handed me a letter from my sister. Shortly after, he told me he'd continue to retrieve and deliver letters for me, and he's done so without a single complaint. Maybe it was the way he kissed me in our bath, or the way he shielded me from the snow this afternoon. In each of those instances, he chipped away at my reservation, carving a place for himself in a heart I thought I'd given away.

"I always find myself wondering what you're thinking about."

I turn around at the sound of his voice, my hand rising to my chest in an effort to calm my raging heart. "I didn't hear you come in."

Felix steps into the room and undoes his coat, letting it drop to the floor. "They call me the Shadow Emperor for a reason, my love."

He walks up to me and gently cups my cheek, and I take a moment to study the golden specks in his eyes. I've never seen anything like it, and each time I look into his eyes, they mesmerize me a little more.

Felix moves his thumb over my lip, his movements slow. I watch as his expression changes from wonder to desire, and I'm reminded of the words he whispered into my ear earlier today.

"I meant what I said today."

I nod. "I know."

"Tell me you want this, too, Arabella. Tell me you crave my touch as much as I crave your body."

I hesitate, the words stuck in my throat, nerves and fear rendering me speechless.

"Tell me no, my love. Say the word, and I'll leave you alone. I won't force my affection upon you any further. I once told you I would never take you against your will, and those words still hold true, regardless of our agreement."

I shake my head, and Felix freezes, misunderstanding me. His hand slips away, but I catch it before he has a chance to step away from me. I cradle his hand in mine and entwine our fingers, holding our joined hands against my chest. The veins on his face move in patterns, revealing a different part of his face every few seconds. A mere few months ago, his face repulsed me, but now I find myself seeking traces of him through the black veins that slither along his face.

"I do," I whisper. "I...I want this, too."

I shouldn't, but I do. I'm tired of feeling guilty about my desire. I'm tired of pretending I don't want more of the feelings he instilled in me, and I'm tired of fighting this.

I rise to my tiptoes and press my lips against his, the moment so awkward that I fear I made a mistake, but before I can pull away, Felix grabs my hair and kisses me back.

He groans against my lips and pulls me closer, until our bodies are pressed together. The way his tongue moves against mine sends shivers down my spine.

Felix's hands wrap around my waist, and I gasp as he lifts me on top of the same dresser he kissed me on. "I've been wanting to do this ever since that time," he murmurs. His fingers trace over the straps of my dress, and he looks me in the eye as he pushes one of them over my shoulder.

He smirks and leans in, his lips hovering over mine. "I wanted to do so much more than kiss you then." His lips capture mine, and I moan as he takes his time with me, kissing me softly, deeply. "I wanted to do everything I told you about today, yet so much more." His lips move to my neck, and I gasp when he sucks down on it, the feeling foreign. It hurts just slightly, but there's something about the roughness of it that sends tremors down my body. "I wanted to mark you as mine."

He leans back and stares at my neck in satisfaction, making me trace over the spot instinctively. Whatever it is he did, the look in his eyes has my heart skipping a beat.

Felix smirks before leaning in again, his lips brushing over my neck. He presses soft kisses on my skin, taking his time with me when I want *more*. I'm uncertain what exactly it is that I want, but I know I need more of him.

"Felix," I murmur in protest, eliciting a chuckle from him.

He wraps his hands around my waist and pulls me closer, our bodies pressed together as his lips come down on mine. I lose myself in his touch, in the way he moves against me and the way he makes me feel. I've never felt so alive, so wanted, so whole.

I'm lifted off the dresser, but Felix's lips never leave mine. He carries me to our bed, and I wrap my legs around him, my skirt riding up until it's bunched around my hips. I expected him to put me down on the bed, but instead he presses me up against the bedpost.

"You drive me mad," he whispers against my lips. "Before the night is over, I want you feeling as desperate as I do. I want you delirious, your every thought filled with me."

I lean back against the bedpost, my eyes on his. We're both breathing hard, lost in this moment. "You already invade my every thought, Felix, whether I like it or not."

I place a trembling hand on his cheek and lean in, pressing my lips against his. Felix groans, his hardness pressing between my legs, alleviating a foreign ache, yet the movement doesn't take my need away. I feel heat simmer around me, and I direct my magic outside, praying I won't set our bedroom ablaze. Already, the flames in our room are burning fiercer than they did before.

Felix kisses me harder, his movements rougher, less controlled. Watching Felix lose his icy control because of me is one of the sexiest things I've ever experienced, and I want more of it.

"I'm trying to take my time with you, beloved, but you make it impossible."

Felix snaps his fingers, and my dress disappears, right along with my corset, both reappearing on the floor seconds later. He glances down and bites on his lip for a second before leaning in, pressing a kiss over my hard nipples through the fabric of my chemise. I inhale sharply, the heat of his lips sending a thrill down my body. Felix leans back and smirks, as though pleased by my response. He looks into my eyes as he snaps his fingers again, and I gasp as I feel my chemise disappear, baring me to him.

I attempt to cover my chest, but Felix shakes his head. "No. Don't hide from me, Arabella. Such beauty should never be hidden."

He cups my breasts and brushes his thumbs over my bare nipples, the roughness of his fingers sending a sharp burst of desire straight to my core. "Felix," I moan, lust overtaking my thoughts.

I let my hands roam over his chest, pulling at his uniform, impatience ruling my every move. Felix looks into my eyes and grins as he snaps his fingers again, leaving him bare-chested. I swallow hard as I take in his strong muscles, at last allowing myself to touch him freely. Thick veins slither over his skin, leaving most of his body as black as ink, his muscles obscured. Despite that, I run my hands over him, eager for the few moments the veins move out of the way, showing me a small part of him.

I almost breathe a sigh of relief when Felix places me down on the bed. I sit up with my legs dangling as he stands in front of me, our eyes locking. Felix snaps his fingers again, and this time, I'm left completely bare.

He kneels down in front of the bed and spreads my legs, my embarrassment and insecurities increasing by the second. "Felix," I murmur, uncomfortable.

He looks up at me, his eyes heated. "Trust me?" he asks, and I nod. "I've been fantasizing about doing this to you again for weeks. Lean back, my love. Didn't you enjoy it last time?"

I do as he says and bite down on my lip when he leans in and kisses my inner thigh, slowly inching closer. I gasp when he presses a soft kiss right between my legs, where I want him most. I feel energy buzz deep in my chest and all over my skin, and once again, I try my hardest to push it out the window, eager to channel it yet scared of setting anything on fire tonight.

A moan escapes my lips when I feel his tongue, the feeling unlike anything I've ever felt before. It's different tonight, perhaps because I crave him with greater urgency. Felix draws circles with his tongue, slowly increasing the pressure I'm feeling, until I do what he wanted me to. I moan his name, over and over again, feeling as though I'm losing control of my body. All the while, Felix increases the pace, until he sends me over the edge, making me drown in satisfaction and desire, his name on my lips.

He pulls away and rises to his feet, his own gaze filled with satisfaction, though I doubt he could possibly feel as good as I do in this moment. He snaps his fingers again, and this time, he's left standing in front of me bare.

I'm a blend of nerves and desire as he lifts his hand and repositions me on our bed so I'm fully lying down. He smiles as he joins me, hovering on top of me. He pushes my thighs apart with his knees and lowers himself so our bodies are touching, and my eyes fall closed when he presses up against me.

Felix grins, and my eyes widen when I feel his fingers move the way his tongue did earlier, yet he hasn't moved his hands. He leans in and presses a kiss to my forehead before pulling away, his eyes on mine as he pushes into me, stretching me almost painfully.

He pauses on top of me, our bodies fully connected, allowing me a moment to adjust. All the while, the feeling of his fingers on me distracts me, the combination of him inside me and his fingers drawing circles drives me insane.

"Are you all right, my love?"

I nod, my cheeks blazing. I stare into his gorgeous eyes, my heart skipping a beat. There's something about this moment that I'm certain I'll always remember. Felix smiles and pulls back, moving inside me slowly, his eyes tracing my every expression. He grins when a moan escapes my lips and increases his pace. "That is music to my ears, beloved."

"Felix," I moan, the sensations almost too much. He increases the pace, his movements slow but hard. Once again, I start to lose control over my body, unable to take the combination of his fingers when I'm already so sensitive, combined with the way he's thrusting into me. "I can't take it," I moan. "Felix, *please*."

He smirks, but I see the torment in his eyes. "Come for me, Arabella," he orders, and I do. I didn't think I'd experience this feeling twice, but this time it's even more overwhelming.

"Fates," Felix groans, his own movements erratic. He takes me hard and fast, the movements adding to the sensations that overtake me, and my eyes fall closed as wave after wave of pleasure crashes through me.

Felix drops his forehead to mine, both of us panting, the two of us still connected. "How could this possibly have been better than my dreams?" he whispers. "Arabella, you are my every dream come true."

He holds me closely and turns us over, until I'm on top of him, his arms around me. Felix hugs me tightly and I rest my lips against his throat, my heart still racing.

I don't dare admit it, but he's my every dream come true, too. When I first got to Eldiria, all I wanted to do was get away. I was desperate to return home, to the life I left behind. Right in this moment, I can't imagine wanting to be anywhere other than in Felix's arms.

Felix turns to look out the window and tenses. "Arabella," he murmurs. "Look outside."

I turn in his arms, my eyes widening when I realize there's no snow on the parts the lights illuminate. It likely won't last long. By tomorrow morning, a fresh layer of snow will be covering the ground, but for a couple of moments, we're rid of it. I bite down on my lip, pride and embarrassment mingling into an emotion I've never felt before.

"You'll see, Arabella... you and I will change the course of Eldiria's future."

I turn in his embrace to look up at him, the conviction in his eyes stealing my breath away. "Yes," I tell him. "We will."

For the first time since we came to an agreement, I truly believe it.

CHAPTER
THIRTY-THREE

Arabella

"We think this might help warm the ground permanently, but there's a lot that's still under consideration. For now, I think it's a good idea to start with a small area on our private grounds so that we can assess if it works, and whether the curse will leave it intact," Elaine says. "The fact that you were able to melt the snow at all inspires more hope than you can imagine. I've been casting spells to melt the snow for years, but the curse is immune to my magic."

I wrap my arms around myself and nod politely, trying my very best to hide my embarrassment. Elaine came to find me earlier today, in shock because months' worth of snow had disappeared around the palace. I scrambled to explain myself and ended up telling her that I'd merely been practicing and lost control, but I worry she saw straight through me.

I nod at the drawings she shows me, anxiety uncurling in my chest. "This will be hard to accomplish, and it's going to be a lot of work for Felix."

"It will be," she admits. "But he's been waiting all his life to make a difference like this. If this works, the burdens on our people would be lifted tremendously. We aren't quite sure why, but you appear to be immune to the curse's effects. It does not haunt you the way it does us. Every magic user within this empire feels its pull. Each time we access our powers, a small part of it leaks away. It feels as though we're giving the curse our location, our own magic working against us to destroy all we try to build."

I bite down on my lip, fear ruling my thoughts as I stare at the plans of underground pipes. It took him days to rebuild the stable the curse knocked down, and now we're asking him to help transform steel into pipes to meet the quantity demands our workmen can't meet by themselves, and then transport them deep underneath the earth. Once that's done, I have to heat the pipes, and hope that it heats the ground's temperature sufficiently for us to grow crops. That is if the curse doesn't wreak havoc; it could destroy the pipes before I have a chance to heat them, or the temperature could drop even further, dousing the heat I create. Then there's every chance that I can't heat the pipes at all. So far, all I've been able to do consciously is set small things on fire. I have yet to do much more than that. Elaine has been working on this plan from the moment I told Felix about my fire powers, but I fear I'll let her down.

I'm startled out of my thoughts by the sound of Felix's voice. "Are you letting your thoughts rule you, Arabella?"

I turn toward the sound of his voice and find him standing in the doorway of the audience room, where Elaine and I have spent the morning. His eyes roam over my body leisurely, and heat rushes to my cheeks as vivid memories of last night come to mind. The way he looked at me as he held himself up on top of me, the way he moaned my name, the way his eyes fell closed when he pushed inside me. My favorite memory of all was the reverence I saw in his eyes all night. He's wearing that very same expression today.

"You'll be able to do it. I have faith in you," he says, his voice soft. Felix walks up to me and wraps his hand around my waist, his head tilted toward me. He's never touched me like this in public, and though it startles me, I don't dislike it.

Thankfully, there's no strangeness between us. I'm certain my cheeks are crimson, and there's a knowing look in his eyes, but there's no awkwardness between us. If anything, this is a new kind of intimacy. One I didn't know existed.

"I have faith in you, too. This won't be easy."

Felix leans in and pushes a strand of hair behind my ear. "I know it won't be, but we'll get it done together."

He keeps his arm wrapped around me as he leans in to look at the schematics on the table. "I've never transformed quite that much metal," he murmurs, a hint of insecurity in his eyes. I lean into him, offering silent support, and he tightens his grip on me.

"I believe in *both* of you," Elaine says. "Between the two of you, we might well gain the upper hand in this fight. We'll start with the atrium at first, and if that works, we move on to larger parts of the city. At each step, we'll pause to assess any damage the curse might inflict, but so far, the curse has not touched the empress. I hope that will extend to her elemental powers, too."

"While this might work in theory, I don't know how to keep a fire going. Each time my concentration wanes, the fire douses."

"We'll train together," Felix promises, his gaze reassuring. "And if it doesn't work, then we'll try something else. Truthfully, it's an idea with a low chance of success and a high dependency on you. We're asking too much of you."

"I'll do whatever is necessary," I assure him, wishing I could offer more certainty.

Felix's thumb brushes along my waist, drawing circles leisurely, and I bite down on my lip. What would it take for me to create permanent heat like the type we'll require? Mere thoughts of Felix are allowing me to call upon my fire, but will that be enough?

I look into Felix's eyes, certain he'll have a training schedule in mind that I will not be able to resist. He once said I'd set the palace ablaze if he took me to bed, and I came close to it last night.

"When is the metal expected to arrive?" Felix asks, barely able to take his eyes off me for more than a few seconds. "I'd rather get started sooner than later. I expect this to be a tremendous amount of work, for all of us."

"A fortnight," Elaine says, and Felix nods.

"Would you like to accompany me to the audience room?" he asks, and I smile. When I first arrived, he'd have said, *You will come with me*, ordering me around like the brute the world thinks he is.

"Yes," I say. "I'd love to."

Much to my surprise, Felix's hand slides down to mine, and he entwines our fingers as he pulls me along. His hand is large in mine, yet it feels perfect. He glances at me and snaps his fingers, my cloak appearing around my shoulders. Heat rushes to my cheeks at the sound, memories of last night flooding me, and Felix chuckles knowingly. "I'll get you your gloves later," he says. "For now, I want your hand in mine."

I bite down on my lip to hide my smile and nod at him, my heart racing. He's different today. I'm not sure what I was expecting after last night, but I suppose part of me feared he would be indifferent. I feared that last night wasn't as special to him as it was to me. I'm far from the first woman he's ever been with, after all.

Felix pauses as we round the corner leading to the atrium, turning toward me with a smile on his face. Something about the look in his eyes makes me take a step back, until I'm pressed against the wall, my heart hammering in my chest.

"I missed you this morning, Arabella," he murmurs, closing the distance between us. "All morning, you've been all I've been able to think about. I sat through countless strategy meetings, finalizing the acquisition of Romtheo, a tiny country filled with gold, but all I could think about was the honey color of your eyes, and the way they darkened when you whispered my name." He leans in, his body pressing against mine. "Do you have any idea how hard it was for me to leave you in our bed this morning?"

My breathing is irregular as I look into his eyes, nervous, eager for *something*. Felix appears to read my mind and smiles as he tilts his head, his lips capturing mine.

A soft moan escapes my lips when he kisses me, and I instinctively wrap my arms around his neck, deepening the kiss. I'm breathless by the time he pulls away, and Felix smirks before pulling his hood over his head.

"Let's go, my love. The sooner I finish today's work, the sooner I can take you back to bed."

CHAPTER
THIRTY-FOUR

Arabella

I lift my hand to my chest as a letter shimmers into existence on the writing desk in our bedroom. I've never seen anything quite like that before. My eyes widen when I see my name written on it in Felix's handwriting, and I open it carefully. Ever since the steel was delivered, he and I have barely spent any time together. I didn't think it possible, but I *miss* him.

Beloved,

Meet me for dinner tonight.
Audience room. One hour.

Love,
Felix

I smile at the brusque tone of his letter. I can almost hear his voice. My fingers trace over the word *love*, and my heart skips a beat. Even in this short letter, I can feel his attempts to be gentle with me. When we came to our agreement, he asked me to give him an honest chance to see if we could break the curse through love. At the time, I gave in because it was the only way to get what I wanted in return. I didn't think I could ever love him, regardless of what I said. Now? I'm not so sure. I'm certain I'm not there yet, but I feel things I've never felt before. I look forward to moments we get to spend together, and I find myself seeking him out on days I know he won't make it to bed before dawn.

A knock on our bedroom door startles me out of my thoughts, and I turn toward it. "Your Excellency," one of the palace magicians says, hovering by the doorway. "My name is Molly. His Excellency sent me to help you get ready for dinner."

I nod for her to enter, and she bows down low in front of me. Her eyes are brimming with excitement when she rises, and I smile back at her. The attitude of the staff here is in such contrast with the way I was treated at home. There they sneered at me, scared I'd infect them with my bad luck, while here they look at me like I'm a myth come to life. It's something I don't think I'll ever get used to.

"It's a great honor to attend to you," she says, trembling just slightly. This is how Serena was always treated, but never me. It's strange how quickly a place can start to feel like home when people seem to *want* you there. Molly takes a step closer to me, her eyes roaming over my face. "You hardly need any beautification, Your Excellency. Your skin is healthy and has a natural glow, and your hair is thick and dark. I can darken your lashes and brows, and perhaps accentuate your cheekbones? What do you think of adding some redness to your lips?"

I nod, unsure what to say. I've never been attended to by a palace magician. Since magic is strictly banned in Althea, I have no experience with it. I've never used anything but the ointments they had in Althea. "Do as you please," I tell her. "I'll trust your judgment."

A tiny squeak escapes her lips, as though she's barely able to contain her excitement, and I struggle to swallow down a chuckle. Molly is exceptionally cute, and she reminds me of Serena.

"I won't let you down, Your Excellency," she promises me. It's clear she takes great pride in her work, and I can't help but smile.

"It's such an honor to be standing in the same room as you," she says as shimmering magic flows from her fingers. She brushes them over my brows, instructing me to close my eyes next. "Eldiria has waited generations for you. His Excellency warned us not to put any pressure on you, but I just wanted you to know that we're all grateful you're here. I still remember when my grandmother first told me of a prophecy about our empress breaking the curse, and here you are. Some believed the emperor made it up and told us about a false prophecy to give us some hope to hold on to, but I've always known better."

I feel her magic flood over my skin, the sensation foreign. "You know, Your Excellency... I thought all hope of me ever having a child of my own was gone. I'd given up, but then you came. I just know you're going to save us all. I can feel it."

I'm glad she's instructed me to keep my eyes closed, because I don't think I can face her. I fear I'm not the savior they all think I am, and I'm scared to let her down.

"The day you arrived is the first day I dreamed of her. I dreamed of being pregnant, of my baby lying on my chest. Then there were scenes of me cooing her to sleep, and me kissing her forehead. The dreams have come every day since you arrived. It's all so real. Sometimes I could swear I can smell her. I don't think they're dreams, Your Excellency. I think they're visions... visions of the future you will give us."

My heart squeezes together painfully, and a shiver runs down my spine. I want nothing more than for her to have all of what she just described, but I do not have the power to grant it. I'm scared I won't be able to break the curse. Felix and I aren't even certain we can heat the ground.

"All done," Molly says, and I open my eyes. She turns me toward the mirror, and I gasp. I still look like myself, except... I don't. I look a thousand times more beautiful than I did on my wedding day. I lift a hand to my face in disbelief. "Magic," I whisper. Even my hair is done perfectly when that shouldn't be possible in so very little time.

Molly frowns at me and nods. "Of course. What else could it be?"

I belatedly realize that the word *magic* isn't used as an expression here, and the questioning look Molly throws my way has me feeling defensive. It's likely that she expects me to be an experienced sorceress myself, and I'm unsure what Felix has been telling his people. It's clear that he's been using me as a beacon of hope, and I can hardly blame him.

"It's just something we say in Althea," I tell her, smiling serenely in an attempt to hide my inner turmoil.

Molly nods in understanding and takes a step back. "Oh! Of course," she says, grinning. "Now, what kind of dress shall we put you in?"

My wardrobe swings open, a golden dress floating out of it. I smile to myself. I've grown accustomed to the palace's quirks, and I've come to trust its fashion sense, too.

"This is beautiful," Molly whispers, grabbing the dress from the air. Several minutes later, I'm wearing the stunning golden dress the palace selected for me. I watch it shimmer in the light with my every move and worry that it's too much for a simple dinner, but Molly looks so excited that I can't bear to say anything.

I find myself wondering what Felix might think of me in this dress as I walk down the long hallway. For the second time today, I find myself thinking about love. If he and I were to fall in love, would that truly break the curse? Would it grant Molly's wishes?

I bite down on my lip and hesitate in front of the throne room. I take a deep breath in an effort to steel myself, but before I've had time to push the doors open, they open themselves.

Felix freezes when he sees me, and my heart skips a beat. In that moment, everything fades away. All I can focus on is the look in

Felix's eyes. It isn't until someone speaks to him that I realize that he's standing next to several men I vaguely recognize as his advisers. I take a step back, worried I'm interrupting, but then Felix hands the documents he's holding to Elaine. "Excuse me," he says. "I can't keep my lovely wife waiting for a moment longer."

He walks toward me, the hood of his cape falling over his face. I can see why they call him the Shadow Emperor. It must have stemmed from the curse initially, but it's also the way he moves and dresses.

"Arabella," he says, offering me his arm. I take it, and he leads me forward. "I apologize. Time got away from me. I hope you'll forgive me."

"I'm thankful you were able to carve some time out of your schedule after all. I feel like I've barely seen you since..."

Felix turns toward me and grins. "Since when?"

I blush as I think back to the night we spent together. Shortly after, the steel we need for our plan was delivered, and ever since, we have both been forced to focus on our individual roles in our plan, practicing and refining our strategy endlessly. I've spent countless hours channeling fire and bending it to my will, until eventually, it required very little thought, and I was able to keep fires lit in all fireplaces in the palace for several days. Felix, on the other hand, has spent all his waking hours helping his men create the pipes we need. His alchemy powers are far swifter than even his best workmen, and though I know he finds it fulfilling to help them, I also know it exhausts him. I've missed him, but admitting that and asking for his time felt selfish when we both have so much on our plates.

"I have somewhere special in mind," he says. His hand slips down to mine, and he interlocks our fingers, his thumb drawing circles around my hand. I glance at him, wishing he'd stop wearing his hood at all times. It's strange, but I miss seeing the gold in his eyes. Even when I catch a glimpse of him during the day, I rarely see *him*.

"Here we are," he says, his voice soft. He takes a step forward and holds the door open for me. I pause in the doorway, my eyes wide as I take in the bright sun and the greenery surrounding us.

"This can't be real," I whisper. I haven't seen sunshine since I got here, and I hadn't realized how much I'd missed it.

"It isn't," Felix says, and I turn to him. He lifts his hood off his face and takes off his cloak, revealing a suit I've never seen before. Even on our wedding day, he wore his usual uniform. The suit he's wearing today is all black, and it looks like something royalty might wear. He usually keeps his physique hidden, but this highlights his strong body.

"It's an enchantment," he adds. "The curse makes it hard to maintain an enchantment like this. Even when it isn't real, it seems we aren't allowed any kind of sunshine. It'll only last a few hours."

"You did this?" I ask, confused. "You created this... for *me*?"

"Technically, I begged Elaine to create it, but I did transmute all the flowers for you. Those are all real." He takes my hand, leading me to a table in the middle of a pavilion. It's got thousands of pink peonies growing all around it, rendering the scene utterly romantic. I glance back at him, finding it hard to believe that the same man who once threatened my life and my loved ones would do this for me.

"I thought you might miss the sun," he murmurs as he pulls my chair out for me. "I know I do."

I watch him as he walks around the table and sits down opposite me. "You could leave, couldn't you?"

He shakes his head. "Not for long. If I stay in the palace, I remain human. The longer I'm away, the less human I become. Physically, my nails turn to talons and my teeth become razor-sharp. My skin changes, becoming rougher, more animal-like. That isn't the worst of it, though. It's the bloodlust. If I stay away too long, my humanity disappears. The palace has a soothing effect on me, undoing some of the worst effects of the curse. The longest I've been able to leave is just under a year. I'm trapped here."

Felix hesitates, and then he looks away, a sigh escaping his lips. "If we don't break this curse, that is the future that awaits me. The change is slower within the palace, but I can feel it deep within. Every day, I feel a little less human. I struggle to experience emotions the way others do... except when I'm with *you*." He looks at me, and for a moment it's as though it isn't me he sees. "I understand that you don't believe me, but I truly believe you were destined to save my people. Pythia, the seer I mentioned, cannot lie. I'm not sure, but maybe, just maybe, you might save me, too."

More than ever, I find myself wishing I could. I don't know how I'm meant to do something like that. I'm startled out of my thoughts when plates appear in front of us, my eyes widening when I realize what I'm looking at. It's a traditional Althean rice dish.

I stare at the food, a familiar ache settling in my chest. These reminders of home are a kind gesture, but it just makes me miss my sister more.

"If we manage to heat the ground and grow crops, you'll let me go back home?"

The words leave my lips before I realize what I'm saying, and for a moment, I fear Felix's response. He looks away, his expression turning guarded. "I never break a promise, Arabella. Do all you can, and I'll let you go, even if we can't break the curse. I won't keep you captive." He turns back to me, his eyes darkening. "But you'd better remember what you promised me. Until I let you go, you're mine. Your every thought, Arabella."

I bite down on my lip as my heart begins to race. There's such profound jealousy in his eyes, and though I should reassure him, I can't help but revel in it. When he looks at me that way, it's like nothing else exists anymore, like he isn't a cursed emperor who needs me—instead, he's just a husband who wants his wife to have eyes only for him. And I do. Fates, I do.

Felix snaps his fingers, and the table disappears. He rises from his seat and throws me a pleading look. "Tell me, beloved. When you asked me if I'd let you go, who was it you were thinking of?" I'm breathing hard, my heart racing as Felix walks up to me. He cups my cheek, his thumb brushing over my lip. "I warned you, beloved," he murmurs, his voice soft. "What should I do with you, my love? How do I punish you for breaking our agreement?"

He moves his hand, using his shadows to lay me down on a bed of pink and red flower petals, my hands pinned above my head by his invisible force. He smiles, but there's no humor in his eyes as he kneels down beside me.

"Felix," I whisper, a thrill running down my spine. I loved the way he made me feel on our wedding night, and I'm tempted to provoke him into punishing me in that same way again.

He leans over me and bunches the fabric of my dress in his hands, pushing it up slowly. "Were you thinking of him?"

I look at him and shake my head, unable to help myself. I don't want to lie to him, but I love the way he's acting. Felix leans in and lifts my leg, placing it over his shoulder. He turns his face inward and kisses my thigh, sending a tremble down my spine. I gasp when I feel his powers brush over my breasts, almost as though the tips of his fingers are caressing me.

"Can he do that to you?" Felix whispers, right before I feel his fingers trace circles up my thigh. He spreads my legs and smiles. "Wet, as expected."

I gasp when Felix pushes a finger deep inside me, using his thumb to tease me. The combination of sensations is almost too much, and I can already feel the pressure climbing. He lets go of me, yet the feelings don't stop. His hands move to his breeches, but I still feel them on me.

"*Felix*," I moan, and he smiles in satisfaction as he settles between my legs.

"Beg for it," he orders. "You want it, don't you?"

I nod. "*Please*," I whisper. "I beg of you, Felix. *I need you.*"

I'm so close, and the feelings he's arousing within me are addictive. I need him with a desperation I can't put into words. The same magic I felt last time buzzes around me, and once more I try my hardest to direct it outside. I vividly imagine the atrium and pray I don't set the flowers around us on fire.

Felix grins at me and lifts his hand into the air, snapping his fingers. All at once, I'm turned over, landing on my knees. I look up to find myself staring straight into a mirror.

"Watch yourself succumb to me. Watch as you beg for it. That little boy will never make you feel the way I can. The pleasure I can give you is unmatched."

He grabs my hip and pushes into me slowly, his eyes on mine in the mirror. Felix pauses halfway inside me and I groan. "No!" I whisper, wishing he'd push all the way inside me, and Felix laughs.

"Beg," he orders again.

"Please, Felix. *Please!* Stop torturing me, husband."

He looks startled, his expression softening. "So you do realize that *I'm* your husband."

Our eyes lock in the mirror, and he pulls almost all the way out, driving me half mad. "You are the only one I've ever wanted, Felix. The only one I will ever desire," I tell him, and deep within my heart, I know it to be true. The feelings I have for Felix are unlike any I've ever known before.

Felix stares into my eyes, seemingly satisfied with what he sees, and at last, he pushes into me, taking me with the same desperation I'm feeling.

I fear the hold he has over me. With each passing day, it becomes harder for me to see a future without him in it. I fear that one day, I truly will lose him to this curse, and I cannot let that happen.

CHAPTER THIRTY-FIVE

Arabella

I haven't been able to stop smiling all day. Memories of yesterday have kept the fire in the library going for hours now, even as I read. It's giving me hope that Elaine's plan might actually come to fruition.

I sigh happily, recalling the room Felix created for me. I noticed how tired he was afterward, but he didn't complain once. The sunshine, the peonies... and Felix. The way he touched me last night, the jealousy and possessiveness in his eyes. He made me feel so wanted. I never expected there to be such power in feeling like you belong with someone, but there is.

"Daydreaming, Your Excellency?"

I slam my book closed and jump at the sound of Elaine's voice, the flames flickering. I only barely manage to keep the flames alive as she sits down opposite me, my concentration waning. Elaine chuckles as she spots the title of the romance novel I'd been reading. "I have a lot more of those in my room. The ones in the library are the tamer ones," she says with a wink.

I chuckle and clutch my book to my chest. "I may have to ask you to lend those to me."

"Of course, Your Excellency. I'll have the very best ones sent to your room."

Elaine leans back in her seat and sighs softly as her eyes roam over the library. "You know, my betrothed loved this space as much as I did. In fact, it was our joint love for reading that brought us together."

"Betrothed?" I repeat, confused. None of the books ever mentioned Elaine being engaged, but then again, there is not much our history books got correct.

"Raphael," she whispers, his name a prayer on her lips. I think back to the conversations Felix and I have had, certain that he's mentioned Raphael before.

"This is something not many people know, but Raphael and I are heirs of rival kingdoms that were both overtaken by Theon. Neither of our kingdoms were prosperous, and both lands benefited from the improvements Theon made, so neither I nor Raphael held any grudges. If anything, we were beyond grateful he saved our people when both our parents had been failing, so when Theon asked, we both joined as his advisers. If anything, I jumped at the opportunity, since I was barely tolerated in my own kingdom due to my strong magic, but here, I was appreciated in a way I never could've imagined. You see, while I inherited my mother's magic, I was always taught to hide it, which only made me want to explore it more.

"Neither Raphael nor I realized the other had joined, and neither of us was pleased to find the other at court. We hated each other."

She smiles to herself then, seemingly lost in thought, and I realize that this is the first time I've seen her so relaxed. In all the months I've been here, this is the first time I've seen true happiness reflected in her eyes.

"We would constantly fight each other, destroying parts of the palace that Theon then had to fix, and at some point, I was certain he would kick both of us out. Except... Theon saw something neither of us could."

She smiles at me then, a knowing look in her eyes. "I finally understand it now. At last, I understand how he could be so certain when neither Raphael nor I could see it."

Her tale sounds so romantic, yet my heart bleeds because I know it must end in tragedy. "So how did reading unite you two?"

"I suspect the reason Theon did not kick either of us out, when we certainly deserved it, is because we had both befriended him, and he valued us equally. So when Theon asked that I read several books about curses to help us prevent some of the damage we were seeing, I agreed. Unbeknownst to me, Raphael had been tasked with reading the same books. We ended up in the library together for hours every single day. Back then, the library was still filled with scholars, so there was no way we could argue with each other the way we usually would. Though it certainly wasn't for lack of trying. Raphael and I exchanged many torn pieces of parchment with insults scribbled on them, but as time passed, the tone of our notes changed, until they turned into letters that allowed us to truly get to know each other."

I smile and sigh happily. "You fell in love."

She nods. "We fell in love. We were so nervous about telling Theon that we attempted to keep our relationship a secret. By the time we gathered the required courage, everyone already knew—we just didn't realize it. Theon gave us his blessing, and that should have been the start of our future together."

She wraps her arms around herself and looks away. "You see, Your Excellency... Raphael had a secret he didn't share with me or anyone else. I suspect he feared it would cause me to see him differently, but I never would. In the end, it was his lycanthropy that made the curse too hard to withstand. It's different for those of us with a regular supply of magic, but even more so for lycans. From what Theon and I have gathered, it appears lycans are worse off than humans. Humans at least have a natural resistance against the curse's pull. Raphael must have fought so hard, yet in the end he lost the fight."

She bites down on her lip, visibly emotional, and my heart breaks for her. This curse has taken so much from everyone around me.

"He is the reason why I stopped you that night in the caves, Your Excellency," she tells me, her voice breaking. "It's just... you are my last hope, and I couldn't... Fates, I hope that someday you'll be able to forgive me for it."

I reach for her hand and squeeze gently. "I forgave you for that long ago. If not for you, I'd have missed out on so many experiences and memories that I wouldn't trade for the world. I'd never have learned to harness my powers, and I'd have gone through life believing I was a cursed being unworthy of existing."

Elaine looks up at me, her eyes shimmering.

I reach for her and swipe away her tears. "How do you maintain the will to fight?" I ask, my voice soft. I can't imagine how much pain she's gone through, how much she must continuously be in due to the curse's pull.

"The only way for me to ever see Raphael again is for this curse to break. When he disappeared, a new rose bloomed in the atrium, and I just have this feeling that he isn't truly gone forever. I keep fighting because it's the only way to get to him."

I hear the unspoken words and lower my eyes. "I'm scared I can't break the curse, Elaine."

She smiles at me, quiet confidence in her gaze. "You're wrong, Your Excellency. I can see what Theon once did. You might not realize it yet, but you're falling for our emperor. I truly believe that love is the most powerful force in this world. In time, you will see that, too."

Her words both surprise and scare me. Falling in love with Felix never seemed like an option, yet within the span of a few days, it has crossed my mind several times.

Could he and I truly find love together? And if we do, will it in turn save those we love?

CHAPTER
THIRTY-SIX

Arabella

I stand under the shelter by the atrium, at the start of the footpath that's always kept as clear of snow as possible. My eyes are fixed on the other end of the atrium, the part I'm trying to get to without the heavy snow bearing down on me.

"Remember," Felix says, "concentration matters above all. Your powers will go wherever your attention directs it."

I nod and glance up at the sky. The snow is falling as heavily as usual, and a hint of insecurity makes me hesitate. I've learned how to fuel my fire, but I have yet to fully master air—though not for lack of trying. For Elaine's plan to work, I must access my air powers. I must be able to feed air into my flames to spread the fire rapidly.

I bite down on my lip and let my eyes fall closed, taking a moment to feel everything around me. The heat of Felix's body, the wind that moves my air, the small disruptions the snowfall is causing in the natural direction of the wind. I wait for the buzzing in the air to become clearer, and then I take hold of the energy around me, channeling it for my own purposes. I push it up, creating an invisible shelf above me, and I breathe a sigh of relief when it works.

I watch as snow collects above me and hold my breath as I take a step forward, willing it to move with me. I exhale in relief when I stay dry, not a single snowflake reaching me.

"Keep going," Felix quietly murmurs, and I nod.

Fire never requires this much concentration. It always comes with ease, flowing where I want it to go without any resistance. Air is different. It doesn't want to be harnessed; it wants to flow freely. When I tried explaining that to Felix, he didn't seem to understand. In his experience, air is controlled purely by alchemy, and it has no will of its own. It has never been like that for me.

I take a careful step forward, trembling just slightly. I need to get this right. I can't let Elaine down. The very least I must do is ensure her plan succeeds.

I gasp when a pile of snow falls on top of me, instantly making me ice-cold. I groan loudly, and tip my face up at the sky. "Fates!" I yell, beyond frustrated.

Felix chuckles and uses his own powers to flick all the snow off me. I let my fire powers warm me up, and a thin trail of fire envelops me briefly. "Have patience, Arabella. It has only been a few weeks. You cannot learn this overnight."

I shake my head and turn to him. "I must," I whisper, desperation rendering my voice hoarse.

Felix walks up to me and cups my cheek, his thumb brushing over my lips. "Why must you, my love? There is time."

I grab his cloak and slide my hands underneath it, clutching the lapels of his uniform. "The people of Eldiria have waited so long already. I cannot fail them. To some, I might be their last hope. I must try harder. I can't... I can't let Elaine down. Isn't it bad enough that we aren't trying to break the curse? How could I live with myself if I don't try my very hardest to adhere to her plan for the atrium?"

Felix nods in understanding. "I was wondering what it is that occupied your thoughts this morning. I suppose she told you about Raphael?"

I nod and look away, my heart aching. "I've been thinking about their story for days now, and I can't think of a way to bring him back. We must break this curse, Felix."

Felix sighs and leans in, pulling me into his embrace. I rest my head on his chest and inhale shakily, unable to keep my chest from aching. I'm filled with sorrow, and it isn't even mine to carry.

"Beloved," Felix whispers. "You might well be the most wonderful thing I have ever come across. Your heart... it's unlike any other." He presses a kiss on top of my head and tightens his hold on me. "Arabella, my love, it is not your responsibility to break this curse. People might have expectations of you, but you need not meet them. They were imposed on you without your consent, and as such, you may step away from them at will. No one could possibly ask more of you than you already give."

I shake my head and lean back to look into his eyes. "It's not enough, Felix. Surely you understand? If there's more we could do, then we *must*. These are our people. They are *our* responsibility."

He stares at me, his eyes widening ever so slightly. "Yes, my beloved Empress. They are our people, but are we not giving them all of us already? Tell me honestly, do you think there's any more we could do?"

I shake my head and drop my forehead to his chest. Felix twists his fingers into my hair and sighs. "Raphael was my best friend, Arabella. Perhaps my only friend, bar Elaine. Seeing them together brought me such joy. They gave me hope that perhaps true love does exist. I want nothing more than to have him back, to shake his hand and drink one of the vile drinks he ferments himself. I miss him, Arabella, every single day. But I also know that I'm doing all I can. You are, too. The only thing we can do for them is to keep learning, to keep growing stronger, to keep fighting. That is all we can do, love, and we do it every single day, don't we?"

I nod and swallow hard. "I'm sorry," I whisper. "This has been so much harder on you than it ever could be on me, yet I—"

"No," he cuts in. "There is never any competition between you and me, my love. You have every right to feel what you do, and I adore you all the more for it."

I nod and pull out of his embrace. "If all I can do is try harder, then that is what I will do."

Felix brushes my hair out of my face and nods. "Very well. I will be here every step of the way."

I smile at him and take a step away, letting my eyes close once more. This time, the air comes to me with more ease. It still resists my call, but not quite as much. It's almost as though it agrees with my intended purposes for it, offering me quiet assistance. I bite down on my lip as I try to keep my snow cover above my head, taking slow steps down the footpath. It stays intact, and I smile to myself in relief as I keep my eyes on the fire at the end of the way. It has been my target all morning, and keeping that burning was far easier than it was to call upon the air around me. I exhale when I reach it and swallow hard. This is the real test… keeping the fire burning and the snow cover above me, while also pushing air into the flames to make it burn bigger.

"*Please*," I whisper, before inhaling deeply. I exhale and channel the air around me, pushing it into the flames the way I envisioned, and much to my surprise, it works.

Felix laughs as the flame grows bigger, and I turn toward him with snow piled high above me, a wide grin on my face. "I did it," I say, my voice soft, as though speaking too loudly might make it all fall apart.

"You did indeed," Felix says proudly.

One step at a time. That is all I can do for now, but I will do it to the best of my abilities. The people of Eldiria deserve that much.

CHAPTER THIRTY-SEVEN

Felix

"Are you ready, my love?" I ask, my heart racing with anticipation. Arabella nods, and I take a step closer to her to tighten her cloak. After weeks of practicing and preparing, we are as ready as we can be.

"Felix," she murmurs, her voice soft. "Even if we fail to place and heat the steel today, we can try again. We'll keep trying, until we get it right."

I smile at her, but the feeling is bittersweet. Once upon a time, I felt as hopeful as she did. I was certain that beating the curse was only a matter of time, but it is not quite that simple. We've been extremely fortunate so far. Every other attempt to stand up against the curse has ended in ruins. Arabella has yet to experience the crushing defeat that follows a near-perfect plan. I pray she won't lose her spirit the way I did—the way we all did. She might be a beacon of hope to my people, but my darling wife is more than that to me. I'm uncertain what I'd do if I were to find her in tears because of this curse. I don't want her to feel the helplessness we all feel.

"Of course," I tell her. I cup her cheek and take in her honeycomb eyes, my heart full with an emotion I can't quite name. My lips brush against hers once, twice, before I kiss her fully. I wish I could preserve this moment. I fear what is to come; I fear seeing disappointment and pain in her eyes, but I see no way to prevent it.

Arabella rises to her tiptoes and deepens our kiss, her hands clutching my cloak, balling it up in her fists. It isn't until we hear gasps around us that we step away from each other. Arabella's cheeks turn rosy, and she pulls her hood over her head. For a single moment, she and I had both forgotten about the people around us, the myriad soldiers and household staff who have volunteered to help us.

The atrium is filled with hope and excitement, and for once, there's no snow falling down on us. I wish I could take it as a good sign, but I dare not be so optimistic. I glance around at the familiar faces surrounding us, feeling uneasy. They're used to defeat, and they've come to accept that even my best attempts only make the slightest difference, but it's different with Arabella. They see her as their savior, and I fear the way they might look at her if we're unsuccessful today. More so, I fear how it would affect Arabella. It has taken some time, but at last, she's come to consider Eldiria home. I hope it remains that way.

"Theon, we're ready," Elaine says, her voice trembling. I look into her eyes and find my own worries reflected back at me. She smiles, but she fails to hide the unease she feels. I nod in reassurance and glance at my wife. Though I know the odds are stacked against us, I'm certain my wife will be victorious. If anyone can go up against the curse and come out on top, it's Arabella.

Arabella nods at me, and I nod back at her before walking away toward my designated position at the opposite end of the atrium. I inhale deeply and turn toward her, countless steel rods in front of me that have already been put in the right position by our men. All I need to do now is transport them deep underneath the surface. I drop to my knees and place my hands on the cold earth, my eyes on the steel in front of me. It's been years since I attempted to use my alchemy powers to this extent, and I worry it will leave me drained, at the curse's mercy. If that were to happen, the entire palace would be at risk. Arabella would be at risk.

I take a deep breath and clear my mind, focusing on the task at hand and letting every other thought fade. I glance up at my wife and find her already looking at me, her eyes filled with quiet confidence. She smiles at me and nods, and I begin to transmute the metal.

The steel rods start to shimmer, and sweat drips down my brow as they become translucent. I fear I can't hold on long enough to get them into the ground. Every second I hold on, I grow weaker.

"Almost there, Felix."

I hear her voice clearly through the buzzing of energy around me, and I hang on to the hope in her voice as I push through. I inhale once more, my eyes falling closed as I visualize the depth the rods must be placed at. Once I exhale, they disappear from sight, even though I can still feel them clearly. I feel sick to my stomach as I push them down, my vision swimming as I lower them just a little farther, until at last, the rods are in place.

I look up at Arabella and nod, giving her the go-ahead. I see the worry in her eyes and force a smile onto my face. She stares at me, as though she's trying to ascertain whether or not to trust my smile, but then Elaine places a hand on her shoulder. I breathe a sigh of relief when Arabella nods at Elaine, and I force myself to my feet, wanting to offer her the support she offered me.

I watch as Arabella closes her eyes and spreads her arms. Fire engulfs her, sparks shimmering all around her as she inhales deeply, focusing her attention. I find myself wondering which memory she chose to fuel her powers today, and I'm intent on finding out tonight. The wind blows through her hair, and for a moment I worry that the weather will turn, the curse bringing us torment we cannot escape, but no such thing happens.

Instead, gasps come from all around me as the snow on the ground starts to melt, revealing the patterns on the stone floor underneath. I stare at the stones in shock, remembering what it looked like in my childhood, before the curse's effects were quite as bad as they are now. For as long as I can remember, these grounds have been filled with ice and snow, bar the walkways we always keep clear. In the last few decades, I have not once seen this entire atrium without a single snowflake on it, yet that is exactly what I am looking at right now.

I look back up at Arabella to find her still standing opposite me with her eyes closed, her cheeks rosy and a hint of a smile on her face. Her long dark hair moves with the wind, and I doubt she's ever looked more ethereal.

Arabella opens her eyes, her gaze instantly falling to me, and she smiles before turning to look around her. I grin when she spins around in a circle, pure joy lighting up her face.

"Felix!" she yells, and my heart skips a beat. She opens her arms wide, as though to say, *Look around*, and I just stand and stare at her in disbelief. Arabella of Althea. I don't deserve to call her my wife, but I'm beyond blessed to do so regardless.

She takes a step toward me before she increases her pace and runs. I rush toward her, meeting her halfway, and Arabella jumps into my arms. I wrap my arms around her waist and lift her up high, spinning her around and eliciting a laugh from her.

"We did it!" she shouts, and I shake my head.

"*You* did it," I correct her, slowly lowering her as her body slides against mine. Arabella wraps her arms around my neck, her lips pressed together, betraying her dissatisfaction.

"I could not have done this without you, Felix. Without you, there would be no steel rods for me to heat. We did this together."

I nod. *Together.* I like the way that sounds coming from her. "Yes. Yes, we did."

She smiles then, seemingly satisfied with my words. Her eyes drop to my lips, and my heart starts to race when she tilts her head, edging closer. For her to take the initiative to kiss me... it makes a special moment even more special.

Her lips brush against mine, and I exhale shakily, impatient for more. I tighten my grip on her, and Arabella finally kisses me, a soft moan escaping her lips. Her kiss is deep and leisurely, and much to my surprise, she doesn't pull away—not even when cheering erupts all around us.

By the time she leans back, my heart is once again full, and I'm starting to wonder whether this emotion I'm feeling might be the one thing I never thought I'd experience. I wonder if it might be *love.*

CHAPTER
THIRTY-EIGHT

Felix

Arabella's smile hasn't left her face since we left the atrium, and her joy is infectious. I can't recall the last time the palace was filled with true joy. It isn't just us—it's every member of the staff.

We have people walking through the atrium barefoot. Some are dancing and singing, while others have brought out our limited supply of liquor. It has been years since my people had hope the way they have it today, and we owe it all to Arabella.

"I knew we could do it," she says. "You didn't believe me. You might not have said it, but I could see it in your eyes."

I pause in the hallway, surprised she managed to see through my attempts to hide my worries. "No one has ever been able to read my mind like that," I tell her.

"I can, Felix." She looks proud and stubborn, a chastising look in her beautiful eyes. There's something so ethereal about her at this moment. She looks at me the way a wife looks at her husband—with intimacy and a level of knowledge only a married couple can share.

"Is that so?" I ask, a smile stretching across my face. "Tell me what I'm thinking of right now, my darling wife."

I let my eyes roam over her body and imagine undoing her corset.

Arabella's eyes widen and her cheeks turn rosy as she turns away from me and takes another step toward our bedroom.

"I have no idea!" she answers, her voice high-pitched. I love seeing her flustered. I think scandalizing my wife might well be my new favorite hobby. Making her blush and seeing her eyes widen... it does something to me.

"Are you quite certain you don't know what's on my mind?" I ask, trailing behind her.

Arabella looks over her shoulder and attempts to glare at me, but I see the thinly veiled desire in her eyes. I chuckle and count the steps to our bedroom as I watch her walk in front of me. Deciding that I can't wait that long after all, I reach for her with my powers, undoing her corset from behind.

Arabella gasps and looks at me over her shoulder. "Felix!" she chastises, and I grin at that wide-eyed look she throws at me. Beautiful.

I continue to undo the laces of her corset, and Arabella giggles. She looks back at me again, and then she breaks into a run.

I find myself frozen in surprise for a moment, and then I grin as I chase after her. Her giggles sound through the hallway, and my heart nearly overflows. When was the last time these halls were filled with happiness?

Arabella escapes behind our bedroom door, and I follow close behind her. "Where do you think you're going, wife?" I need her with a desperation I can't contain, and I'm running out of patience.

Arabella laughs as she runs up to our bed. She leans against one of our bedposts and looks at me, her breathing uneven. Her eyes are dark with desire, and my heart skips a beat when her gaze roams over my body.

I rest my back against the door and watch her, lifting my hand to undo the rest of her corset. Her lips fall open, wiping the smile off her face, and I chuckle. "Hiding from me, my love?"

"Maybe," she whispers, her voice husky. I twirl my fingers and swallow hard when her corset comes undone. I look her in the eye, wondering what she'll do, and I tense when she lets it drop to the floor.

I'm breathing hard as I undo the tie at the top of her skirt. Arabella lets this garment, too, fall to the floor, her eyes filled with the same desire I'm feeling.

She stands before me in her chemise and leans back against the bedpost, facing me. Her eyes are on me as I send a sharp tug through her chemise, ripping it apart. I move it off her shoulders, and that joins the rest of her clothes on the floor.

Arabella raises her arms to hide her naked body, but I shake my head as I close the distance between us. "No. You're too beautiful to hide away."

I pull her arms apart and pin them above her head, making her gasp. "Felix!" she whispers, and I smile.

"I like the way my name sounds on your lips, beloved. I'd rather enjoy making you scream it."

The way she looks at me has me straining against my breeches painfully, yet what I want more than anything else is to take my time with her. I want to please my wife and drive her as crazy as she makes me. I want my name on her lips, over and over again, until tomorrow's responsibilities tear us apart.

I walk up to her and pinch her chin, tilting her face up so I can kiss her. I take my time with her, entwining my tongue with hers in the way I've learned makes her tremble with need.

"Felix," she whispers against my lips, her tone pleading.

Arabella pushes against my shadow, and much to my surprise, she unravels it, undoing my hold on her wrists. No one has ever been able to do that. I smile as her hands roam over my chest, tugging at my uniform. My beautiful wife has no idea just how strong she is. I can't imagine how much stronger she'll get.

"You've teased me quite enough," she tells me as she pulls my uniform open. I'm startled when she leans in, pressing a kiss to my neck. Never once has she been this brazen, and I'm enjoying every second of it. While her body has always betrayed her desire, this is different.

Arabella pushes against my chest, and I take a step back, curious. She grins and pushes me toward the bed, until she's got me standing right in front of it. "Not so fun being thrown around, is it, husband?"

I smirk as she pushes against my chest again, making me fall backward onto our bed. I lean on my elbows to look at her and shake my head. "On the contrary, wife. I'm rather enjoying this."

"You see," she tells me. "Elaine loaned me some of her romance novels. They were quite a bit more graphic than the ones we had in the library."

I wonder if she realizes that she refers to everything as *us* and *we* now. She calls my people hers, and my palace is granted the same treatment. I wonder if she considers *me* hers, too. I've never found myself jealous of my own citizens before, but today that's exactly what I am. I'm jealous.

"Elaine, huh? I have a feeling I'm about to be grateful for whatever wicked books she gave you."

Arabella chuckles, the sound making my heart overflow with feelings I don't dare name. For so long, I've associated love with the curse; now I don't dare taint what I feel for Arabella.

"I think you might just be. I'm not so sure. It all seemed so appealing in the books, but it might not be quite as easy in reality."

"Good thing we have plenty of time," I murmur, wishing it were true. "I would be happy to subject myself to what I'm certain will be torturous practice events."

Arabella bursts out laughing, and I can't help but chuckle in return. I've never experienced anything like this: joy entwined with lust, humor entwined with desire.

"Torturous... if I do this well, it might just be." She leans over me and runs her hand over my chest.

"Beloved," I whisper. "I'm not quite that patient. If you want my clothes off, just say the words."

She looks at me through lowered lashes and nods, an enticing smile on her face. I snap my fingers, and my clothes end up on top of hers, leaving me bare and entirely at my wife's mercy.

She kneels in front of me, palming my erection without hesitation, and I moan. "Fates, Arabella..."

She looks at me as she lowers her head, and I almost lose it when she wraps her lips around my cock, her mouth wet and hot. Arabella moves her head up and down, her touch hesitant and determined all at once. She'll drive me insane, which I'm certain was her objective all along.

She swirls her tongue the way she loves to kiss me, and I groan, unable to take it. "My love," I tell her. "Keep going like that, and I'll mess up your pretty little mouth."

She has no idea what she's doing to me. No idea what she looks like, her breasts on display as she takes me in so deep.

I lift her up into the air, repositioning her so she's on top of me. "Felix," she protests, but I shake my head. I can't take another second of the torment she's putting me through.

"Grab it," I order, and she obeys, guiding me inside her slick wet heat. "Ride me, my love. Use me however you want to."

She starts to move on top of me, and I smirk as I use my shadows instead of my fingers, teasing her, until I feel her muscles contract all around me.

I can't get enough of her. I agreed to let her go if we manage to mitigate the curse's effects, but I'm not certain I can. Losing her isn't something I can survive.

CHAPTER THIRTY-NINE

Felix

I can't shake the deep unease I feel as I walk toward the east wing, the chilling wind cutting against my skin. It's almost as if I've been existing in two entirely different universes lately, one of which allows me to lose myself in Arabella the way I wish I could consistently. She soothes my restless soul, and she does it with nothing but her wit and smiles. The more she gives me, the greedier I become, and the more I fear losing her to the curse.

I draw a shaky breath as my eyes roam over the tattered canvases that I took a knife to many years ago, venom stealing away the remnants of peace waking up next to Arabella granted me. When I ruined them, I'd wondered if the palace would repair them, the way it does most other things of value. Part of me had been quite certain it'd want to preserve anything related to my mother, and this was, after all, her wing.

The curse has mostly contained itself to this wing, almost as though it isn't able to extend to other parts of the palace as easily as it's spread through my empire. Whenever tendrils of darkness do spread, I often manage to send the energy back to the east wing. It's at its strongest here, yet the damage I've done has not been undone.

I grit my teeth as the Mirror of Pythia comes into view, distaste rushing through me as I take in the delicate floral golden ornaments. When Pythia appeared at my palace nearly fifty years ago, begging for refuge from the curse in return for a prophecy that could save my people, I offered her a binding spell, binding her to the mirror and the mirror dimension, and thus keeping her safe from the curse. Pythia sees different versions of the future, and in all but one, she saw herself succumbing to the curse. Offering me the prophecy in return for the binding spell was the only way she could keep herself safe. In hindsight, I wish she'd chosen anything but this mirror—the one my mother allegedly loved and had handcrafted.

"Pythia," I call, the usual dread rushing down my spine as she appears. "The plans Arabella and I have laid—will they succeed?"

She's silent for a moment, more trepidation in her body language than usual. "In every version of the future I have seen, you will fail to break the curse with this plan. It is, however, a necessary step you both must take."

I nod and look away, used to my attempts failing. I'd have been more surprised if she'd told me this was indeed how we'd break the curse. It'd be too simple. "Will it make the lives of the Eldirian people better?"

I raise a brow when she seems to hesitate. As part of our binding spell, she is compelled to answer me provided her answers don't negatively influence the future, but even so, she often tries to fight the compulsion. "Though it is a temporary reprieve, it is all part of a grander plan. Your efforts will inspire hope, and they will greatly and positively impact the lives of the Eldirian people, but it will come at a great personal cost."

My heart sinks as a new type of fear takes hold of me. I've never had anything to lose—not truly, but I do now. The thought of losing Arabella to the curse shakes me to the core, leaving me feeling true terror for perhaps the first time in my long existence. "Show me."

Pythia disappears, and a vision of me appears. Except my eyes are fully black, as though the curse has taken hold of me. Denial surges within me, and I grit my teeth as I vow that this will not come to pass. The visions she shows me don't always come true—the future is fluid, and nothing is set in stone.

"How long can I stay away?"

Pythia appears. "It varies in each version of the future I've seen, ranging from weeks to months. It is your proximity to the empress that expedites your vulnerability to the curse."

I nod and run a hand through my hair. This means I'll have to closely monitor myself. The second I begin to notice myself losing control over my own strength, I'll have to distance myself from Arabella. I can't ever let her see me turn into the monster I become when the curse temporarily takes hold over me, as it has on battlefields in the past. I can't show her the bloodlust, the mania.

I clench my jaw and run a finger over the edge of the mirror, watching the ripples underneath, though the surface feels solid and impenetrable to me. "I will have to take you with me," I warn her. "So I can continue monitoring the way the future changes as we lay pipes. I won't risk my wife's life."

"You've come to love her," Pythia says, her tone both mocking and gleeful at once. "The wheels of destiny are spinning, and not even you can stop them."

I grit my teeth and slam my fist against the edge of the mirror, then use alchemy to remove all sharp edges from the shard I broke off. Pythia's face blanches, and I grin, pleased to have caught the seer by surprise. With each year that passes, she resents me more, and I can hardly blame her. If not for me, she wouldn't have to remain trapped in this mirror, and the curse wouldn't have targeted her as it did. It must have known that she held a clue to breaking it, and as a result, her village was buried in an avalanche, taking her home and her family with it. It nearly killed her, too, but dying wasn't what the

Fates had in store for her. Not then. Not when she had a prophecy to convey.

"Nor can you," I remind her. "You will, however, help me attain the best future possible, and it will be one in which both Arabella and my people are happy." I lift the mirror shard and watch the displeasure in her eyes as I let it slip into my cloak. "You will answer when I call, no matter where I am, and you will guide me. No harm will come to Arabella."

Pythia's expression turns stormy for a moment before she disappears. I'm tempted to call her back, just to make a point, but I know better than to further aggravate a seer. She might be compelled to answer me, but the more I call upon her, the more cryptic and unhelpful her answers become.

"Theon?" I look up when I find Elaine standing by the entrance of the east wing, as though she was waiting for me. "Tell me this will work."

I think back to Pythia's words and nod. "It will greatly and positively impact the lives of our people," I tell her, leaving out every warning Pythia gave me.

Elaine's shoulders sag in relief, and she stares up at me with such hope in her eyes that I instantly feel remorseful. I'll need to do everything in my power to ensure this plan succeeds.

CHAPTER
FORTY

Arabella

I bite down on my lip as I put aside my quill, my heart aching. It's my sister's birthday today, and it's the first time she'll have to spend it without me. Usually, the day would be filled with festivities Father arranged for her, but she and I would always find a moment to escape together. I'd sing to her, and we'd share a slice of cake, just the two of us. We'd stand by the window and reflect on the year behind us and all she wished to accomplish in the next. Those moments we shared were filled with hope and joy, and they belong among my favorite memories.

The pain of leaving home is not as intense as it initially was, but today the loss weighs heavily on me. I miss Serena, and I miss the lead-up to her birthday, the talk of dresses and color schemes, the trips we'd go on to find her the perfect bakery and the perfect outfit. I miss her.

"What's wrong?"

I look up at Felix, startled. "Nothing." I shake my head and clutch my letter to my chest. "Felix, would you please deliver this to my sister?"

I hand him the letter with a sigh, and he takes it from me with a frown on his face. He's been delivering my letters for me for weeks now, never asking me about them, but today he looks curious.

"It's my sister's birthday today," I murmur, my melancholy leaking into my voice. "I can't be with her today, but I'd like to wish her a happy birthday nonetheless."

Felix takes a step closer to me and cups my cheek, his touch gentle. "Of course, beloved," he says. "I'll see to it that it gets to her at once."

I watch as the letter shimmers bright gold before it disappears and sigh. I hope this will bring a smile to her face. I hope it lets her know that I'm thinking of her today.

"You miss her," Felix murmurs.

"More than you could ever know. My little sister is everything to me. She's all I had in a life that I never belonged in. She was my confidante, my best friend."

Felix looks away, his expression conflicted. "Once the curse has been managed, you can go see her," he tells me, and I nod. Thoughts of returning home don't come to me as frequently as they used to, but days such as today make it hard to resist the desire.

"Having said that," Felix adds, his tone hesitant, "the atrium was filled with snow this morning."

My eyes widen, disappointment flooding me. All morning I've felt heartbroken, and this just adds to it. I run a hand through my hair and inhale shakily. "How could that be? It was fine for so many days!"

Felix nods and brushes my hair out of my face, tucking it behind my ear instead. "Take a moment to feel out your powers, Arabella. Do you feel the connection you forged to the flames in the atrium?"

My eyes widen when I realize that I don't. Feelings of sadness consumed my every thought this morning, pushing aside the flame I kept in the back of my mind. "Oh Fates, Felix! I did this!"

He smiles, a hint of relief in his eyes. "Arabella, my love... it's hard to consistently sustain energy flow of any kind. You did incredibly well. The pipes are already in place, aren't they? It's just a matter of reheating them. I suspected it was the curse, that the pipes may have been destroyed altogether, but that doesn't appear to be the case. As we hoped, your elemental magic renders anything it touches immune to the curse. That's good news, beloved."

I nod, but I fail to hide my disappointment. I was so certain that we'd succeeded, that we were a step closer to fulfilling our plans. If the flames go out every time I get distracted, then how are we meant to make this work? If sorrow pushes aside the emotions that fuel my fire, then how do I sustain it?

"Come on," Felix says, his hand finding mine. He entwines our fingers and pulls me along. He snaps his fingers once we get to the hallway, and both of our capes appear around our shoulders.

"Gloves?" I ask, and Felix nods.

"Yes, my love," he says, before closing his eyes for a moment. When he opens them again, he's holding both of our gloves.

"Why is it that you often snap your fingers when you call upon your alchemy powers?"

Felix shakes his head. "I'm not quite sure. It helps me concentrate my powers. Concentration is of paramount importance in alchemy, or the item being transported or transmuted could be damaged. When I first started learning, I lost things entirely. I'm uncertain where items go while they're in transit. I suspect it's some kind of limbo."

I bite down on my lip, guilt settling deep in my stomach. I never considered how hard it must be for Felix to constantly use his alchemy. I always took it for granted, in part because he makes it look so easy. "Is it hard for you to send my letters?"

He looks at me then, hesitating. "It would be harder for a messenger to get through our woods to hand you her replies."

I suppose that's as clear of a yes as Felix will give me. I've been asking him to send and retrieve letters for me every single week since he offered. How much must it have drained him to do this for me?

"Thank you," I tell him. "I'm sorry for not saying this sooner. My sister's letters have made my stay here bearable. I would be terribly lonely without them."

"Bearable, huh?" he repeats, and I pause.

"I didn't mean it quite that way. You know what I meant."

Felix stops walking and turns toward me, his expression guarded. "No, Arabella. I don't."

I hesitate, unsure what to say. I might not be as lonely as I used to be, but no matter how much I enjoy being with Felix, in the back of my mind there's always a niggling thought reminding me I was forced to come here.

"Let's go," I tell him. "We should heat up the pipes as soon as we can."

Felix nods, his hands disappearing into his pockets. I've grown so accustomed to him reaching for my hand that it startles me, and I instantly feel guilty for being unable to answer him in a way that might set him at ease. Lying didn't feel right, and I'm certain Felix would see straight through it.

"Your Excellency!" Elaine says, rushing over when we reach the atrium. "Please, is there anything you can do?"

The desperation in her eyes fuels my guilt. I may have been taken from my kingdom, but Elaine lost *everything*. If she can fight the way she does every single day, then I must, too. Feeling sorry for myself for even a moment isn't acceptable, not when so much is at stake.

"I'll try my best, Elaine. I swear it."

She nods, but I see the way she trembles. I've never seen her display a moment of weakness, not once. I never realized just how much hope our success in the atrium gave her. A quick glance around the atrium makes it clear that it isn't just Elaine whose faith is shaken. This happened because I lost control over my emotions, because I allowed my self-pity to overwrite the memories that fueled the fire.

I sink down to the floor, my hands pressed upon the icy ground that felt warm against my fingers just a day ago. My eyes fall closed, and I let my favorite memories of Serena and me fill my mind, until my heart overflows with happiness instead of sorrow. I smile to myself when I feel the threads of fire all around me, and I pull them toward me with a grateful heart.

I let the energy run through me, letting my body be a conduit for the fire I'm sending deep down to the pipes, and I breathe a sigh of relief when I feel it hit its target. I sit there, on my knees on the floor, letting memories of my childhood fuel my fire. I think of Serena and I sneaking away, discovering parts of the palace we never knew existed. Those memories turn into ones of us sneaking into town and trying mead together for the first time. Then there's us dancing and laughing together, but perhaps my favorite of them all are the memories of Serena and I just sitting together, dreaming of the future.

I open my eyes when I'm certain the pipes are fully heated, my heart filled with happiness of a bittersweet kind. "Happy birthday, Serena," I whisper. The quickest way for me to get back to her is to complete Elaine's project. Once we do, I'll be able to see her and wish her a happy birthday myself. I might have missed this year's festivities, but I won't miss next year's. If I can have it my way, Felix and I will attend together.

CHAPTER
FORTY-ONE

Felix

I walk through the dozens of wagons filled with steel pipes, inspecting every batch we're taking with us. It took weeks of preparation to prepare a sufficient amount for our trip.

"I'm worried, Felix."

I turn toward Arabella and lift my hand to her face, the back of my fingers stroking over her cheek. "Don't be, beloved. You've kept the atrium heated for weeks now. Have you not seen the plants Elaine and the other sorcerers have been growing? I don't recall the last time something grew in Eldiria, and *you* made that happen. If you could do it in the atrium, you can do it in the rest of our empire, too."

She shakes her head and clutches my cloak in her hands. "The atrium is one part of the palace where the curse's effects are largely mitigated. The rest of the country won't be the same."

She's right, but for once, I'm certain we'll be victorious. "Have faith, beloved. I do. I have faith in you, in us. We've come further than ever before, and I suspect we have much further to go still. Walk this road with me, Arabella, and we'll change more lives than you ever thought possible."

She nods, but I see the insecurity in her eyes. It astounds me that she doesn't seem to realize how powerful she is. Within a few months, she's harnessed powers that were thought to be extinct, teaching herself more than I ever could. Her control over fire is unlike anything I've ever seen, and her control over air is growing rapidly. She's now able to lift me into the air for a few seconds at a time, when a mere few weeks ago, she could barely lift snow. I wish she could see herself through my eyes.

"Let's go, my love."

Arabella takes my arm and I wrap my hands around her waist to lift her on top of Sirocco, my touch lingering. She and I haven't had many moments alone recently. Every waking moment that I'm not working is spent executing Elaine's plans and preparing for the trip we're about to embark on. Countless regions of the empire should be receiving steel within the next few days, accompanied by soldiers that will dig up the ground and place the pipes so Arabella and I can move through the country at a quicker pace. I expect there to be many instances where the pipes won't have been placed yet because of the ice or the curse's effects. From what I've observed, the curse doesn't go near anything Arabella's magic has touched, but before then, it might go rampant.

My wife and I have done our best to be prepared for the unexpected. This trip could last a mere few weeks, or it could last months. While we have prepared for both scenarios, I know she's still filled with fear, and I'm uncertain how to take those fears away.

"It's beautiful," Arabella says, as we ride past empty fields filled with snow, and I try to see it through her eyes. The stars above us illuminate the fields, and I suppose there's some beauty to it.

"Many years ago, those were rice fields."

She tenses, her back rigid against my chest. "I'm sorry, Felix. I . . . I didn't realize."

I smile to myself and wrap one arm around her. "One day, I'll show you what they looked like. One day, you and I will restore those fields to what they once were."

She turns her head to look at me, her eyes finding mine. I miss her. The last couple of weeks have been filled with late nights and early mornings. I miss lying in bed with her in my arms. I miss having her bare body against mine, and the way she whispers my name late at night. I miss the way her eyes shimmer with need, her pleas silent but effective.

I lean in and kiss her, startling her. Arabella freezes for a moment, and then she lifts her hand, threading it into my hair as she kisses me back. It's been over a fortnight since I last had her lips against mine, and the distance that has grown between us since makes me deeply uncomfortable.

I push aside the ache and deepen our kiss, losing myself in her for a moment. I fear that the memories we'll make throughout this trip might be the last ones I have of her. I hoped to change her mind, but I suspect she still has every intention of leaving me the moment we return to the palace. This trip might well be my very last chance to win her heart.

Arabella pulls away, her cheeks flaming, and I smirk. It's been so long since I made her blush. "Beautiful," I whisper into her ear. "I love the way your cheeks redden, beloved. It's been too long."

"Felix!" she chastises, but the tone of her voice puts me at ease. Arabella has been different lately. Ever since her sister's birthday, she's been absentminded. I used to be able to read my wife with ease, but lately she's a mystery to me. I can't tell what she's thinking, and I fear her thoughts are on Althea. I've been tempted to read the letters she exchanges, for fear that in truth it's the boy she communicates with, but I've been giving her my trust. I hope I don't come to regret it.

"We're here," she says, her voice a nervous edge to it. I glance around at the square in the first town on our journey. The town's people have gathered to welcome us, their faces lit with hope.

Snow starts to fall as our horses come to a stop, turning to hail the very moment my feet hit the ground. I look up, my heart sinking. Arabella was right. The curse won't let us intervene with the same ease we experienced in the atrium.

My mood is grim as I lift her off Sirocco, my spirits falling by the second. I can't stay away from the palace for long. Each time I've tried, the curse entangles me, suffocating me so slowly I barely realize what's happening, until it's too late and the damage is done. Our plan fails without me, and recuperation periods at the palace will set us back endlessly.

"It's okay, Felix," Arabella says. She slips her hand into mine and smiles at me. "We're going to be just fine."

I nod as I follow her, willing myself to believe her words. Arabella has never seen me lose control—few people have and lived to tell the tale. I fear what I might do to her if we stay away too long. Fates, she and I will never recover if it gets that far. She might be able to see beyond my monstrous exterior now, but once she sees the beast within, I'll lose her.

"Felix?"

I look up at my wife, my heart aching. She's so heartbreakingly beautiful. It isn't just her stunning face or that body I can't stop fantasizing about; it's her heart.

"Are you ready, Felix?"

I nod and glance at the steel pipes already laid out for me. Moving them will take so much of my energy... how many times can I do it before I'm depleted? How much can I do before I become a danger to everyone around me?

CHAPTER FORTY-TWO

Felix

I glance at Arabella as she's bent over her makeshift desk in our tent, writing so furiously that I can see specks of ink on her cheeks from where I'm standing. Her eyes shimmer with contentment as she pens a letter to her sister, and I wonder if I'll ever be able to make her smile the way she does tonight.

I've made her laugh, and there have been moments where I brought her happiness, but it's always been fleeting. Could I ever make her as happy as a letter from her sister does? Arabella sighs, her smile dropping for a mere moment before she shakes her head and continues to write. I wonder what thought just crossed her mind.

I've never before felt curious about a woman, but I wish to know every single thing that consumes her. I want to know her every stray thought, every reason behind her sighs. I suppose it's only fitting that setting my people free means losing her. I've been cursed from the moment I was born, and I'll die feeling its effects. It is fortunate that I'll be surrounded by memories of Arabella in the end. I'm fortunate to have had her for as long as I may.

Arabella looks up, her hand rising to her chest as her eyes widen. "Felix," she whispers. "I didn't see you standing there. How long have you been there?"

Far longer than I'll admit to. "Not long," I tell her. She stares at me, almost as though she's trying to read me, but then she shakes her head, the movement so subtle I almost miss it.

"I know I'm asking a lot of you, but would you be willing to send this letter to Serena? I promised her I'd stay in touch even while we're on the road. She's worried. I hate the thought of her sitting there filled with anxiety. I just know she'll struggle to sleep until she hears from me. No matter what I tell her, she's certain I'll freeze to death or—" She stops speaking abruptly, her cheeks rapidly turning rosy.

"Or what?"

Arabella looks away and shakes her head. "It's nothing. She fears you, and she's convinced you'll harm me someday. No matter what I say, she can't be dissuaded. I suppose it has something to do with the way you handled Father on our wedding day. That's all she's ever seen of you."

"What do *you* think?" I ask, hesitating. "Do you think I'll hurt you, Arabella? Do you fear me?"

She looks up at me, wide-eyed. "You have never hurt me, Felix."

That's not an answer, and she knows it. I suppose I should be grateful that she isn't lying to me outright. I wish I could set her at ease and swear to her that no harm will ever come to her, but the longer we're away from the palace, the more restless I feel. With every day that passes, I can feel my control slip away. I feel the darkness pull at me, luring me with thoughts I can't keep at bay. From experience, I know I'll only be able to resist for so long, but I expected to last far longer than I have.

It's almost as though the curse is sentient and aware we're close to defeating it. Its pull is stronger than ever before.

"Felix? Will you send the letter for me?"

I nod and walk up to her, taking the letter from her carefully, and all the while resisting the urge to touch her. My need for her grows every second, but I fear being with her when I have so very little control.

"Of course, beloved." I stare at the letter as I focus on the memory of the long table in Althea's throne room, where I've been sending all of Arabella's letters. The letter shimmers bright gold before disappearing, and Arabella smiles.

"Thank you, Felix."

I nod and turn to leave, but Arabella grabs my hand and stops me in place.

"Where are you going?" Her voice is soft, sweet, and entirely irresistible.

"I need to check on the progress of the pipes. The soldiers are still digging, and I'm wondering if perhaps it would be better to utilize alchemy again after all. This is the third town that hasn't had the pipes in place for our arrival. It's slowing us down considerably."

Arabella nods in understanding, but there's a hint of a smile on her lips. "Or you could just leave them to do their job, and we can enjoy our evening together. We haven't taken an evening off yet. Aren't you tired?"

I hear the unspoken words, the longing. She misses me as much as I miss her, but I cannot push aside my fears. "I'll just go check up on them. I won't be long."

"Felix," she says, my name a plea on her lips. She rises from her seat and lets her hands slide up my chest, until she's got them wrapped around my shoulders.

She looks into my eyes, her gaze searching, though I can't tell what for. She hesitates, and then she rises to her tiptoes, her lips finding mine.

I groan when she kisses me and thread my hand through her hair, pulling her closer to me with a desperation I struggle to contain.

She moans against my lips and I lower my hands to her waist, lifting her up higher, until she wraps her legs around me.

I push her against the wall, rolling my hips against her the way I've been dreaming of. Her moans fuel my desire, and I'm tempted to take her right here and now. I feel my control slip for a single moment, my vision going black as the shadows pull at me, taking away my consciousness. It takes all of me to fight it, to remain right here with Arabella.

I pull away from her and drop my forehead against hers, both of us breathing hard. She's entirely unaware of my internal torment, and though I wish to keep her in denial, it isn't safe.

"Arabella," I murmur, my eyes falling closed. "I can feel it. I feel the curse's allure, and it's hard to resist. It pulls at me, tempting me to give in to the darkness. I'm not as strong as I wish I were, beloved. While you might win this fight against the curse, I might lose it. And if I do... I can't tell you what the consequences would be, but I can tell you I have never opened my eyes after one of those blackouts without being surrounded by casualties. I can't risk you being one of them."

She places her palms flat against my chest and shakes her head. "You won't hurt me, Felix. You won't."

I cup her cheek and force a smile onto my face, in awe of the trust I see in her eyes. It's that same trust that'll make it hurt so much more. "You don't know that, my love. I'm just going to check on the soldiers, all right? I just need some fresh air."

She looks at me as though she wants me to stay, and there's nothing more I'd rather do... but I can't. Not tonight. Not when the curse's allure is so strong.

Arabella's expression haunts me all the way into the woods, and with every step I take, I resist the urge to go back to her, to fulfill the needs she left unspoken.

My hands tremble as I take a shard of the Mirror of Pythia out of my pocket, holding it up in the moonlight. "Pythia," I whisper. "Show me the future."

Her face appears in the mirror, and she nods before her image is replaced by the same flashes of the future I've become accustomed to, the very same ones I've come to despise. I watch as Arabella rides away on Sirocco, my palace fading into the background the farther she gets away. I see her embrace her sister, and I watch her sitting down on her father's throne, a crown on her head. The image shifts to the one that pains me most, and the darkness calls to me as I watch her rest her head on Nathaniel's shoulder, his arms wrapped around her intimately.

"These are all visions I've seen before. Has any part of our future changed?"

Pythia appears in front of me again, her face serene. "Perhaps it is not a change, but a new image came to me. I don't believe it to be wise for you to see it."

My heart twists painfully as the images shift, until I'm looking at myself, infected by the curse. My eyes are fully black, black tendrils of smoke surrounding both me and Arabella beside me. The images are moving so quickly I can barely make sense of them, but the one thing I see clearly is the cuts on Arabella's skin and the blood that flows from her wounds. The images fade away, until it's only Pythia I see in the mirror.

"I'll hurt her," I whisper, my heart wrenching. My stomach tightens, and I begin to feel sick. "Tell me there's a way to prevent that version of our future, Pythia."

"I can't, Your Excellency. This happens in every version of the future I have been shown."

"There must be something you can tell me, something you can do."

She shakes her head and bows, disappearing before I can question her further. I clench the shard in my hand, coating it in my black poisonous blood.

I stare at my hand, realization dawning. It's only a matter of time before I infect Arabella, too.

CHAPTER
FORTY-THREE

Arabella

I glance over at Felix standing in the distance, every instinct telling me that something is wrong, yet I can't quite figure out what it is. I'm certain Felix has been ignoring me for close to two weeks, hiding behind the excuse of needing to help with placing the pipes in every town we've visited.

"Is everything okay?" Elaine asks, and I turn toward her, unable to wipe the frown off my face.

"I'm not sure. Felix...he's been different. Has he ever told you about the darkness calling to him?"

Elaine freezes and looks up at me, a hint of fear in her eyes. "It's happening so soon? He's usually capable of keeping its lure at bay for weeks at a time. We must move quicker if that is true."

I bite down on my lip, unable to ignore the niggling feeling that I'm not getting the full story from either Elaine or Felix. "What happens when he gives in?"

Elaine looks away and wraps her arms around herself. "He is never harmed. The curse envelops him, but it never hurts him. It's everyone around him that suffers. Before I joined the cause, Theon would often let the curse take him to aid us in conquering other surrounding countries. He'd go by himself and return victorious.

Theon would decimate an entire army in a matter of hours, and he'd never remember a second of it. All he saw was the blood on his hands when he eventually took back control, without any indication of what might have happened. It hasn't happened much in the last decade, but once, when he was going up against an army of tens of thousands of men, Raphael and I followed him with our best soldiers in tow, despite his warnings. I'll never forget what we saw."

She shudders and closes her eyes for a moment, as though the memory is too vivid to bear. "He loses himself, truly. The curse transforms his entire body into a creature unlike anything I've ever seen before. His eyes turn black, and he becomes a demon in every sense of the word. I've never feared Theon, but I fear him when he's like that. When the battle was over and he was the last person standing, Raphael and I tried approaching him. We thought it would help him fight the curse's hold on him, but it didn't. We lost several of our men, and we nearly lost our lives, too. When he's like that, he's not himself. It's almost as though he's possessed. He didn't recognize us, and he couldn't discern who did or didn't wish to harm him."

I look at Felix, unable to even imagine what Elaine is describing.

"We cannot let it get that far, Empress. You must warn me if it looks like he might be losing control, so I can arrange for us to return. Our plans can wait."

I nod in agreement and watch as Felix helps the soldiers lift and place the metal. I've noticed that he's minimizing his use of his alchemy, and I wonder if it's because he's starting to fear that using it will make him lose control.

I walk over to him, noting the way he tenses, yet he doesn't look up. It's odd, but I feel like he's barely been looking at me. That's an entirely strange thing to notice, but I doubt I'm mistaken.

"I can help with that," I tell the soldiers. They pause what they're doing, and almost as though in sync, they bow. "You really need to stop doing that," I tell them. They don't bow to Felix; they treat him like one of their own, yet they won't treat me the same. The soldiers look at me with reverence, and it's unnerving.

"Our apologies, Your Excellency," one of them says. Simon, I believe his name is. "It's instinctive. Most of us have waited for you our entire lives, and to have you here among us is an honor. Rumors of a prophecy have been whispered from one generation to another, starting with my grandmother."

I smile as best as I can and raise my hands the way Felix taught me to, lifting the steel into the air before lowering it into the ground the soldiers dug up, taking minutes to do what would take them hours. In each area we visit, Felix places the largest pipes as quickly as possible, and I push my fire through just as quickly, before the curse has a chance to disrupt our work. Once the main one is in place, it appears to give us a safe radius from which our soldiers can operate, placing additional pipes that warm the ground more than just the single one can, after which Felix connects them, and I channel my fire through them all.

The soldiers murmur excitedly among themselves, but my eyes are on Felix. He's facing his men, and he has yet to acknowledge me. I've been making excuses, telling myself that it was just the workload that was getting between us, but I'm uncertain how much longer I can deceive myself. Felix is avoiding me.

His back straightens when I walk over to him, betraying his awareness of me. "Felix," I murmur. When he turns toward me, he looks impatient, as though he doesn't want to be anywhere near me and I'm merely inconveniencing him. "Let's retire for the night," I murmur nonetheless.

He looks at me, his expression guarded, and I find myself wishing there was a way of knowing what he's thinking. For a while, I was certain that he and I were growing closer, turning our marriage into a real one. The moment we embarked on this journey felt like the start of the end, and with every day we're away from the palace, that feeling is reinforced.

"Very well," he says, nodding politely. He gestures toward the tents behind us, and I tense. I expected him to take my hand or offer me his arm at least, but he's keeping his distance from me.

I smile tightly and turn to head back to the tent we share, Felix right behind me. "Won't you walk by my side?" I ask, my voice soft.

Felix responds by falling in step with me, his cloak brushing against mine. It hurts that I have to ask him for something so simple.

"You're pushing me away, Felix. I want to know why. Is this truly all because you think it'll keep me safe?"

He stares straight ahead, avoiding my gaze. "I've merely been busy, Arabella. We all have been."

"Why are you doing this to us?" I ask, my voice breaking. "It wouldn't hurt you to treat me with kindness, would it? Are you behaving this way because you've now accomplished your goal of mitigating the curse's effects? Now that I'm near useless to you, you're dismissing me?"

My worst fears escape my lips without conscious thought, and I wrap my arms around myself in an attempt to shield myself from the vulnerability I'm feeling.

Felix is quiet for a moment, and I regret saying anything at all. I feel exposed and foolish.

"Does it matter?" he asks, his tone uncaring. "Once we finish heating the ground, you'll return to Althea."

I look up at him in surprise. It is what we agreed on when he asked me for help, but somehow I expected him to ask me to stay nonetheless.

"What if that's no longer what I want?"

He looks at me then, a hint of an emotion I can't identify flashing through his eyes. "You'll return home, Arabella. You'll have all you've ever wanted, everything I've promised you. That was our agreement, was it not?"

"It was, but that was before..." I bite down on my lip, unsure how to finish my sentence. It was before he and I became a couple, before he took me to bed and showed me who he truly is, beneath the monster he portrays.

Felix smiles, but it doesn't reach his eyes. "Before I took your innocence? What is it you're worried about? I'm certain the boy will take you back the moment you return."

I stop walking then, and so does Felix. For so long he refused to even let me think of Nathaniel, and now he's seemingly accepted me being with him after I return to Althea? It can't be.

"I assumed you were staying away from me because of the curse's effects on you. I see the torment you're in, Felix, and I've tried to be patient...but perhaps I was wrong. Perhaps I was just another woman in the long life you've lived. Someone who has fulfilled their purpose and ceased to be of interest to you. Perhaps I was seeing things that weren't there."

He looks away, as though this conversation is a tedious matter he must sit through, and it hurts. "What is it you'd like me to say, Arabella? As part of our agreement, we tried finding love together, and we failed. We've found a different way to mitigate the curse's effects, so naturally, our priorities must shift in line with that."

Arabella. He hasn't called me *my love* or *beloved* in so long. I stare at him, wondering whether I can trust his words. I can't tell if this is the curse's doing, or if I'm merely being naïve.

"Don't do this," I whisper, one last plea.

Felix smiles at me, regret in his eyes. "Our fate has always been sealed, Arabella. We might fight it, but we only delay the inevitable."

"Do you truly believe that?"

Felix looks up at the sky and nods. "I know it."

I stare at him and take a step away from him before turning and walking away. Part of me hoped that he'd follow me, but he doesn't.

CHAPTER
FORTY-FOUR

Felix

Arabella's words haven't left my mind since she spoke them. They resound in my mind, taunting me with all I wish I could have, day in and day out.

I lean back and watch her from the shadows at the tent's entrance as she sits and writes yet another letter to her sister. I'm unable to resist my need for her. No matter how many times I consult Pythia, our future never changes. I end up hurting her and she leaves me, reuniting with the boy I tore her away from. I fear what I'll do to her if I go near her, but I can't stay away, either.

She smiles at the parchment in front of her, and I try my hardest to recall the last time she smiled at me. When was the last time I heard her laugh? It's an unsettling experience to miss her when she's right in front of me.

Every day, the distance between us increases. I can feel her slipping away, and it's hurting me more than this curse ever will. I didn't think happiness existed before her. I thought it was a myth, or something elusive at best, a thing people convince themselves they must achieve in an effort to make life more bearable. It wasn't until Arabella walked into my life that I understood why humans go to such great lengths to find what Arabella and I did. Despite my long life, I don't think I was truly alive before her.

Arabella sighs as she folds her letter, her touch gentle as she slides it into an envelope, sealing it with wax. Her control of fire has become so strong that she manages to do it without needing to concentrate, and once more, I'm in awe of her.

How many times have I stood here, watching her as she writes? I've lost count. It's the only moment she takes for herself, my only chance to watch her without the mask she wears for my people.

She rises from her seat, her envelope in hand and a dreamy expression on her face. I wonder who it is that put that smile on her face. It certainly wasn't me. The boy, perhaps? Lately it's taking her longer to write her letters, and instead of asking me to send them for her, she's requested Elaine's help. Elaine has been sending an enchanted carrier pigeon on her behalf, and many times, I've been tempted to intercept it to find out who she's writing to, but how could I stand in the way of her happiness after all I've already done to impede it? I've taken so much from her, and if Pythia is right, I'll bring her more sorrow before she finds happiness of her own.

"Felix!" She freezes in place when she finds me leaning back against the wall. Her eyes find mine, but the intimacy I've grown accustomed to is missing. She forces a smile for me, and all it does is anger me.

I push away from the wall and walk up to her, my eyes dropping to the letter in her hands. "Who is the letter for?"

Her eyes flash as she tightens her grip on it, a stubborn tilt to her chin. "Does it matter?"

It shouldn't, but it does. "Our agreement still stands," I say against better judgment. "I have yet to let you go, Arabella. Until the day I do, you're *mine*."

She grits her teeth as she looks up at me, anger lighting up her eyes. "Am I, Felix? Am I yours? You can't control who I think of, who I dream of."

I take a step closer to her, expecting her to take a step back, but she doesn't. My body brushes against hers, and she looks up at me, her eyes filled with defiance and fury. "I once told you I have no problem reminding you who you belong to, and that still stands."

"You *do* remind me every single day," she tells me. "Every time you brush me off or ignore me, you remind me that I never meant anything to you. You remind me that all I ever was to you was someone to use and discard. Nathaniel never once made me feel that way. *Not once.*"

I grit my teeth and thread one hand through her hair, my touch rough as I cup her cheek with my other hand. "I don't want his name on your lips, Arabella." My thumb brushes over her lip, as though that might wipe away the words she just uttered.

"Too bad, Felix... because Nathaniel is all I've been able to think about. Every time you dismiss me, you remind me of the gentleness he showed me. When you make it clear you don't want me, I find myself wondering if he'd ever—"

I lean in and cut her off, taking her lips the way I've been dreaming of. She moans against my mouth and kisses me back, her hand roaming over my body with the same impatience I'm feeling. I pull away from her and lift her into the air, until her back hits the wall behind us. Arabella's eyes are dark with desire, and the way she looks at me undoes me.

I walk up to her and smile as I reach her, my hands wrapping around the top of her chemise before I rip it apart, the sound of the fabric tearing loud in our quiet tent. I inhale sharply when her chemise falls away, revealing her breasts. "I doubt that boy of yours has the strength to do this," I murmur as I yank her corset off her, letting it drop to the floor. I lean in and suck down on her nipple the way I know puts her at my mercy, and she moans loudly in protest when I pull away. I smirk and snap my fingers, her eyes falling closed when the feeling is mimicked by my powers while I move my touch lower.

"He certainly can't do that, can he? Even if you're ever with him, it won't feel as good as it does with me."

I tear her skirt off her and let it fall to the floor, smirking when I slip my fingers between her legs. "Let me guess... you're already wet for me. Do you think he'll ever make you feel this way? Even if you ever let him touch you, it'll be me you think of."

I slip a finger into her, enjoying the sounds she makes for me. "Do you really think so, Felix? Do you think I'll remember you when he's making me forget my own name?"

A low growl escapes my throat, the sound inhuman, an omen of the evil we'll unleash if I don't walk away. I let go of her and take a step away, needing space and distance to collect myself. I move to walk away from her, but she's got me trapped and unable to move.

Arabella's eyes are ablaze with anger when my gaze lands on her, and she shakes her head. "No," she says. "You don't get to touch me like that and walk away."

She lifts her hand and before I realize what's going on, she's got me pressed against the same wall I just held her up against, her control over the air around us formidable. "Arabella," I warn her.

"No," she repeats. She snaps her fingers, and my clothes burst into flames, the flames eating at the fabric yet leaving me completely unharmed. I try to resist smiling, but I fail. I'm in awe of her. As she stands before me, her clothes ripped and her lips swollen, her eyes blazing with anger and desire... I don't think my beloved wife has ever looked more beautiful.

"Be glad it was just your clothes this time, Felix."

I chuckle and rest my head against the wall as the fire takes away my last remaining clothing, revealing just how badly I desire her. I watch her through my lashes, unable to resist her. One hour... if I can fight the darkness for a single hour, I'll get to see her look at me the way she used to. I'd give the world for one more memory of her.

Arabella rises to her tiptoes, her lips finding mine. Her touch is gentler now, more hesitant. I kiss her back, and her body relaxes against mine. She releases her hold over me, and I push away from the wall. "Arabella," I whisper, and she shakes her head as she presses her finger against my lips.

"Don't say a word, Felix. Not now."

I pull on her hand and turn us over so I've got her pressed against the wall. She moves her arms around my neck, and I lift her, my hands on her waist. Arabella wraps her legs around me, and I breathe a sigh of relief when my erection brushes against her wet heat.

"I need you, beloved." She nods and reaches between us, guiding me into her. "Oh Fates," I murmur as I slip deep inside my wife. "I missed you more than you'll ever know."

I pull back almost all the way, my eyes on her as I thrust back into her. I watch the way her eyes widen, the way her lips fall open when she moans, the fire in her irises. I try my hardest to commit this image of her to memory.

"More," she whispers, her hands threading through my hair. She pulls me closer, her lips finding mine, and I lose myself in her. I've never wanted a woman more than I do her. I'll never get enough of her. I take her harder, giving her what she's asking for, and the way she moans has me losing it.

I feel the darkness claw at me, and I close my eyes for a single moment, exhausted from fighting and wanting just a single moment with my wife.

When I open my eyes again, Arabella is on her knees on the floor, blood staining her skin red. She looks up at me in fear and horror, and I take a step away from her. This. This is what I saw in the mirror of Pythia. There are cuts all over her skin, blood flowing freely from her wounds.

I did this. I knew I'd hurt her, and I let myself go near her regardless. "Elaine..." I whisper. "I need to get Elaine."

CHAPTER FORTY-FIVE

Arabella

"I can't believe we managed it," Elaine says. Our soldiers are packing up around us, and I look around in awe. It took us several weeks, but we placed pipes in the most important parts of the country.

"Your wounds are healing nicely," she remarks, and I lift my hand to my throat. Memories of Felix's eyes turning black come to mind, and I shudder. For a moment, it wasn't my husband whose eyes I was looking into. The way he smiled was terrifying. Felix has never scared me before, not truly, but in that moment I feared for my life. Before I could even scream, darkness enveloped me, thick and sticky, suffocating me. The next thing I knew I was on the floor, cuts all over my skin and flames engulfing me protectively, chasing away the darkness.

Color returned to Felix's eyes, followed by panic when he found me lying on the floor, drenched in blood. Within minutes, he'd brought Elaine to me, begging her to heal my wounds. I've never seen him that panicked before, that terrified. He disappeared as soon as Elaine bandaged my wounds, the cuts immune to her magic. I haven't seen him since, though each town we passed through informed us that Felix had already placed the pipes we needed.

He's been ahead of us by a few days, so I suspect that he's already back at the palace by now. I can't help but wonder if he pushed me away early into our trip because he feared the curse's pull. He warned me he felt it, but I failed to realize it was to this extent. I'd gotten so wrapped up in my own insecurities and fears that I failed to support him with his.

I'm lost in thought as I lift myself on top of Sirocco. The horse and I have become reluctant allies, united by our mutual abandonment.

"He's okay, Your Excellency," Elaine tells me. "I'm certain he's waiting for you at the palace. I think he might just have needed some time to process what happened. The curse...it's hard on all of us, but it's different for Theon. While you and I can acknowledge that he wasn't himself in that moment, Theon can't make that same distinction. He'll blame himself endlessly, and he'll fear hurting you again. I beg of you, Your Excellency, don't let him unravel the future the two of you have woven. Don't let him untangle your lives. He will, if he's given the slightest chance."

"Arabella," I tell her. "I've told you countless times that my name is Arabella."

She nods, but I know she'll refuse to call me by my name. She insists on formality and propriety.

Elaine sends me a pleading look, refusing to let me change the topic, and I nod. "Don't worry," I tell her, unsure what else to say. I can't make her false promises. I don't fear Felix, but I fear what he became. Can I protect myself if it happens again? I believe I might be able to, but what I saw was nothing compared with what Elaine has described in the past. Was it Felix who pulled himself out of the darkness's clutches, or was it the flames that expelled it?

I'm lost in thought the entire way home, for once grateful for Sirocco's inhuman speed that allows me to reach the palace long before the others do.

I'm tense as my feet hit the floor, unsure what I should do or say.

"Where is Felix?" I ask as I cross the palace's threshold, confident that the palace will lead me to him.

Candles flicker on, illuminating a path toward the east wing. I follow the path the palace lays out for me, chills running down my skin as the temperature drops. The palace is always kept warm, but it is ice-cold here. I glance at the covered golden portrait frames, curious what's underneath, yet certain this place is best left undisturbed. I've never felt such strong evil magic, and I finally recognize it for what it is—the curse. Not even my father's torture devices felt this vile. This must be where the curse originated. What would bring Felix here?

I pause in the hallway as I realize that the Felix I might find could be the one that haunts my nightmares. I bite down on my lip and shake my head, reminding myself that Felix told me the palace restores his magic and soothes the curse's worst effects.

I climb the stairs toward a tower eerily similar to the one I've so often been held captive in, my heart hammering in my chest. In the final weeks of our trip, I've replayed our last few moments together countless times, wondering if there's anything I could have done. If I'd called upon my fire, would that have kept Felix safe?

I'm nervous as I push open a door that was left ajar, the hinges creaking. I find Felix throwing a cover over what looks like a mirror before turning to me, and I breathe a sigh of relief when I find his eyes the same turquoise color I love.

For a moment he looks at me as though I'm a mirage, but then his eyes clear, and his shoulders straighten. "You can't be here."

He walks past me, his expression as haunted as mine must look. "Felix," I say, my voice soft. "It wasn't your fault."

He pauses and turns to look at me. "It was, Arabella, and it'll happen again. You aren't safe around me. You never will be. You have to leave."

"I can protect myself. I'm no longer the girl you brought here from Althea. I can defend myself from the curse's effects if I need to, Felix."

He runs a hand through his hair and looks up at the ceiling. "You know you can't, Arabella. There's no escaping it. It'll always be there, and you'll always be at risk."

He looks at me, his gaze sorrowful as he cups my cheek. I feel him tense, darkness slithering into his eyes. The whites in his eyes disappear, black slithering in, taking over. I step back defensively, gathering my magic around me as his expression changes.

He laughs, the sound shrill, and a shiver runs down my back. "You can't fight me," he says in a voice unlike his own. "You can't stop this. His soul was always mine to take. He's fought all his life, but once he sees his precious little wife bleed out, dying at his own hands... he'll give in, and this world will be bathed in darkness at last."

I stumble back, feeling sick to my stomach. Felix takes a step toward me, his movements inhumanly fast. Before I can call upon my powers, he's got his hands wrapped around my throat, the black veins on his skin moving, slithering onto my body, as though it's trying to infect me.

I can feel the spark of fire, yet I can't reach it. I can't reach beyond the darkness that's rapidly enveloping. "Felix," I choke out, trying my hardest to call upon the elements around me and failing.

Felix freezes and lets go of me, his eyes clearing. He looks at me in horror and takes a step back, stumbling. "You... you aren't safe around me, Arabella," he whispers.

I sink to my knees, tears in my eyes as he rushes away, the door slamming closed behind him. I held on to hope for as long as I could, but I have nothing more to give. Felix might be right, and I truly might not be safe around him. What's worse is that I doubt he's safe from the curse himself. The more we worked to mitigate the curse's effect on the land, the more it appears to have targeted *him*.

"Arabella of Althea."

I look up when I hear a woman's voice. She sounds far away yet close all at once.

"The mirror."

I rise to my feet, my heart racing in fear. My hands tremble as I pull off the cover I saw Felix place over the mirror when I walked in, revealing a woman in a white gown. Her eyes are milky white and unseeing, but she's mesmerizing, and she's undoubtedly the woman I thought I saw in the mirror the first time I walked into the east wing.

"My name is Pythia," she says. "Along with the people of Eldiria, I have been awaiting your appearance."

"Pythia," I repeat. "You're the seer that prophesied our marriage, the one that said I'd break the curse."

She nods. "The future is fluid, never written in stone. Your future has changed countless times from the moment you stepped foot in this palace. Most people have a general path that was pre-written and that they cannot diverge from, but you do not."

I stare at her, unsure what to make of her words. "If my future is not pre-written, does that mean I might never break the curse?"

She nods. "I can only see the future as it is presented to me. In the current version I see, you will be in torment until the day you die, never finding the love and happiness you crave. Your presence here was a direct result of my vision, and though I cannot take back the words I spoke as a result, I urge you to heed the Shadow Emperor's words. If you stay, your blood will spill on these very floors, and your life will be lost."

"I don't—"

Before I can finish my sentence, she disappears, the mirror only reflecting myself. I stare at my reflection, the scars on my skin, the haunted look in my eyes. The vision Pythia had will never come to pass. I will never break the curse, and I will never be able to set Felix free.

CHAPTER
FORTY-SIX

Arabella

Pythia's words keep resounding through my mind, keeping me awake in the bed I expected to share with Felix.

Your blood will spill on these very floors, and your life will be lost.

I'll die here without ever breaking the curse. I had so many more questions for her, and after she vanished, I waited for hours in the hope of her returning, but she never did.

How do I die? Do I die at Felix's hand? Will the curse concentrate right here in the palace now that I've made so many parts of the country inaccessible to it? How will it adapt to our efforts to fight it? Were our attempts to mitigate the curse's effects doing more harm than good?

There is so much I need to know, so many questions unanswered. Oddly enough, the thought of dying doesn't scare me. What I fear more than anything else is what it'll do to Felix if I were to die by his hand, even if not by his choice.

I understand it now. I understand why he became more distant the longer we were away from the palace. If I'd known that he pushed me away in an effort to protect me, I'd never have provoked him the way I did.

I sigh and slip out of bed, my eyes roaming over the bedroom I've come to consider mine. Tonight isn't the first night I'm in Felix's bed without him being here with me—this is exactly how we started our marriage. I still remember his words, his plea to give our marriage an honest chance in case it might break the curse. It was a foolish notion, and it seems even more so now.

I lift my hand and let my robe float through the air until I step into it. I was powerless when I arrived here, and despite all I've learned, I'm still powerless today. I can't save my marriage, and I can't break the curse that will eventually take my husband. If Pythia is to be believed, I can't even save myself.

I step out of my bedroom, pausing when the candles in the hallway light up, clearly trying to guide me somewhere. I smile to myself, at ease with the palace's quirks now when once it terrified me.

The doors to the library swing open as I approach it, and I pause in the doorway. Felix is seated behind his desk, his eyes filled with profound torment as he looks up. "Arabella," he whispers.

I suspected he was still at the palace, but I wasn't certain, since he's made every effort to avoid me in the last three days. I smile tightly and walk in, noting the way Felix's eyes roam over my body. It isn't just desire I see in them; there's a different, deeper kind of longing, too.

He drops his quill and leans back in his seat, the sadness in his gaze resonating with the aching of my heart. "I thought you were asleep."

I pause in front of his desk and shake my head. "No. I've been unable to sleep for weeks now." He tenses, guilt flashing through his eyes, and I shake my head. "I've grown so accustomed to being in your embrace that I struggle to sleep when you aren't there."

His eyes roam over my face, as though he can't quite believe I'm standing in front of him. "What are you doing up so late?" I ask, my eyes dropping to the papers on his desk.

Felix inhales deeply as he pushes a piece of parchment toward me. "This is what you asked for when we came to an agreement. I'm ready to grant it to you now."

I lift the document, my heart stopping. "Annulment papers," I murmur. I look up at him in shock. "Why?"

"I received reports from the cities we've visited. The ground is heating, and the snow has melted in most places. There are no more reports of natural disasters or misfortune. Your fire is keeping the curse at bay, just as we suspected. I've asked the sorcerers in our safe havens to visit the affected areas and help grow crops, and the results have been promising.

"When I asked for your help, I told you I'd let you go if you were able to help me lessen the curse's effect on my people, and you've done just that. There's nothing more I can ask of you. I took you from your kingdom, from the man you love, and despite that, you've given my country more than we ever should have asked for. The only thing I can offer you in return is freedom."

I stare at him, anger rising from the pit of my stomach, until I can feel the pressure in my head. I set the parchment on fire and watch it burn to dust before brushing my hands off.

"I didn't mean a word I said to you about Nathaniel, Felix. I was angry that you'd been pushing me away. I was hurt, and I set out to hurt you in return. You may have told me that you struggled with the curse's effects, but you never told me how bad it'd gotten. Instead of continuing to confide in me, you pulled away, leaving me to make assumptions about what might be on your mind."

He nods as he pulls out another sheet of parchment. "I suppose I'll have to draw up another document," he says, his voice devoid of emotion.

"You may if it pleases you, but know that I'll set that ablaze, too."

"Arabella, this is what you asked for, isn't it?"

I look away. "Felix, that's what I asked for before I even got to know you. My dreams and wishes have evolved since then. Our marriage has become a true one. You once asked me to give our marriage a chance, and I now ask the same of you."

"I have," he says. "I gave it a chance, and we were unable to break the curse. I don't see the point in continuing this charade. You're young, Arabella. You have a whole life ahead of you, but not here, not with me. You aren't the only one who looked into the Mirror of Pythia and asked what our future holds."

I freeze, a chill running down my spine as I recall Pythia's words.

"If you stay here, you'll die, Arabella. I've seen what your future holds if you leave, and your happiness lies in Althea. I suppose you and I always knew that. You were always meant to return home to the life that's waiting for you there. I can't be around you. Even as you stand here in front of me, I feel the darkness rise within me. I suspect that it knows you're the one reining it in, and I can't protect you from it, not when it resides within me."

Your blood will spill on these very floors, and your life will be lost.

No matter how badly I want to stay, I can't. For a moment I felt like we'd defeated the curse, giving our people some relief from the damage it causes... but with every win comes devastating personal defeat. I should have known that we couldn't win. Not truly.

I look into Felix's eyes, his expression unreadable. I inhale deeply as I drop my gaze to the stack of parchment on his desk and turn around, snapping my fingers as I do so, engulfing his desk in flames as I walk away.

It doesn't soothe my aching heart, but it brings me peace to know he'll struggle to draw up new papers tonight.

CHAPTER FORTY-SEVEN

Arabella

I wake up to noise in my room and sit up in shock, only to find my clothes flying through the room, folding themselves and dropping into open suitcases. I look around, but it doesn't appear to be Felix's doing.

My heart races as I lean back against the headboard, keeping still as my belongings float through the room, packing themselves. It takes me a moment to realize what's going on.

"You too, Palace?" I whisper. "You want me gone, too, huh?"

Everything stops in place and my belongings slowly lower to the floor, and for a moment I could almost swear I feel the palace's sadness. I smile when my curtains swing from the left to the right, almost as though the palace is trying to shake its head.

"Then why are you packing my belongings when I haven't even decided if I'm leaving?"

I raise my hand to my heart when magic concentrates in the middle of the room, shimmering gold until a woman stands before me, her skin translucent. What is she? An apparition? I stare at her in shock, unable to look away. She's beautiful, with long golden hair and beautiful emerald eyes, a golden dress making her look ethereal.

"Who are you?" I ask, my voice trembling.

She smiles at me. "You've always referred to me as *palace*, and that's all I am. A physical manifestation of the walls that surround you. I'm packing your things because I want you to live, Arabella. I want Felix to be free of torment. If you stay here, I'll lose you, and in time, I'll lose Felix, too. So long as you're alive and happy somewhere in this world, that's enough." She pauses as her skin becomes more translucent, almost as though she's fighting to stay corporeal. "If you die, the curse will take Felix. It's trying to take root in him, and if it succeeds, that will be the end of the world as we know it. Felix will be gone, and we'll never get him back. If you stay, you'll both die."

She fades from view, and my belongings rise back up into the air as she continues to pack my suitcases. I sink to the floor beside the bed, my heart aching. I don't even know when my wants and needs shifted. When did going home stop being something I yearned for?

The candles near the bathroom flicker on and I rise to my feet, taking the hint. I never knew the palace could take on a form, and I'm left with even more questions than I went to bed with.

By the time I step out of the bath, all my belongings have been packed and a riding outfit lies on the bed, the gloves Felix gave me beside it. My heart breaks as I get dressed in Felix's colors, the gold on my coat shifting patterns, from Eldiria's crest to Felix's, over and over again. I used to love watching this, but today it hurts my heart knowing I won't belong to either once I step foot out of this palace.

I'm startled out of my thoughts by knocking on my door, and the door swings open before I can even call upon my air powers. Elaine steps in, her eyes filled with the same ache I'm feeling.

"You're leaving."

I nod and she walks up to me, taking my hands in hers. "I must, Elaine."

"Felix told me what Pythia said," she whispers. "I understand that you must go, but I'll miss you more than you could know. I just... I truly believed love would break this curse. I believed it with all my heart."

I look down, unable to face her. "I'll keep training, Elaine. I'm going to do everything in my power to grow stronger, to keep the fire in the lands going. I'll keep researching as much as I can. I might be leaving, but I'm not giving up. If I can bring Raphael back to you, I will."

She inhales shakily and wraps me in her embrace, startling me. I smile and hug her back, resting my head on her shoulder. "Don't go," she whispers.

I tighten my grip on her. "I wish I could stay." My voice trembles, and I squeeze my eyes closed. "Every time I'm around Felix, the curse puts him through torment. If I die... I fear he'd let the curse take him, and we both know that cannot happen."

She pulls back and grabs my arms. "You write to your sister," she says, hesitating. "Would you... would you consider writing to me every once in a while, too?"

In the time I've been here, Elaine and I have grown closer, and though no one could ever take Serena's place, I've come to love her as a sister. I'm not sure I could have gotten through the last couple of weeks without her. I smile shakily and nod. "I would love to, Elaine. You kept me together after I fell apart throughout our journey, and I'll always be grateful to you."

She shakes her head. "Eldiria and I owe you a great gratitude of debt. Thank you... Arabella."

I grin at her. "At last you're calling me by my name. Did you know that I used to idolize you when I was younger? You're so much more, so much better than I expected you to be. Someone once told me to never meet my heroes because they might let me down, but you never have. I'll miss you, Elaine."

My suitcases lift into the air, hovering by the door, and I shake my head. "That's my cue," I tell Elaine, and she nods, her expression sorrowful as we walk through the long corridor she once guided me through when I first arrived.

She and I both pause when we find Felix standing beside Sirocco. "Don't take a carriage," he tells me. "I'll see to it that your suitcases arrive to Althea before you do. Take Sirocco. He'll keep you safe, and he'll get you back to Althea in very little time."

"How do I return Sirocco to you?"

He shakes his head. "Don't. He's yours to keep. I'm certain he's grown more fond of you than he is of me."

The edges of my lips tilt up into a reluctant smile, and Felix stares at me for a moment. I'd give the world to know what he's thinking. He leans in and wraps his arms around my waist, his hands lingering as he lifts me on top of Sirocco. That's as close to me as he's gotten in weeks.

Just as he's about to speak, Felix freezes and yanks his hands off me. I watch as darkness slithers into his eyes, and he takes a step away.

The more I took away the curse's effects, the more it's started to affect him. I'm poisonous to him, to the point that he and I can't coexist. I wrap my arms around myself for a moment, trying my hardest to keep from falling apart. "If my love for you could have broken this curse, it already would have," I murmur.

Felix looks up at me, my heartbreak reflected in his gaze. "I love you more than words can convey," he whispers, almost like he doesn't want me to hear it, but can't quite keep the words in. "You are my sun, Arabella. The mere thought of you fills me with warmth on the coldest days, and forevermore, my world will revolve around you. I love you, but you must forget about me, Arabella. Build a life for yourself you can be proud of, find happiness of your own. Knowing you're out there in the world, chasing the happiness I know I'll never give you... that is all I could ask for."

My stomach twists painfully, and my throat tightens with unshed tears. My grief flows from my eyes, and I reach for him, wishing I could kiss him one last time, but knowing I can't risk it. For so long, I wished I could return to Althea, and now that the time has come, I want nothing more than to stay right here with him.

We thought we'd won when we realized our plan to heat our ground had worked, but in the end, the curse is demanding the ultimate price for our intervention. We might have saved our people, but we're losing each other.

CHAPTER
FORTY-EIGHT

Arabella

I stare ahead as the castle I grew up in comes into view, trying my hardest to latch on to the sliver of happiness I feel at the thought of seeing my sister again. The closer I get to the castle, the more lonely I feel. I miss Felix already. I miss the palace itself and all her quirks, and then there's Elaine.

My eyes widen when I see my father's entire court standing outside the castle, and then realization dawns. I arrived here unannounced, riding Sirocco. My father's relief is palpable as Sirocco comes to a stop in front of him.

"Arabella," he says, a hint of surprise in his voice. I watch my father for a moment, seated atop Sirocco. It's clear he never expected to see me again. When he sent me off, he sent me to die.

My eyes instinctively trail up toward the tower Serena and I had been in when Felix first arrived here. While I can't see her from here, I just know she's standing there today, too. I take my time dismounting Sirocco, leaving everyone in suspense. They have no idea what brings me here, and I'm unsure what to say.

"I assume you've missed me, Father?"

He snaps out of his stupor and looks from me to the woods behind me, as though he expects Felix to appear at any second. "You've come alone?"

I nod. "I thought it was time to visit. It's been months since I last saw Serena. It was unfortunate that I had to miss her birthday, but I couldn't step away from my duties."

He nods at his advisers, and they return inside. It doesn't escape my notice that they failed to greet me properly. None of them curtsied the way they would have done for Felix.

"The Shadow Emperor sent you here alone? Without any servants or protection?" I hear the disbelief in his voice, and for a moment, I wonder if he's worried about me. "Did he send you away? What have you done? This had better not affect Althea."

Ah, there we go. "And here I thought you'd be happy to see me, Father." I turn toward Sirocco and stroke him between his brows, easing some of his tension away. Though Sirocco has stood beside me quietly, it's clear to me he dislikes my father. I can hardly blame him. "Do you think he'd send me away on his beloved horse?" I ask, my voice calm despite my inner turmoil.

I'm well aware that our marriage is over, but I refuse to acknowledge that to my father—in part because I haven't given up hope yet, even though Felix has.

He looks at the horse, and the fear I see in his eyes brings a smile to my face. When I was younger, my father always seemed all-powerful. I was desperate for the love and approval he gave Serena. I saw the way he treated her and always knew he had kindness in him. It just took me years to realize that it would never be directed at me.

Because he was so clearly capable of it, I always assumed that I must have been doing something to make me unworthy. Standing in front of him today, I can finally see what I failed to for so many years. He's just a man who fears what he doesn't know and cannot control. That's what I've always been to him. It's what I'll always be.

"Tell me the truth, Arabella. Did he tire of you as I expected he would?"

I smile at him. "Why don't you try asking my husband that question? I'd love to see how you fare."

I walk past him and take Sirocco to the stables. "I know," I whisper when he neighs. "He's always been like that. I just never realized it." I take off Sirocco's reins and saddle, grooming him the way Felix always has. "If you want to go back to him, you can. You know the way home, Sirocco. I might be stuck here, but you don't have to be."

Sirocco neighs angrily, and I grin despite the tears that gather in my eyes. Sirocco brushes his nose against my shoulder, and I wrap my arms around him. "We're going to be fine, aren't we?" I whisper. He nudges me, and I take that as agreement.

"Arabella!"

For a single moment, joy overtakes the heartache I feel, and I turn toward Serena as she comes running up to me. I open my arms wide just as she crashes into me, nearly sending us both flying into the haystack behind us.

"I can't believe you're back," she says, her eyes filling with tears. "Oh, Fates, I was so scared I'd lost you. If not for the letters, I'd think you were gone. I missed you every single day. I can't believe you're truly here!"

I hug her tightly, resting my head against her shoulder. "I missed you too, little one. *So much.*"

She strokes my back, letting me hold on to her for a moment. "What's wrong, Arabella?"

I sigh and shake my head, blinking away my tears before I pull back and force a smile onto my face. "I've just truly missed you, Serena. I'm so sorry for missing your birthday. It was the first one we didn't spend together, and you have no idea how lonely I was all day, how much I thought of you."

"Me too," she murmurs, grabbing my hands. "It wasn't the same without you at all. I always thought it was the party I enjoyed, but in truth, it's all the preparations we did together, the time we got to spend together every year, without any other obligations."

I nod and wrap my arm around her shoulder as we walk toward the castle. It looks foreign to me now, when it was once my home.

"How long will you stay? Your luggage appeared in the throne room moments before you arrived, and it looks like it's a lot. It actually looks like it's all of your stuff."

I smile at her as brightly as I can. "Felix told me to stay for as long as I want. He realized how lonely I'd gotten after your birthday and told me to spend some time at home while he's inspecting the empire. That's the amazing thing about alchemy. He was able to send me all my things so I wouldn't have to worry about leaving anything behind."

Serena nods in understanding. "I always hate it when I forget things, or when I can't take everything I want." She hesitates before looking up at me. "So he... *Felix*, he treats you well? Are you happy?"

I pause, unsure how to answer that question. For a while, I experienced true happiness, of a kind I've never known before, but with it comes devastating agony. "Yes," I tell my sister. "He treats me very well. Our marriage didn't start off that well, considering I'd just tried to run away with another man, but we got through it, and eventually we found happiness together." It didn't last, but we found it.

Serena pauses and bites down on her lip. "Nathaniel," she whispers. "One day he was just released and reinstated without a word of explanation. I spoke to him, and not even he understands why."

I nod. "I asked Felix to have him released," I admit. "Nathaniel was merely trying to help me, and I didn't want him to suffer for his good intentions."

Serena frowns, her gaze searching. "You asked, and he just agreed?"

I smile at her disbelief, reminding myself that all she's ever seen of Felix is what he showed everyone on our wedding day. "Yes, my darling," I tell her. "Of course he did. I'm his wife, after all."

It wasn't quite so simple, but Serena doesn't need to know that. I can't justify to myself what I'm doing, pretending that everything is okay between Felix and me. At some point, the truth will come to light, and my reputation will suffer for it. Even so, I prefer that over acknowledging that Felix truly did send me away.

"Oh!" Serena says. "There was a letter on top of your luggage. There's something in it, I believe? It was heavy. I asked the staff to move your things to your old bedroom, so it'll be there for you."

A letter? Who could have possibly sent a letter? Felix, perhaps? I'm reminded of the annulment agreement he attempted to draft, and my heart sinks.

My heart races all the way to my room, scared of what I'll find when I open that letter.

CHAPTER FORTY-NINE

Arabella

I breathe a sigh of relief when I recognize the handwriting on the parchment, and I smile as I run my finger over it. Elaine.

I'm impatient as I tear it open, eager for a piece of home even though I've only just left. Much to my surprise, a sharp, jagged piece of glass slips out alongside the letter. I hold it up, my eyes widening. It's a piece of a mirror. If I'm correct, it's not just any piece... it's a shard of the Mirror of Pythia.

My hands tremble as I unfold Elaine's letter, my thoughts racing. Why would she send me a piece of the mirror? Could it show me Felix?

Dear Arabella,

This letter won't reach you until you arrive at Althea, but as I'm writing this, you've only just left. It has been a mere few minutes, and the entire palace already mourns your loss—though none more so than Theon. I stood beside him as he watched you ride off on Sirocco, the two of us staring into the distance until you disappeared from sight.

Before you entered our lives, I was certain that the only human part of Theon was lost alongside Raphael. I watched as you thawed his heart, and I sat back as he became fascinated by you, watching you when he thought no one was looking. Slowly but surely, you won him over, stealing parts of a heart he was certain he didn't possess. Watching you two together was one of the most glorious things I've ever had the honor to witness, and I'm certain this is not where your story ends—just as I'm certain that my story with Raphael is far from over.

 Enclosed you'll find a piece of the Mirror of Pythia. It's Theon's, and he's unaware that I took it from him, but I'll gladly bear his wrath. It's near impossible to make her appear at will as she answers only to Theon, but I have a feeling she'd come to you if you call for her. I refuse to believe that your fate is to separate from Theon, and I hope that the future will shift. I hope that one day, Pythia's answer changes, and you'll return to us.

 In the meantime, I've instructed the staff to keep all parchment away from Theon unless I'm present. Interestingly enough, they informed me that the palace has already seen to that. It appears that I'm not the only one who wants to keep him from creating an annulment agreement. Perhaps it is a touch childish, but I do not regret my behavior, and I will see this through till the end. This is not how your story ends, Arabella. I know it.

With all my love,
Elaine

 I clutch the letter to my chest, my heart aching so terribly that the pain spreads through the rest of my body. I miss Felix and Elaine,

A CURSE OF SHADOWS AND ICE

and I even miss the palace. Had I been home right now, I'm certain my clothes would have already unpacked themselves, making me feel welcome without a word.

My hands tremble as I place the letter on my bed and pick up the mirror instead. "Pythia," I murmur.

The mirror mists over, and I tense when she appears. "Your Excellency," she says.

"Has our future changed?"

She pauses for a moment before speaking. "If you remain where you are now, you'll live a long life, filled with glory."

"I don't want glory," I whisper. "Will Felix be able to get the curse under control while I'm away? Will I be able to return to him?"

"In the future I see before me, you cannot return to Eldiria. In every version of your future that has been shown to me, returning to Eldiria results in your death, and the subsequent absence of your magic combined with the Shadow Emperor's loss of control fully unleashes the curse. That is as far as I can see, Your Excellency. My inability to see beyond the moment the curse is let loose is an omen that should not be ignored."

It's clear. I cannot ever return to Eldiria. "Can you show me Felix?"

Pythia disappears, the small shard filling with Felix's face instead. I watch him as he sits on our bed, his hand brushing over my pillow. I see the sorrow in his eyes, and it matches my own. Before I've had a chance to truly commit his image to memory, he disappears, the mirror becoming ordinary once more.

"Pythia!" I call, but she doesn't return, no matter how many times I repeat her name. I bite down on my lip harshly as I place the mirror on top of Elaine's letter, my eyes burning from unshed tears. I gave my all in an effort to save Eldiria, and in return I lost the person I love most.

I glance around the room I grew up in, finding not a single memento. The room looks untouched, as though it was never mine.

It could've easily passed as a guest room. That's how much of an impact I made while I lived here. Just like I used to be, this room is unassuming and quiet, wary of standing out. Felix never once made me feel the way I felt while I lived here. Even when we were at odds with each other, I never felt unwelcome or insignificant. I never felt silenced.

The room I shared with Felix is so unlike the one I'm in right now, and it makes me miss home even more. There were memories all over Felix's room. They were in the small burn marks on the curtain from a fire I accidentally started, and the damaged bedpost from when Felix took me against it, neither of us aware of our strength. I miss the tattered rug by the fireplace, where Felix once laid me down and undressed me, and I miss the way the palace laid out outfits for me and supplied me with my favorite meals, the way I imagined a mother would.

Our room in Eldiria holds so many memories, though I've spent so very little time there compared with this one. I inhale shakily as I walk over to the desk in my room, finding an untouched quill in the drawer. It looks as though everything I've ever used has been replaced.

I let my eyes fall closed for a moment before I pull myself together to write a letter to Elaine. Felix always used to collect my letters from Serena from the audience room at four in the afternoon exactly, giving me thirty minutes to pen a reply.

Dear Elaine,

I wish I could adequately convey how grateful I was to find your letter waiting for me when I arrived. It's strange, since this is where I grew up, but I'm terribly homesick already. Though it shouldn't be, it's a consolation to hear the palace mourns me. This morning, as I prepared to leave, she turned corporeal. You've never told me that the palace could take on a form, nor did I know that she's so incredibly beautiful. It was an honor to be sent off that way.

I'm equally grateful for the mirror you sent me. It won't come as a surprise to you that I've asked already, but the future hasn't changed. If I return to Eldiria, I'll be walking into certain death. You are right to say that the future shifts, and I will keep asking, hoping for a better answer. In the meantime, I too will continue to find a way.

I refuse to let our stories end this way, both yours and mine. We came so close, and I'm still hopeful we'll be able to defeat the curse someday, somehow. I won't stop until I find a way to return to Eldiria. Until I do, please keep an eye on Felix. The curse is affecting him more than it ever has before, and I'm endlessly worried.

As for the annulment, I have not informed anyone of the state of our marriage. I have every intention of returning to Eldiria, to Felix. I'll fight to make it happen every second of every day.

All my love,
Arabella

P.S. I failed to mention that I set all his parchment on fire when he first mentioned the annulment, and you have my full permission to do the same should he mention it again. I'll happily take the blame.

Though the heartache isn't gone, writing a letter to Elaine soothes my restless spirit. I find myself smiling as I fold the parchment, filled with renewed motivation to return to Eldiria. There must be a way, and I'm intent on finding it.

CHAPTER FIFTY

Arabella

I browse through the countless books in the library, not finding a single one that could teach me anything about curses that I don't already know. The information here is outdated and elementary, at best.

"Arabella."

I pause at the sound of Nathaniel's voice and turn around, finding him standing in the doorway. He stares at me as though he can't quite believe I'm truly here, and I smile, the feeling bittersweet.

"It really is you," he whispers, walking up to me. Nathaniel pauses in front of me, and then he wraps his arms around me, embracing me. I tense for a moment, and then I hug him back, finally at ease with my feelings for him. What I felt was never romantic love—it was a combination of comfort and the acceptance I so badly desired, wrapped in years of friendship. Years of insinuations about the two of us made it easy to assume that everyone must be right, that we were in love, but I know better now.

True love is all-consuming and maddening. It's selfless, yet selfish, all at once. It's unconditional and uncontrollable. I've never felt that kind of love for anyone but Felix.

He pulls away, placing his hands on my shoulders. "You're wearing *his* colors," he says, his voice laced with disgust, and I frown.

"I'm his *wife*," I tell him, straightening the dark cloak I've grown accustomed to wearing.

Nathaniel takes a step away from me, his eyes roaming over me. "So you are." We both fall silent for a moment, neither of us sure of what to say. "I suppose I owe you my gratitude for the unexpected release and reinstatement," Nathaniel says, his voice soft.

I shake my head. "It was Felix who gave the order. Besides, I'd never let you suffer for attempting to help me. I never should have agreed to go with you in the first place. I knew we wouldn't get away with it, but I was scared and tempted by hope."

"*Felix*," he repeats, his expression filled with venom. "Arabella, I can't stand the idea of you being with him. Do you have any idea how worried I've been about you? Countless times I've considered chasing after you in an attempt to free you from him. I've thought of the two of us running away and creating a life of our own, one where no one knows who we are. I've dreamed of it so often that some nights I woke up, certain I'd find you by my side."

I take a step away from him and look away. "You've always been my best friend, Nathaniel... but that's all you and I ever really were. I believe you know that, too. If you felt differently about me, you'd have proposed marriage when I came of age, but you didn't. You didn't act at all until you felt it was the only way to keep me safe."

He looks into my eyes, startled. "No, Arabella. No, of course not. You were the crown princess of all Althea, and I... I was merely the son of a duke. I didn't feel qualified to ask for your hand. I didn't dare."

I smile at him. "If you'd truly loved me, you wouldn't have cared. Someday, Nathaniel... Someday you'll understand. When you find someone you truly love, you'll know that what we shared was never romantic love. It was love, and it still is, but it was love born out of friendship."

He stares at me, a hint of anger making its way into his expression. "Surely you don't... you can't care for that beast. You can't truly believe you *love* him. Arabella, did you not see what he did to your father? He's a monster, a brute."

I grimace, wishing Felix had reined in his temper that day. All my people have ever seen of him is his ruthlessness. Because of his actions on our wedding day, I feared him, too. It took me weeks of getting to know him and seeing the way his people loved him before I changed my view of him. I can't expect anyone in Althea to understand.

"Nathaniel... he's my husband," I say instead.

His eyes roam over my face, his gaze searching. "You're different," he says. "He must have you bewitched. You're colder, and though you try to hide it, I see your sorrow. Say what you will, but it's clear to me you aren't happy."

I look away, wishing I could explain that I'm unhappy because I'm *away* from Felix. No one outside of Eldiria knows anything of the curse, and it must stay that way for Felix to remain in control of our vast empire.

"You don't have to go back, Arabella. I'm not asking you to be with me, but I can help you disappear if that's what you want. I might not be the Shadow Emperor, but I have connections that can help you stay off his radar. There's nothing I won't do to take away the pain I so blatantly see in your eyes."

I smile at him, unable to help myself. It's no wonder I thought I was in love with him. "Trust me when I say that it's not possible to evade Felix, and I wouldn't even if I could." One single glance in the Mirror of Pythia and he'd find me. Though I suspect he wouldn't even need to do that much. I firmly believe that he'd be able to feel my presence, the way Elaine feels Raphael's.

"Arabella..."

I shake my head. "I know that it's hard for you to understand, but I swear he treats me well. I'm happy in my marriage, Nathaniel. He hasn't bewitched me, for such a thing is not remotely possible, nor am I his prisoner. I'm here now, aren't I? He let me go home because I missed Serena so terribly." The white lie falls off my lips with such ease that it astounds even me. "I don't need you to save me, Nathaniel."

He looks into my eyes and I can't hold his gaze, vulnerability washing over me. "If you're happy in your marriage, then why do you look so miserable?"

I look up at him, not wanting to hurt his feelings yet unable to lie to him. "Because I miss my husband more than I missed Althea. I'm here now, and all I want to do is go back, but I can't. I can't return so soon after arriving here, because Felix will just worry that I was made to feel unwelcome."

It isn't the entire truth, but there's enough truth there for me to speak with sincerity.

"He truly treats you well?"

I nod. "He treats me like the empress he made me."

"Empress," he repeats softly. "I suppose that's what you are now. Empress of Eldiria."

I smile, the title feeling foreign to me. Though our empire is vast, we spent all our time in the parts that made up Eldiria before Felix conquered half our world. I was always treated with reverence, but there was a certain kind of familiarity with the people, all of us united through joint suffering. I never felt like I was their empress— I never felt as untouchable as my father always has. Instead, I took pride in the bond I developed with everyone I met throughout our journey through the country.

"I can't tell what it is you're lying to me about, Arabella, but I know there's something you're keeping from me. I won't rest until

I know what it is. I won't stop worrying about you until the pain in your eyes disappears."

    I smile at him, but I struggle to push down my fears. How long will I be able to keep smiling and pretending everything is fine? I can't keep up this charade forever, and I'm terrified of facing a life without Felix in it.

CHAPTER
FIFTY-ONE

Felix

I sigh as a cup of tea flies in my direction, landing on my desk. "I don't want tea," I say, my face tilted up to the ceiling. Ever since Arabella left, the palace has been accosting me, forcing food and drinks on me.

The teacup rattles on my desk, and I've learned the hard way that it won't stop until I take a sip. Lately the palace has become more temperamental, almost as though it's trying to lessen the pain caused by Arabella's absence.

I sigh and raise the cup to my lips, taking a small sip. Everything I do reminds me of her. Something as simple as this reminds me of every time she's brought me tea while I was working, the memories flashing through my mind, keeping me in torment.

I sigh and rise to my feet, unable to spend a moment longer in this room that's filled with memories of her. I try to resist temptation, but I fail. Every day since she left, I've found myself standing in front of the mirror with the same request.

"Pythia, show me her."

The mirror turns milky white before clearing, and I smile as Arabella comes into view. My heart skips a beat as I watch her walk through the castle in Althea, a cloak that matches mine around her shoulders. It's far too warm for Althea, yet I'm glad to see her wearing it. Her wearing the cloak I gave her means she still holds me in her heart. One day, I'll look into this mirror, and I'll find her in someone else's embrace.

"Has our future changed?"

"No. The day she returns to Eldiria is the day her life comes to an end."

I nod, having grown accustomed to Pythia's words, yet I can't keep myself from asking in the hope that someday she'll tell me that the future has shifted, and Eldiria no longer poses a threat to Arabella.

I long to go see her, but I can no longer step foot outside the palace without losing control over my hold on the curse. If I were to see Arabella, I'd put her in danger.

Even as I stand here, watching her in the mirror, I feel the darkness within me trying to claw its way out. I know that I only have a few more moments before the weight becomes too much to carry, yet I cannot look away.

She's beautiful, and though there's sadness in her eyes, there's strength in the way she holds herself. She's a sight to behold, a far cry from the scared girl she was when I first met her.

I groan when my vision blurs, pain shooting through my body. From the corner of my eye, I can see my hands turning black, and I take a step away from the mirror. Removing the curse's access to our lands has made its effects on me far worse than I admitted to Arabella. Each time I see her in the mirror, I lose consciousness for a few moments, the curse so eager to get to her that I can barely control it. I drop to my knees and clutch my head, trying my hardest to push down the feeling of dread and horror climbing its way up my throat.

I lift my face to look into the mirror and watch as darkness slithers over my body until it reaches my eyes. I fight to hold on to my consciousness, but it's a fight I'm doomed to lose. The last thing I feel before the world goes dark is my body hitting the floor.

CHAPTER
FIFTY-TWO

Arabella

"You've been cooped up in the library for days now," Serena says, pulling out a chair beside me. "You're here, but it's like you aren't here at all."

I look up from the book in front of me, regret rendering me speechless. She's right. I've been working on finding a way back to Eldiria without taking a moment to enjoy the time I have here. For months I missed my sister terribly, and now that I'm here, I've barely taken any time to be with her.

"I'm sorry, Serena," I murmur, my hand wrapping over hers.

"What's going on with you? You haven't been the same since you got back. You've always been reserved and quiet, but never with me. You're right here with me, so how come I still miss you?"

I bite down on my lip, a fresh wave of guilt washing over me. "You're right," I tell her, closing the book I was reading. "I'm sorry, sweetness. I'm yours for the rest of the day, okay?"

Her eyes drop to the book on the table and she grimaces. "Why do these books about Eldiria's history fascinate you so?"

I look away, unable to look her in the eye as I lie to her. "I thought it would be good to learn more about the country I call home now. I know what Eldiria is like currently, but I wonder what it used to be. The way it's grown is fascinating, and I was hoping to learn more about the evolution from the small country it once was to the empire it is today. Besides, I suppose I'm a little homesick."

"*This* is your home, Arabella," Serena says, sounding offended. "What is going on with you? That monster took you from us, breaking Father's fingers before taking you away without giving us a chance to say goodbye. You tried to run the day before your wedding, and now that you're finally back, you're dreaming of Eldiria? Of him? What has he done to you?"

I look her in the eye, unable to push aside the discomfort and anger I feel. "The question you should ask is what has he done *for* me," I tell her, my voice soft despite my anger. "Did you ever stop to think about *why* he reacted the way he did on our wedding day? Felix has never hurt me, Serena. All he's ever done is stand up for me against those who *have* hurt me. I stood there on our wedding day, in excruciating pain, because our own father whipped me until I passed out, leaving me lying on the cold stone floor, locked in a tower. Yet you're surprised I'd favor the man who'd avenge and protect me over the people who have always condemned me?"

Her face blanches, and she looks away, her arms wrapping around herself. "Arabella," she whispers. "Magic is illegal in Althea. It always has been, and you know that. I don't condone Father's actions, but he told me he did it because he was certain you possessed magic. It's the law."

I stare at her in disbelief. For years, I thought she was simply unaware of the extent of my punishments, and I was always happy to keep her blissfully unaware. "You knew what he'd been doing to me throughout the years, and you never spoke up. Not even you would stand up for me."

Serena looks away, her expression betraying her torment. "I couldn't, Arabella. I'm powerless against him. We both are."

"If you couldn't stand up for me, then the very least you can do is appreciate that someone will."

Serena rises to her feet, tears in her eyes. "It isn't like that, and you know it. Fates, Arabella. All I wanted was to spend some time with you, perhaps sneak into town now that Father's court is in session, the way we always used to. I don't understand why you're so antagonistic these days. What have I done to deserve your wrath?"

Father's court is in session, and I wasn't notified? I rise from my seat and shake my head. "Nothing, Serena. You did *nothing*."

I used to think that she couldn't help it, that she was unaware, or that she was merely young, but she isn't. "You are a princess of our country, Serena. It is your duty to stand up for those who cannot stand up for themselves. It is your plight to be the voice of those who are silenced. It's about time you take those duties to heart."

I grab my cloak and wrap it around my shoulders, my heart softening as I tie it closed. I've had months to learn and grow, to see the suffering of my people, and to fight against injustice. I can acknowledge that Serena has never seen any of that—but that does not absolve her of her responsibilities.

"I love you, sister. I admit that my time in Eldiria has changed me, but in my opinion it's for the better. I'll make more time, all right? In return, you must promise to think of what I just told you. This is no longer the Althea you used to know. Althea is part of Eldiria now. Magic is no longer prohibited, and one of the strongest sorceresses I have ever known commands our army. There is a place for you in our empire, if you dare step up to the role."

She looks startled, the gears in her mind turning. I smile at her as I walk away, leaving her alone with her thoughts. I can only hope she leans into her potential. I may be able to push her in the right direction, but I can't make her act.

"Where are you going?" she calls as I reach the large library doors, and I look back at her with a smile on my face.

"The throne room. How could I possibly miss Father's court session? I am, after all, the Empress of Eldiria."

CHAPTER
FIFTY-THREE

Arabella

My cloak trails over the floor as I walk to the throne room, the hallway quiet. Sunlight streams through the windows on my left, and I glance at it, taking a moment to appreciate what I used to take for granted.

I wish Felix were here to see this. I'd love to see the sun turn his dark hair a brown hue. One day. One day, he and I will find ourselves bathing in sunlight. I smile at the mental image, my heart longing for it with such vehemence that I have to pause for a moment, letting my eyes close as I swear to myself that I'll find a way to make it happen.

I take a deep breath and pause in front of the throne room. It's taken me some time to get used to the loss of the palace's cute quirks. The doors here don't open by themselves, and every single reminder of the palace makes me more homesick.

I let my air powers loose, using them to open the door forcefully. The room falls quiet when I walk in, and my father's eyes widen. For a moment, he looks surprised, but that surprise quickly makes way for anger.

"What do you think you're doing?" he asks, his voice controlled, though it in no way hides his anger.

I smile at him sweetly. "I'm sitting in on this session with our court," I tell him as I walk toward the long table in the room, taking a seat nonchalantly. "Proceed," I add with a wave of my hand.

My father looks infuriated, and oddly enough, it amuses me. I stare at him, taking in the wrinkles, the graying hair. He isn't even a particularly tall man, and over the years he's become severely overweight. Yet not too long ago, I feared this man more than anything.

He looks at me, clearly attempting to decide whether or not he's going to ask me to leave, but after a moment or two, he decides to leave me be. The look in his eyes tells me this is far from over, and I clench my jaws in anger. I'm more angry at myself than I ever have been at him. It's surreal to me that I let him terrify and hurt me throughout my childhood, simply because he feared I *might* have powers beyond his comprehension.

Father nods at one of his advisers, and the man rises to his feet. Thomas, I believe his name is. He's been a member of my father's court since I was a child, but that's as much as I know about him. Despite being a former princess of this country, the information I was exposed to was carefully controlled. "We've given a quarter of our kingdom's proceeds to Eldiria," he says, sending me a furtive glance. "Per your request, I've created a plan that will keep more of our gold in our coffers."

I tense and look at my nails, pretending to be bored in an effort to keep them talking. My father is attempting to evade Felix's tax requirement.

"Due to the increased trade contracts we were given, we have, in essence, become a transit city for many of Eldiria's carriages. This increased traffic has also increased our own income. However, there is every possibility of us understating the additional coin we earn, as I suspect that Eldiria will at most compare our numbers from before..." He swallows down the remainder of his sentence, and I glance around the room to find everyone tensing. Looks like my father is none too happy about the conquest, despite the benefits the country has received. I never realized just how selfish he is. He's only interested in filling his pocket, potentially at the expense of his people.

"How much additional coin has Althea earned over its previous average since it became part of Eldiria?" I ask.

Father's head snaps up, and he slams his palm against the table in anger. "I allowed you to sit in on this meeting because I'm indulging you, Arabella. I did not give you permission to take part. Be quiet lest I have you removed."

I lean back in my seat, my eyes meeting his. He looks startled, as though he expected me to cower, and a hint of insecurity crosses his eyes.

"*Your Excellency*," I tell him. "You will refer to me as *Your Excellency*. I did not permit you to call me by my name." My voice is calm, without a trace of the fear I thought I might feel. Compared with all Felix and I have had to face, my father seems inconsequential.

"Guards!" he shouts. "Have her removed at once! Escort her to her bedroom until I have time to deal with her impudence."

My father's royal guards jump into action, two of them approaching me without a moment of hesitation. Everyone present knows that I'm Felix's wife, yet they dare treat me this way. I suppose that in this moment they fear the man in their presence more than they fear Felix. It's a terrible miscalculation on their part.

I sigh and call my air powers to me, gripping my magic tightly as the guards are lifted into the air forcibly. I leave them hovering in the air and cross my arms over my chest, my gaze dropping to my father.

"I'll forgive you for misspeaking on account of our familial relationship. I will not condone this behavior ever again."

His eyes are wide with shock, and something I've never seen before crosses his eyes. Fear.

I turn back to Thomas and nod. "I asked you a question. I expect an answer."

"I...I...we..."

I frown. "Words, please, Thomas. Speak in full sentences."

He looks down and nods. "Our income has tripled, Your Excellency."

"And how much of that has Felix asked you to contribute to Eldiria?"

"A quarter, Your Excellency."

"So even if you pay what Eldiria is due, you have gained a considerable amount from the trade Eldiria has facilitated?"

"Yes, Your Excellency."

I nod and lean in, resting my chin on my elbow. "And what is the punishment for non-compliance?"

He swallows hard. "Death. The punishment is death."

"For who?"

"For every member of the court, Your Excellency."

I look around the room, my gaze slowly roaming over every single member of my father's court. "You'd all risk your lives to save a quarter of the proceeds? You would do so at the risk of losing all additional trade, costing the country endless opportunities? In the end, it's the people of Althea who would suffer. None of you are competent or qualified for your roles. I wonder what my husband will have to say about this."

The hush that falls over the room would amuse me if I weren't so deeply unhappy. The state of my country saddens me, adding to the torment I feel. I rise to my feet and tighten my cloak, the gold on it sparkling with my every movement.

"I'll be reconsidering your roles. I want a description of your job roles and the value you've added to our kingdom in the last twelve months. You have one week to prepare it. I expect to receive your reports at the next court meeting."

Some of them nod, but most of them stare down at the table as though they're chastised children, and it astounds me that they're in charge of our country. I sigh and turn to walk away, my gaze meeting my father's as I walk away.

I recognize the venom I see in his eyes, but I don't have it in me to care. I have bigger battles to fight.

Chapter
Fifty-Four

Arabella

I trace my fingers over Elaine's handwriting before opening her letter. I expected a reply far sooner, and I admit I was starting to get restless and worried. Countless times I've asked the mirror to show me Eldiria, but each time life was as usual, dismissing my fears.

An old yellowed piece of parchment slips out of the envelope, and I freeze when I recognize the woman drawn on it. My mind is racing as I unfold Elaine's letter, its contents short this time.

Your Excellency,

Forgive me for the late reply. It took me several days to find a portrait that Theon hadn't destroyed. Is the woman in the illustration the one you saw the day you left?

If that is the case, then it is Theon's mother you saw—the caster of the curse that plagues us. Powers we are unaware of might be at play. If she sent you away, she must want you far from Eldiria. Theon's condition has been deteriorating rapidly since you left, and I'm uncertain if you being away is beneficial to him or not.

I fear what your response might be. Please, Arabella, write to me at your earliest convenience. I have asked Felix to check for letters from you at dawn.

With all my love,
Elaine

I think back to the woman I saw in my bedroom, her energy the same as the palace's. She looked vaguely familiar, but I mistakenly assumed it was her energy I recognized, rather than her face. I've seen a torn image of her in the east wing once. It was a mere glimpse, but it should have been enough.

Guilt courses through me as I pick up my quill to reply to Elaine. How could I possibly not have realized something of such importance? What have I done? Did me leaving put Felix at risk?

My hands tremble as I seal the envelope, my gaze trailing to my window. We're several hours away from dawn. Now, more than ever, I wish I possessed Felix's alchemy powers.

My heart races as I walk over to my bed, reaching inside the drawer beside it. The shard of the mirror of Pythia glimmers in the moonlight before she appears, her eyes milky white.

"Show me Felix," I say, my voice breaking.

Pythia nods and fades away, her image replaced by one of Felix. I watch him as he sits behind his desk in the library, staring out the window. He rises to his feet and walks over to the sofa I used to read on, his fingers trailing over the fabric. He sits down, his eyes falling closed, and I sigh. There's nothing I wish for more than to be in his embrace right now.

"Pythia, has our future changed?"

She appears and shakes her head. "No, Your Excellency."

I nod and put the mirror away with shaking hands, feeling utterly powerless. The more powerful I become, the more I lose. I'd give up every bit of magic I have if it means I get to spend the rest of my life with Felix.

I inhale shakily, a tear dropping down my cheek as I lie down, imagining that I'm back home in the bed I share with Felix, his arm wrapped around me. I lie in bed like that, my thoughts on Felix as I await dawn.

The sound of a soft click startles me not much later, and I tense, expecting it to be Serena. Instead my sheets are pulled away, and handcuffs close around my wrists before I have a chance to react.

"We're sorry, Your Excellency," one of the soldiers says, his expression betraying his fear. "We have no choice. The king would condemn our families if we were to refuse his orders."

Panic engulfs me, and for a moment I struggle to breathe. Memories flood my mind, each of them featuring the cuffs I'm once again trapped in. My breathing turns shallow as the soldiers pull me to my feet, forcing me to the door. I have no doubt they're attempting to take me to the tower my father has always used to punish me.

The hallway is lined with soldiers, my father and members of the court standing at the end. "I wish it didn't have to be this way, Arabella. We cannot risk you reporting back to the Shadow Emperor. There is no doubt in my mind that he will not let us live."

I look him in the eye, my heart filling with venom. "What do you intend to do with me?"

My father grimaces and looks away. "You're my daughter. I won't kill you, but I cannot let you return to the Shadow Emperor."

I laugh, the sound betraying the panic I feel. "And you think he won't find me? Your punishment will be so much worse once he does."

Father smiles and shakes his head. "He won't find you. I've made sure of it."

He turns and walks toward the tower I suspected he'd take me to, and with every step I'm forced to take, I try to call upon my powers.

It's different now. I'm able to call upon my powers rather than having them flood me in response to my emotions. I feel them deep within, but usually I can also feel the flow of energy around me. This time I can't. I try to struggle against my restraints as I'm led up to the stairs, but to no avail. No matter. Unlike sorceresses, I don't channel my powers from the ether. I can channel from within.

"We renovated the tower," my father tells me proudly. "Since the Shadow Emperor declared that magic is no longer forbidden in Althea, I expected trouble and prepared for it."

He opens the door, and I look around in shock. The tower has been turned into a large golden cage that hums with magic, complete with metal bars where there used to be walls, cold wind roaring through the room. I've never seen anything like it.

"You don't even need those cuffs," he says, smiling as he closes the door behind him. The two soldiers step away from me and join my father. "The tower itself will contain your magic. It will keep you from calling it to you."

I look around, a shrill laugh escaping my lips. "You built this for Felix, didn't you?"

My father looks caught off guard, and I burst into laughter. "Do you truly believe this could ever contain him? Father dearest, I doubt it can even contain *me*, let alone my husband."

"It will, Arabella. I'm sorry it had to come to this. I'll see to it that food and water are brought to you every day. If you behave, I'll let Serena come visit you someday. In time, I might consider letting you go, once I'm certain you won't go back to the Shadow Emperor."

I stare at him in disbelief and shake my head. "I'm afraid that won't work for me. I have a letter I must deliver to Eldiria at dawn, so I cannot stay here."

My father smiles. "It appears you fail to understand what is happening, Arabella. I'm not giving you a choice."

Elaine is expecting a reply, and I need to ensure it gets to her. I cannot stay here too long or Eldiria will be in danger. I can already feel the flames that burn throughout our empire waning due to my turmoiled emotions, and I have no doubt the cage and the cuffs make it worse.

"The only reason I've indulged you is because I was rather curious about what you'd do," I tell him. I look around, disappointment filling me. It astounds me that he and I share the same blood. "You know nothing of my powers, and had you simply asked me how I've been, and what the last few months have been like for me, I'd have told you all about them." I sigh, my heart aching. "Had I been a regular sorceress, you would indeed have been able to trap me here. Unfortunately for you, I'm *not*. This room does not take away my ability to compel the elements. Cutting me off from the energy in the ether is not sufficient—my powers come from within."

I smile at my father then and let the air in the room lift my shackled motionless arms, before I let it rip the cuffs apart. The winds rise outside the castle, making the bars of the cage rattle. I tilt my head when the wall starts to crack as the first bar is yanked away by the wind, breaking the cage.

My father takes a step back, but I shake my head. "You fail to understand that I'm no longer the daughter you sent away. You sent her to die, and she did."

I inhale deeply as several more bars fly away, taking chunks of the tower's wall with them. I don't feel an ounce of remorse as I lift my father into the air and send him flying through the gap in the wall. I let him fall, his screams loud and far more satisfying than I could have imagined, the sound reverberating.

I turn my attention to the two soldiers who are desperately trying to open the door behind them, but the wind keeps it shut tight.

"Don't worry. I didn't kill my father. I merely left him hanging mid-air. I would never let him get away with such a brief punishment. He has never granted me the same courtesy, after all."

I smile as I lift my hand, sending them flying out of the window, too. My anger is barely contained as I whip the door open, letting it slam into the wall. I don't have long before dawn, and I have every intention of making every second count.

CHAPTER FIFTY-FIVE

Arabella

I place the letter on the table in the throne room seconds before dawn and inhale shakily, terrified I missed the time window. I stand back and watch the letter, praying it gets to Elaine safe and sound.

Just as I'm certain that I'm too late, the letter glimmers gold before it turns translucent, disappearing entirely within seconds. I breathe a sigh of relief and take a step back, my attention shifting back to the task I put on hold. I considered adding today's predicament to my letter, but the last thing I want to do is worry Elaine and Felix over such an insignificant matter. A moment of panic aside, I didn't feel like I was in any true danger.

I sigh as I walk toward the large, heavy wooden doors at the entrance of the castle, pushing them open with a blast of air. I didn't even realize that I'd refrained from using my powers since I got to Althea, subconsciously scared of upsetting my father. I haven't heated my own baths to keep them warm for longer, or fueled the fireplace in my room, though those are things I've become accustomed to doing. He was never deserving of my thoughtfulness, yet I gave it to him out of familial obligation.

My father's calls for help seem to have attracted the entire court's attention, and I smile when I recognize several faces that were lined up outside of my bedroom not too long ago. I snap my fingers the way Felix always does, sending them into the air, too, keeping them immobile.

Several of the people still on the ground take a step back, and I take my time to look around, noting the fear they exude.

"Those currently suspended in the air are guilty of treason. They conspired against their emperor and empress, attempting to imprison me in an effort to hide their plans to embezzle money from our empire." I hear some people gasp, and I commit to memory those that look guilty.

"My father built a cage meant to contain those who possess magic, but like many of you, he failed to understand that magic is not inherently evil. You need not fear what you do not know. Instead, take steps to educate yourselves on the new world we now live in. Times are changing in Althea, and those of you who adapt will thrive. Joining Eldiria has opened up many new avenues of trade—it has given us connections to parts of the world that would otherwise be entirely inaccessible to us. What you make of the opportunities you're granted is entirely in your hands. Will you and your family thrive, or will you act out of fear, punishing not only yourself but also your loved ones? The choice is up to you, but it is a choice you must make."

I lower my father and his men to the floor, keeping them a touch above the ground and entirely immobile. "Let my father's behavior be an example to you. There is a price to be paid for fear and ignorance. For years Althea has punished those who are different, and it ends now. Effective immediately, I am implementing a prison sentence for anyone who attempts to harm an innocent sorcerer or sorceress, or any other supernatural being, for that matter. An office will be opened where cases can be heard, and a Truthseeker will be employed. Truthseekers cannot speak a lie, and they discern truthfulness and falsehood with ease. Should you be found to be lying when your case is heard, your sentence will double."

I hear the grumbles around me, but I ignore them. Without protection, magic cannot flourish in Althea. Those who grew up fearing their power as I did will continue to hide their talents, robbing Althea of what it could be.

"By my royal decree, my father, Rynhelm of Althea, is officially stripped of all titles. He will be imprisoned for his crimes, and the same punishment awaits those who aided him tonight."

Shocked gasps erupt all around me as I turn and walk back into the castle, my father and his men floating behind me. I walk straight to the gallows, not hesitating for even a moment.

I flick the door to a large cell open with a sharp gust of air and lean back as the men float in. I drop them to the floor seconds after I push the door closed.

My father rises to his feet and pushes against the bars, trying to rattle them, it appears. "Release me at once, Arabella. I'm your *father*. I'm your *king*."

I stare at him, wondering how it ever got this far. Has he always been irresponsible as a ruler, and if so, why did the members of his court let him get away with it? Althea has always had elected officials that are meant to act as an opposing force to the monarch, creating balance in the way the country is governed. We appear to have failed our people in multiple ways.

"No," I tell him. "You severed all ties with me the moment you attempted to imprison me, and no, Father, you are no longer the King of Althea. As of today, you are barely an ordinary citizen—you've been convicted of treason. You'll never see daylight again."

He has no idea what he almost did. If my connection to the elements outside had been fully cut off, the fires in Eldiria would have doused. I can still feel them burning brightly, but for a moment, they waned. Thousands of people have started to grow crops, and countless towns are still intact due to the presence of my magic. That could all have become undone, simply because my father wanted to get away with stealing from his country. Felix and I have had to sacrifice so much to get Eldiria to where it is, and he nearly undid months of work.

"You cannot convict me," he says. "There was no official judgment. I've not been given a chance to plead my case." His voice wavers now, as though reality is finally sinking in.

I reach between the bars and lift his diamond-and-ruby-encrusted crown off his head, placing it on my own instead. "I'm the Empress of Eldiria," I tell him. "I can do what I want."

It's obvious there's no talking reason into him, and I will not expend any energy trying. Throughout my life I've repeatedly given my father chances he did not deserve. I can no longer continue doing so, not when I can clearly see that it's not just me suffering from his actions—it's our people, too.

"Arabella?"

I look up to find Nathaniel standing in the doorway, his expression guarded as he looks past me and into the cell. "What are you doing? What is all this commotion?"

He genuinely looks confused, and it gives me a moment of consolation. At least he was not conspiring against me, too. It would pain me to imprison one of my oldest friends, but I'd do it if I had to.

"They've been convicted of treason. They'll remain there until I decide otherwise." I follow his gaze, realizing that his father is in the cell, too, standing right next to mine. "Until I decide on a better monarch, I'll be taking over my father's duties myself."

He walks past me and pauses in front of the cell. I watch him, considering him for a moment. I can't risk him or anyone else setting these men free.

"Stand back," I warn him, and he obeys. I look my father in the eye as I snap my fingers, engulfing the metal bars in flames until they burn bright red, before adding a sharp layer of air in front of it that'll be impossible to penetrate—in case any of them are smart enough to realize that heated metal bends easier than regular metal. The only part I've left unaffected is the food window.

"Just like the cage you tried to imprison me in, this cell is nearly impossible to escape. I invite you to try it, but know that you'll be doing so at the risk of your lives."

I take one more hard look at my father before walking away, a small part deep inside finally at ease.

CHAPTER FIFTY-SIX

Arabella

I'm weary to the bone as I walk into the throne room, hoping that at last I'll receive a letter from Elaine. I've spent days reviewing my father's documents and speaking to his advisers. My father always seemed so certain of himself that I'm surprised to find how much of a mess Althea is in. We're spending coin we barely have on things that do not matter. Just last year, my father spent half the coin that came in on events and renovations, when that money should have gone toward rebuilding our economy. With the new trade routes Felix has opened up for us, we'll be able to recover quicker, but there's a lot of work to do, and I need to find someone capable of doing it. My intentions haven't changed. I can't stay here. Someday, I'll make my way back to Eldiria.

I breathe in shakily as I sit down on my father's throne. For days now, Pythia has refused to answer my calls. If not for the fires I can still feel burning deep within, I'd go mad with worry. I suppose, in that sense, the mess Althea is in has been a welcome distraction.

"I compiled the reports you asked for and identified our most profitable exports," my sister says as she walks up to me, handing me a stack of papers. I smile at her before browsing through them. Serena appears to have taken my words to heart. I can tell that it pains her to see Father imprisoned, but not once has she questioned my decision. If anything, she's shown a great depth of understanding.

"This is good, Serena. Tell the treasurer to invest in supporting the merchants with our most profitable exports. There are more routes for them to explore now."

She nods and hands me another report. "These are the industries I believe have great potential for growth, provided we have the funds to support them. I believe investment in our people could help Althea grow, and in turn, we could become more valuable to Eldiria, resulting in further support and growth."

I take the report from her with a smile on my face. Though I don't dare reveal my hopes just yet, I envision her as Althea's future monarch. She has a lot to learn, but she has it in her. The work she's put in from the moment I took over from Father has proven it. She has tremendous insight and a strategic mind that rivals Elaine's. All she needs is some training. I'm blessed to have witnessed Elaine and Felix performing their respective duties, learning a great amount from each. Once my sister has been given similar opportunities, she could become the kind of monarch my father should have been, if she so chooses.

I look up when I see gold shimmering from the corner of my eye, and I rise from my seat when an envelope appears at the other end of the table, the papers I was perusing falling to the floor as I take a trembling step forward.

My hands shake as I pick up the letter with Elaine's handwriting on it. At last. I've been worried endlessly. My heart races as I tear the envelope open impatiently and unfold the parchment inside it.

Dear Arabella,

Following your confirmation, I questioned Theon about his ability to keep the curse at bay within the palace. From what I understand, he has been able to contain the curse to the east wing using alchemy, displacing every hint of ill intent, but that does not explain how you were able to see the former empress in your bedroom. I have spent several days attempting to unravel this development of the curse, but was unable to do so.

I was told that the palace's enchantment developed over the years and was fully in place by the time Theon reached age ten. I have never felt malicious intent from it, so I failed to recognize it as part of the former empress. In doing so, I have failed both Theon and you.

Theon and I both assumed that the palace's enchantment was part of the balance that must be part of everything we do; we assumed it was the remnants of positive magic being trapped in the palace at the time the curse was cast.

It worries me that she sent you away, for I do not know what her purpose is. From the moment you left, the curse has been haunting Theon in a way it never has before. The curse has never before attempted to leach Felix's magic, but it is doing so now. I believe removing the curse from the lands has weakened it sufficiently for it to act in an attempt to preserve itself, but it appears it has chosen Theon as a target, attempting to concentrate around him in an effort to inhabit him. Once before, it succeeded in doing so for several moments before Theon was able to push back. He still has bruises on his temple from the way the curse clung to his body in black tendrils, as though it became personified. If the curse were to find a host, the results would be unimaginable, and I fear Theon would be forever lost to us.

I have asked Pythia to show me Theon's future and

mine every week for years now, in the hope Raphael might appear in either. Neither of our futures has changed in as long as I can remember, but yesterday Theon's did. It changed for the worse, Arabella.

I'm uncertain how to proceed, or what to say. Pythia warned me not to say anything to Felix lest it accelerate his new fate, but I cannot keep this from you.

I plead that you reply at your earliest convenience, so we may reevaluate the choices we made. I fear that you leaving has condemned us all. I fear that we played into the former empress's plans. I cannot ask you to return, for I know what the cost would be, but I need guidance, Your Excellency.

*I await your reply,
Elaine*

I clench the letter in my hand as I turn and rush toward my bedroom, my thoughts spiraling. I, too, felt no ill intent from the apparition I saw. But then again, she's had years to mask her energy and match it to the palace's. Was I sent away for a reason?

I pick up the mirror with trembling hands and sit down on my bed. "Pythia," I say. "As your empress, I command you to appear."

The mirror turns milky white, and after days of silence, she finally appears, her expression carefully blank.

"Show me Felix's future."

She appears to hesitate before she nods, and the mirror turns milky white once more before visions flash through it.

I watch as darkness attacks Felix, turning his skin black, until at last his eyes are fully black, too. His posture changes, and it's clear that the man looking back at me in the mirror is not Felix. Not anymore.

The figure tenses and looks down, the black color draining away from Felix's eyes as his white shirt rapidly turns red, a sword pierced through his chest.

"No!" I yell, unable to keep my agony contained. I watch as he drops to the ground, blood rapidly staining the wooden floors.

The mirror turns milky white before clearing, and I shake it in desperation. "Pythia!" I yell. "When does this happen? Tell me when!"

"I cannot tell exactly when this will be, Your Excellency."

Pythia disappears, and I find myself staring at my own reflection. When I saw Felix's face just now, he had a bruise on his temple, similar to what Elaine described. The visions I just saw must be coming to pass soon.

I grab the mirror and slip it into my cloak as I head out the door, my heart strangely calm as I pause in front of the throne room. My sister looks up when I walk in, her brows rising.

"What's wrong, Arabella?"

I shake my head. "I must return to Eldiria at once. While I'm away, I'm leaving Althea in your hands."

Her gaze is searching before she nods. "I won't let you down."

"I know you won't." I take in my sister, knowing this might be the last time I'll ever see her. "I love you, Serena."

She bites down on her lip and shakes her head. "You'll be back soon, won't you?"

I smile and turn to walk away. I don't want the last words I speak to my sister to be a lie. Returning to Eldiria will cost me my life, but it'll be worth it if I can save Felix's life.

CHAPTER FIFTY-SEVEN

Arabella

"Please, Sirocco," I murmur as the horse speeds toward Eldiria, the pace otherworldly fast yet not swift enough for me. I can feel it deep in my soul—danger is looming. I can feel it creeping in, almost as though it's moving along my skin, slowly suffocating me.

I breathe a sigh of relief when we reach the woods that separate Eldiria from the rest of the world. Sirocco charges straight ahead, and the trees part for us, daylight fading as we get closer to the palace.

The snow-covered building I now consider home comes into view, and I inhale shakily. "Please, Felix," I whisper. "Please be safe."

CHAPTER
FIFTY-EIGHT

Felix

With each day that passes, the shadows become harder to fight. If I could end the pain and take the curse with me, I would. Each day without Arabella is more difficult than the last. I spent a lifetime without her, never truly feeling alive, and part of me wishes I could go back to those days, back when my heart was as cold as my country is.

The doors slam closed as I walk up to the east wing, and I sigh. For a few days now, the palace has been trying to keep me away from this wing, where the curse is at its strongest... but I can't stay away. The curse's pull is too strong, and each time I lose control, I find myself here.

I inhale deeply and push against the doors, my magic counteracting the palace's, until they swing open. The curse has gotten so strong within these walls that I can see black smoke pulling at the mirror, attempting to leach some of its magic. I raise my hands and push my magic against it until it slides back onto the walls, hiding away in natural shadows.

"Pythia," I say, my voice rough. "Show me Arabella."

Pythia appears in front of me and shakes her head. "Forgive me, Your Excellency. I cannot do that. Each time you see her, the darkness overtakes you for a moment. The curse is at its weakest right now—never before has it been this fragile. It is trying its hardest to concentrate its power, and it has chosen you as a vessel. Each time you see Arabella of Althea, you seem to give in to it, letting it possess you. If the curse were to gain access to a vessel as powerful as you are, the world as we know it would end. Everything would be cast in darkness and ice, and every remaining magical being would be lost. It wouldn't just be the people of Eldiria that would suffer, and I cannot let that happen."

I stare at her, my brows raised. "You are compelled to obey me and mine," I murmur, the gears in my mind turning.

"The binding spell between us was meant to keep me alive and safe from the curse. The curse has weakened sufficiently for it to no longer be a threat to me, and you are no longer strong enough to keep the binding intact."

She smiles and takes a step forward, stepping out of the mirror. I freeze in surprise and take a step back, my eyes widening when I notice the dagger in her hand.

"I cannot be killed, Pythia," I tell her, my voice soft. I've tried several times, thinking it might set my people free, but it's all to no avail.

She shakes her head and raises the dagger. "I cannot risk the curse embodying you completely. The future I see is one that cannot come to pass. I've tried, Your Excellency. For days I've scoured every possibility, every version of your future, and in each one of them you let the darkness possess you fully. In turn, it possesses our world. You must die to rid the world of this curse. It's you who keeps it alive. To break a curse of this magnitude, a life must be sacrificed. This will end when your bloodline does."

I raise my arms, my thoughts whirling. If what she says is true and death truly is upon me, then what I regret most is that I did not get to say farewell to Arabella. Perhaps in a different life, she and I might find our way back to each other.

Pythia pulls the dagger back, her hand trembling. She inhales deeply and strikes, but before the dagger reaches me, her wrist is held in place.

"No!" a loud scream resounds through the room, the windows in the tower shattering as the spirit of a woman appears in front of me, her hand on Pythia's wrist. "Run, Felix! There is no escaping death this time," she shouts as she pushes Pythia away, flickering out of existence moments later. Pythia falls to the floor and scrambles for her dagger, her resolve seemingly strengthened.

"Felix!"

I turn to find Arabella in the doorway. She runs up to me, pushing me aside just as Pythia strikes again. I pull all my magic together to push her out of harm's way, but it's too late. Pythia's blade pushes through her chest, and Arabella falls to her knees, her eyes on mine.

"No, no, no," I murmur, taking her into my arms. I try my hardest to take her wounds away, to absorb them within me, but it's to no avail. Nothing I do makes a difference, and for the first time in decades, I feel completely powerless. "Arabella, *please*. You cannot leave me, beloved." My voice breaks, and tears rapidly gather in my eyes. "I'm begging you, *please*. Hold on for me, my love."

I take her into my arms, and she lifts a trembling hand to my cheek. "I'm sorry," she whispers, her voice so soft it's hard to make out her words. "Th-This isn't how our story was meant to end, but I...I'm grateful I don't have to live a life without you." She smiles weakly, and that look in her eyes...it's as though she knows this is the last time she'll ever see me, and she's trying her best to savor the moment. "I...I love you, Felix." Arabella inhales shakily, and then her eyes flutter closed, her body collapsing in my arms. I cry out as I feel her fade away, her magic fading from our lands slowly, until its subtle hum is gone.

Time seems to still as I hold my wife, countless pleas escaping my lips without conscious thought. I pray to every god I have ever known, but my words go unheard.

Rage slowly begins to overwhelm me, and at last, I give in, letting the curse take me, in the hope that I might join my wife in death. My strength is leached away as the curse drains me, and I hold my wife tighter as the curse takes control of me. Its first aim is Pythia, a sharp sliver of darkness going straight through her heart, mimicking Arabella's wounds.

I start to lose consciousness as darkness slithers into me, my control over my limbs slipping. Dread settles in my stomach as I look down and watch dark, sticky tendrils of pure malice radiating off me, extending through the windows quickly. Bile rises up my throat when my ears are pierced by the screams of souls the curse is taking all over my beloved country, their magic coursing through my body, one after the other. With each soul lost, the curse gains more sentience, more autonomy, and my body begins to move against my will. I watch in horror as I turn toward the mirror, only to find something akin to a demon smiling back at me.

Just as my vision begins to blur, my body is turned to face Arabella, and I watch in shock as she is lifted into the air by magic so pure that it chases away the malice, more of my consciousness returning with each second that passes. An inhuman scream tears through my throat, the curse fighting to cling to me, but I feel it losing strength as water circles around Arabella, shortly followed by circulating air. I watch as vines rise from the floor, circling her, too, the three circles moving over one another. Fire erupts around her body, forming a fourth circle.

Feeling returns to my limbs when the sky around us lightens, until sunshine illuminates the room through the windows, chasing away the last remnants of darkness. "The curse," I whisper, feeling it drain out of my body despite its best efforts to cling to me.

Arabella opens her eyes, each of the elemental circles disappearing one by one, until she's lowered to the floor, her wounds gone. She inhales sharply, and my heart starts to race.

I reach for her and run my hands over her body, terrified I might be hallucinating. "Felix," she says, her voice breaking. Could this be true? Or have I truly lost my senses?

"Fates, Arabella," I murmur, pulling her into my embrace. Her floral scent brings me peace of a kind I've never known before, and the way her chest rises and falls against me chases away my lingering disbelief. "I thought I lost you, beloved."

She looks into my eyes, her gaze roaming over my features as she cups my face. She looks as much in disbelief as I am. "Felix," she whispers. "The black veins... they're disappearing."

I watch my wife as she stares at me in wonder, her hands moving over my face just as I feel the last remnants of the curse drain from my body. A tear runs down her cheek, but even so, she laughs as she traces her finger over my brow. "I didn't think you could get more handsome," she whispers, the tip of her finger trailing to my cheekbone, and then my lips.

I swallow hard, overwhelmed by emotions as she pulls me closer and kisses me, her movements desperate, as if she, too, didn't think we'd ever get to experience this again. I kiss my wife the way I've been wanting to from the moment she left, and not once does evil reach for me. I lose myself in her, relishing her touch. For a moment, I thought I'd lost her forever.

The salt of her tears mixes with the taste of her, and I pull away to kiss her tears, only to be mesmerized by the way the sun kisses her hair and colors her skin golden. She draws a shaky breath as she pulls my forehead to hers with a smile on her face. "We broke the curse, Felix." Her words are soft, almost like she's scared to believe it, to say it out loud, and I hug her tightly to me, equally in disbelief.

"You came back of your own free will, and a life was freely given out of love," I whisper, realization dawning. I'd always known that breaking the curse would come at the cost of a life, since a life was given to cast it, but I'd always assumed it'd be mine. "You broke the curse."

"We did," Arabella tells me. "*We* did."

CHAPTER
FIFTY-NINE

Arabella

Felix holds my hand as we walk through the atrium, the two of us in shock as roses shimmer gold, only to transform back into people one by one.

"All of these people," Felix murmurs, his eyes roaming over the palace filled with embraces and rejoiced tears. "They were all lost to us throughout the years, taken by the curse."

I nod as I watch couples reunite, my heart racing as I try to find Elaine. "There," I whisper. I watch her standing in the corner, her eyes on the same rose I've seen her nurture. It begins to glow gold, and I watch breathlessly as a man appears.

"Raphael," she says. She takes a step closer and runs her hands over his body.

He looks at her, mesmerized for a moment before his eyes clear. Raphael grabs her wrists and holds them in place. "Who are you?"

His voice is loud and clear, and I recoil just as Elaine does. "Raphael?" she whispers, her voice breaking.

Felix walks up to her and places his hand on Raphael's shoulder while I wrap my hand around Elaine's waist. She leans into me, her eyes meeting mine. I recognize the sorrow I see in her expression and tighten my grip on her. "It's okay," I whisper. "Give it time."

"It's good to have you back," Felix says, but there's no recognition in Raphael's eyes.

"Where am I?" Raphael asks, looking around.

Elaine tenses and looks at him as she straightens her shoulders. "We're in Eldiria. Do you know who you are?"

He nods. "Raphael of Iridea, Crown Prince of Iridea."

From what I understand, Raphael lost his titles when Felix conquered his country. "Take him to a healer," I tell Elaine. "It looks like his memory has been affected."

Why is it he remembers who he is, but he doesn't remember Elaine? From what she told me, the two of them knew each other before they arrived here.

"Yes, Your Excellency," Elaine says as she leads him away.

Felix and I watch the two of them, and my heart sinks as they turn the corner. "He doesn't remember her," I murmur. "How could that be possible? Look at all these people around us, all embracing and rejoicing. Why is it that Raphael doesn't remember Elaine or you?"

Felix wraps his arm around me and shakes his head. "I don't know, beloved, but we'll figure it out. If we could break the curse, we can resolve that, too."

He tightens his grip on me as he leads me out of the palace. We both freeze in shock as we walk out the doors. As far as we can see, our empire is bathed in sunlight, green grass and flowers growing everywhere. In the distance, I can see a stream flowing that has always been frozen, and I turn to look at the palace itself, its limestone bricks exposed at last.

"It's beautiful," I whisper. Felix nods, and I smile at the emotion in his eyes. "You once told me you'd show me Eldiria in all its glory, and you did."

He smiles at me and cups my cheek. "*You* did, beloved. You did the impossible and set us free."

I grin at him and rise to my tiptoes to wrap my arms around him. "I suppose true love broke the curse after all."

Felix chuckles then, leaning in to kiss me. "I love you, Arabella of Althea. Let the world you see around you be proof of it. I love you more than words will ever convey."

My lips meet his and I can't help but smile. I thought I'd lost him, and that I'd never get him back. Yet here we stand together. "I love you more, Felix Theon Osiris."

CHAPTER
SIXTY

Felix

"Felix."

I freeze at the sound of the distant voice and look up to find my mother's apparition standing by the window in my bedroom. Agonizing heartache mingles with deep-rooted hatred, rendering me speechless.

"Felix," she repeats, her eyes filled with sorrow. "With the curse broken, my time here is limited. My magic has fused with the palace, but my soul must move on, at last."

She approaches me with such tenderness in her gaze that I find myself standing motionless, uncertain how to respond. Her hand rises to my face, and I let my eyes close for a moment.

"My beautiful boy," she whispers. "Throughout the years, I've watched you grow up, Felix. I've always been by your side. I was there when your father whispered lies into your ears, turning you against me even after I passed. I was there when you fought against the curse that was never meant for anyone but your father. Watching you suffer the consequences of the hatred I felt toward your father was the ultimate punishment. I've always been told that a price must be paid for a curse as cruel as mine, but I never thought it'd be one so high. Watching the only person I have ever truly loved suffer decade after decade, powerless... it tore me apart. I'm so proud of you, my son. I know how heavy the burdens you carried were, yet you never wavered, you never stumbled."

I stare at her in disbelief. "You didn't curse *me*?"

She shakes her head as a tear drops down her face. "Never, my darling. I swear it. It was your father I cursed—I cursed him to live a life without love, one in which he'd never experience any kind of warmth, not even in the moment he took his last breath. Unbeknownst to me, my curse extended to his entire bloodline... to my own son. The moment I first laid eyes on you, I felt love so intense that every emotion before it paled in comparison. There is nothing I wouldn't have done for you, Felix. Even then. The second I felt the curse latch on to you, I used my last breath and every remaining drop of life-force to reverse it, but it was too late. I couldn't protect you, and I've spent the last two hundred years atoning for it.

"My attempt to reverse the curse instead merely kept it from killing you, like it did your father. Even worse, it allowed the curse to take on a form I never intended it to take, and it became sentient. A curse of this magnitude has to be cast with clear intentions, and mine changed the second I realized what I'd done. I tried my best to protect you throughout the years, Felix, but you still suffered so much, and words will never be able to convey the depth of my regret."

"I..." I'm uncertain what to say to her. If she's been here all along, she must have heard me curse her, hate her. She would have seen me rip apart every single one of her belongings, removing every trace of her from my life.

She smiles reassuringly, as though my thoughts are written all over my face. "All that matters to me is that you're happy, Felix. Now that you are, I can be at peace. But I couldn't move on without asking you for forgiveness. Everything you've been through... the pain you suffered... perhaps this curse was not meant for you, but you were the one that bore the consequences, and for that, I am eternally regretful."

"If I don't forgive you, will you stay?"

Her expression shifts into one that is a blend of sorrow and love. "My sweet son, if I could, I would never leave you. However, I must. The Fates are calling me, and I cannot resist them."

Her body shimmers, as though she struggles to stay corporeal. I reach for her, my hand going straight through her.

"I love you, Felix."

She smiles at me, and heartbreak unlike anything I've ever known rushes through me, tearing my very soul apart. "I forgive you," I whisper.

My mother fades from view, and the energy in the palace changes, almost as though it's mourning her loss. I sink down to my knees and inhale shakily, my mind reeling. Could it be true? Was my hatred for her misguided all along? I never heard her words myself, I've only ever heard them repeated back to me as a child... by my *father*.

"Forgive me," I whisper into the empty room, knowing deep in my heart that her words ring true. I knew it the moment she appeared and protected me from Pythia.

"Felix, my love?" I inhale deeply and rise to my feet, vowing to honor my mother's memory the way I always should have. I turn toward my wife, meeting her concerned gaze. "Arabella," I murmur, my voice breaking. "Shall we have a portrait painted of my mother?"

She smiles at me then, her whole face transformed with pure joy. "I would love that."

I walk up to her and take her into my arms, my lips coming down on hers. Happiness... we found it at last.

EPILOGUE

Arabella

Molly pauses casting her beautification spells and tenses as her baby starts to cry in the basket. "I'm so sorry, Your Excellency," she says. "I think she's hungry."

I shake my head and place my hand on her arm. "It's okay, Molly. You go and feed your little one. I think this is quite enough for today's event," I murmur as I look into the mirror.

She nods gratefully and picks up her daughter, my heart warming as I watch the two of them.

"She looks cute, but she torments me, Your Excellency. You'll find out soon enough how exhausting these tiny little things are."

I place a hand on my stomach and smile to myself. My pregnancy is showing now, and there's not much time left until our own child makes it into this world.

"I can't wait," I tell Molly. I glance into the mirror, taking in the maroon dress the palace selected for me today. It drapes perfectly over my stomach, neither drawing attention to it nor hiding it. Molly matched the color of my lips perfectly, and I can't wait to see how Felix might respond when he sees me. A golden crown with rubies sits atop my head, completing the outfit.

I glance back at Molly and her little one as I walk out of the room, mouthing *thank you*. She smiles and attempts to curtsy, but I shake my head. Seeing her with her daughter is one of the greatest joys I've been granted. Eldiria changed so much in so very little time, and it astounds me every single day.

I pause atop the large staircase, my eyes dropping to the portrait of my mother-in-law. Her spirit might be gone, but her magic lives on in the palace, keeping it enchanted. Felix refuses to speak of her still, but the fact that he had such a large and stunning portrait of her hung in the palace speaks volumes. He's slowly been renovating the east wing, recovering many of her belongings. Though he might not talk about her, I know he's processing her role in the curse in his own way.

"Arabella."

I turn toward him when I hear his voice, a smile tipping the edges of my lips up when his eyes widen. "Ethereal," he whispers when I reach him. "You are beyond beautiful, beloved."

I stare at my husband, my heart racing. I still haven't gotten used to seeing him without the poisonous veins trying to obscure his appearance. I take in his strong jawline and cheekbones, his straight nose and the slight stubble on his skin. He's beyond handsome, even more so than I imagined.

I rise to my tiptoes to kiss him, and Felix wraps his arms around me, deepening the kiss. I pull away reluctantly and sigh. "We're going to be late to Elaine and Raphael's wedding," I whisper against his lips, and he sighs.

"Very well," he mutters reluctantly. "Hold on tight." He closes his eyes.

I gasp, and moments later, we're standing in the palace in Iridea. Without the curse to battle, Felix's powers have become stronger, as have mine.

"Are you certain this is a good idea?" I ask Felix, referring to the way he has pushed Elaine and Raphael together.

Felix shrugs. "He wants his country back, doesn't he? The only way I'll give him that is if he marries Elaine. We'll let their countries join together, as the two of them will."

I sigh and shake my head. "He still doesn't remember her. I'm worried for her, Felix."

He looks at me and smiles. "Don't be, beloved. Their love was like ours is. While I don't know why he doesn't remember her, I know that in time he will. Besides, don't we owe it to Elaine to help in any way we can?"

I nod as we walk into the chapel, everyone around us rising to curtsy. Felix and I take a seat in the front row, alongside Elaine's family, my heart racing as music begins to play.

I turn to watch Elaine walk in wearing a stunning white gown with a train suited for the princess she is. She looks beautiful, but also terrified. Her eyes roam over the room, and her shoulders relax when her gaze settles on me. I nod at her, offering her a reassuring smile, and she nods back as she straightens her shoulders.

Elaine looks ahead, and I follow her gaze. Though there is hatred in Raphael's eyes, there's also blatant desire. He might not admit it to himself, but even if he doesn't remember Elaine, a small part of him wants her. I have faith that Elaine will win him over the way she once did. I just wish she didn't have to.

"They'll be okay," Felix whispers as he wraps his arm around me, and I nod. They will be. I have faith that they'll find their way back to each other no matter how slim the odds are, just like Felix and I did.

We watch as they exchange vows and then rings. My heart stops for a moment when the priest pronounces them husband and wife before ordering Raphael to kiss Elaine. He hesitates, but then he leans in and captures her lips, cheering erupting around us, though my own cheers might well be the loudest.

I see what Elaine once did. Though it might take time for them to find their way back to each other, I know that they will.

Felix presses a kiss on top of my head as we watch the newly wedded couple turn toward us. "I love you," he whispers.

I look up at him with a smile on my face. "I love you more."

Want a little more of Felix and Arabella? Gain access to exclusive bonus content, including a deleted spicy scene, by scanning the QR code below.

DON'T MISS ELAINE AND RAPHAEL'S
ENCHANTING STORY

COMING IN FALL 2026

ACKNOWLEDGMENTS

First of all, I'd like to thank you, dear reader, for choosing to spend a few hours with me. There are countless amazing books you could have chosen to read, and I'm beyond honored you chose one of mine. Thank you for supporting my dreams by picking up one of my books—I truly couldn't do this without you.

Second, publishing a book takes a village, and I wouldn't be anywhere without mine. Thank you endlessly to my Kittens; Team Cat; my agent, Thao Le; my amazing Forever team—especially Junessa, Jordyn, Estelle, Dana, and every team member I have yet to meet at the time of this writing. Thank you for making all kinds of magic happen behind the scenes. Without you, this story wouldn't exist in its current form today.

Most of all, thank you to my sweet husband, for always supporting my dreams, and for believing in me like no one ever has before—not even me. I love you endlessly.

ABOUT THE AUTHOR

Catharina Maura is a *USA Today* and Amazon #1 bestselling author. She writes angsty, fast-paced contemporary romance novels that break your heart before they lead you to a hard-won happily ever after. Cat lives in Hong Kong with her husband and a dozen houseplants that all have names. When she isn't daydreaming about future characters, she's exploring the world and seeking out new adventures.

You can learn more at:
Catharinamaura.com
Facebook.com/CatharinaMauraAuthor
Instagram @catharinamaura
TikTok @catharinamaura

ABOUT THE AUTHOR

Catharina Maura is a *USA Today* and Amazon #1 bestselling author. She writes angsty, fast-paced contemporary romance novels that break your heart before they lead you to a hard-won happily ever after. Cat lives in Hong Kong with her husband and a dozen houseplants that all have names. When she isn't daydreaming about future characters, she's exploring the world and seeking out new adventures.

You can learn more at:
Catharinamaura.com
Facebook.com/CatharinaMauraAuthor
Instagram @catharinamaura
TikTok @catharinamaura